PERSONAL
EFFECTS

Personal Effects

E. M. KOKIE

CANDLEWICK PRESS

First edition 2012

Library of Congress Cataloging-in-Publication Data is available.

Library of Congress Catalog Card Number pending

ISBN 978-0-7636-5527-3

BVG 17 16 15 14 13 12
10 9 8 7 6 5 4 3 2 1

Printed in Berryville, VA, U.S.A.

This book was typeset in Scala.

Candlewick Press
99 Dover Street
Somerville, Massachusetts 02144

visit us at www.candlewick.com

For Mom and Dad,
who told me I could do anything

And for K.T.,
who helped me believe it

one

Of all the lame shit on Pinscher's backpack, his *War Is Not the Answer* sticker pisses me off the most — even more than his *Practice Nonviolence* button, which makes me want to practice some violence on his face.

It's not enough that I have to listen to him run his mouth all the time. But to have to see all his slogans and crap on his backpack, watch him strut around and show off, laughing like it's all a big joke — it's almost too much to take. Especially on Monday mornings. Especially on a Monday morning after an even more shitastic than usual weekend.

Pinscher catches me looking. One side of his lip curls up, showing his teeth, making him look even more like the dog we named him for in fifth grade.

T.J. would wipe that sneer off his face.

"Matt?" Shauna's hand waves in front of my face. "Hey. You OK?"

"Yeah." Pinscher says something, and the others all look at me, then laugh. "Fine."

Shauna pries my fingers off the locker door and curls her hand around my fist. My hand throbs like I'm still strangling the cold metal, the hard edge still digging into my palm.

"Forget about him," Shauna whispers. She moves into the space between Pinscher and me, so close I have to blink and refocus to see her face as more than a bunch of shapes. I can't even see him around her. Her fingers slide over my knuckles, back and forth, until my hand relaxes. "Seriously, he's not worth it."

We stand like that, so close I can't see anything but her. Her fingers are warm and smooth. I'd forgotten how good her hands feel. Heat races through me. I yank my hand back, remembering why I started avoiding her hands. Touching leads to bad thoughts, which can only lead to total mortification. No benefits with this friendship.

"Yeah, I know." I rub at my neck, try to shake it off—all of it—the tension left over from Dad's glare, Pinscher's stupid laugh, how I can still feel Shauna's fingers and smell her herbally clean hair.

"What's going on?" She's got that worried look again, like she can't figure out how to fix me, or if I'm worth the effort this time.

"Nothing." I shrug. "The usual."

She's not buying it. Means I'm in for an interrogation. I reach into my locker and push my books around, hoping she'll wait until later or that we can at least get out of the hall first. But when I look up, ready to negotiate, she's not even looking at me.

She's pointedly *not* looking at Michael, who's hovering down the hall, obviously watching her. Hanging near enough to Pinscher to pretend he's paying attention, but watching Shauna. Could be we're heading for another round of their on-again, off-again drama.

Maybe she'll be too busy to interrogate me.

If I have to watch Shauna get back together with Michael—here, now—I really will put my fist through the wall.

"Are you going to be OK?" She's already hoisting her backpack to run, but her forehead is creased with worry. "I can't be late for homeroom again. Señora Rosenfeld will make me *muerta*."

"Yeah." I force a smile. "Go." I close my locker door carefully, like it's made of glass.

"See you later?" Her brown eyes are squinty and dark. "Matt?"

"Yeah. No, I'm fine. I'll meet you at your car after eighth."

I'm late for homeroom, but Mrs. Rahman just waves me to my seat. Pinscher's two rows over, playing around with the shit on his backpack. He makes a big show of peeling the paper off a new bumper sticker and pasting it onto the side of the bag. I make myself look at the wall.

The morning crawls by. Through bio and most of English, I wonder what the new sticker says. He was extra careful with it, like he was extra proud.

I make it through lunch, but take the long way to algebra

to avoid, well, everyone, jumping across the threshold just as the second bell rings.

"Nice of you to join us," Mrs. Tine says, waving me past with her bright-green review-o-rama folder. Like I've got a choice.

She practically dances around the room in full-out math love. It's all review, and I actually get most of it, but Mrs. Tine is cool enough to skip past me when I'm sunk down low in my seat. She only calls on me when I look at her. Today I don't look at anyone.

Pinscher's two rows over and up. His backpack is on the floor next to his desk, the new sticker pointed right at me: *Not in My Name,* the words like a strobe light throbbing behind my eyes. Like any of them are over there for him.

All his talk and buttons and crap. His bracelets, like a girl, with the names of dead soldiers, who would have kicked his ass if they ever got the chance. And ever since Pinscher went to that rally in Philly, all he can talk about is Bush and the war. They made him stop wearing his *Bush Lied* crap in school, but he just tripled up with the antiwar stuff — buttons and shirts and stickers about the war, about the "troops," like he gives a damn about them or what they believe.

Every week some new shirt, paraded around like *he*'s won something.

Bullshit, radiating off his backpack even when his freaking mouth is shut. *War Is a Waste. Not in My Name. Iraqis Are People, Too.* What the hell does that even mean?

The bell makes me jump, banging my knee on the desk. Everyone starts moving, but Mrs. Tine hovers next to me. I slack back and wait. Once the room is empty, she taps the blank page of my notebook, where my notes from class should be.

"Barely hanging on to a C right now, Matt. Don't blow it."

She drops my quiz from Friday on top of the blank page and walks away. A green 70 cowers next to my name in the upper right-hand corner of the page. When the school year started, Dad was pushing for all Bs. Now he'd flip for a C. But since I haven't exactly been paying attention, I'm gonna need a miracle to get through the final and hang on to a C for the year.

The halls are too loud. I cut out the side door and walk around the outside of the building.

When I get to my locker, Pinscher's still at his, holding court. He pulls his sweatshirt over his head. The T-shirt underneath is pristine, bright white with red letters on the front and red and black on back. Has to be new. The red words on front shout at me: *Support OUR Troops: Bring Them Home* . . . He turns, showing it off. All the black type on back is too small to read from across the hall, but the large red *And not in Pieces* screams off the shirt.

Not.

In.

Pieces.

My books scatter on the floor.

Pinscher turns and flattens back against the lockers. He's talking, but I can't hear him over the roaring in my head. Someone grabs my arm, but I shake him off and pull at Pinscher's shirt.

I need to see.

I spin Pinscher around, shove his face against the lockers. My hand slaps flat against his back. Everything stops except for both of us heaving in air. I hold my hand over the words I couldn't read from across the hall. Up close they're huge.

I'm gonna tear them off him.

"It's a waste, dude," Pinscher says over his shoulder. "Don't you see that? The money, and all the innocent —"

"Shut up."

"I'm supporting them." Fucking asshole. "It has to end before —"

"You have no right —"

"I have every right. It's my —"

He struggles. The shirt rips. I've still got a piece of it. Not enough.

"Get off me!" he yells.

Other voices. Someone pulls me away. I shove back, but then they're between us, someone holding on to Pinscher.

"Put your sweatshirt on," someone says to Pinscher. Pinscher sputters. "Put it on," he — Michael — says again.

"You ripped it?" Pinscher snarls.

I leap at him. Someone forces me back. We wrestle until Michael shoves us both farther away.

"Pete," Michael says, "just go."

Pinscher edges around Michael and starts backing toward the office, holding out a piece of the ripped shirt. "Don't you get it? Bush lied. It was all lies. Every time we torture—"

I break free, slam Michael into the wall, and charge. Pinscher tries to get away, but I've got him. We stumble into the lockers. I wedge my arm into his throat and tear at the shirt until I get another chunk.

Pinscher kicks and twists.

I won't let go.

The shirt rips all the way to Pinscher's neck.

The others grab at me, but I shake them off and swing.

"My nose!" Pinscher clutches his face. Blood seeps between his fingers, floods his mouth and chin. "You broke my—"

My fist misses his jaw, gets his shoulder. T.J. wouldn't have missed.

He swings back, but I punch the side of his head, then his neck. We fall.

I swing wildly, both fists. Blood everywhere.

Hands grab at me, pull me. I clamp my knees around Pinscher and keep swinging.

Pinscher covers his face.

T.J.'s voice tells me to go for his ribs. Dad eggs me on.

A roar, and I'm knocked off Pinscher, slammed into the wall. My head bounces off the floor. I spring up, the way T.J. taught me to, aiming for the nearest body. A crash, then glass everywhere.

Pinscher's crawling. I dive for his legs.

Words keep coming. Dad's words.

Wuss.

Show him.

Make him.

Fight.

Harder.

Hoisted up by my arms, I kick out, but I can't find the ground.

I fight, but they're too strong.

I'm hauled back until my feet hit the ground hard, vibrations running up my legs. Ears buzzing.

"Cut it out." Coach Simpson. "You're not going anywhere."

"Stop." From the other side. Mr. Lee. "Matt, stop."

I suck in air. Can't breathe. Gulp in more. Like I was drowning. Now I can breathe.

"Get him out of here."

They pull me down the hall.

Pinscher's *Practice Nonviolence* button is on the floor. I kick it as they drag me by. It skitters all the way down the hall.

two

My ass is numb from the hard plastic chair across from Principal Pendergrast's office. He parked me here to wait for Dad. Two hours ago.

With nothing to do but wait, I can't get the feel or sounds of the fight out of my head.

That first perfect punch in slow motion, a hazy comet trail following my arm all the way to Pinscher's face. The sound of my fist hitting his nose, the crunch, like smashing crusty ice with my foot. Every drawer or door closing sounds like my head hitting the floor. The tangy, metallic smell of Pinscher's blood surrounds me, making me thirsty and sick.

But when I roll my shoulder or flex my hands, it feels good, like the burn after working out so hard your body is at its limit and you know you're alive. I haven't felt this alive in months — since last April, when T.J. was home on leave.

It felt good to hit someone. I can't say that out loud, but it's the truth.

The door to Principal Pendergrast's office opens. He mutters all the way to the lead secretary's desk and then back around the counter to where I'm sitting. He waits for me to move my leg out of the path of his scuffed-up loafers before continuing past to the cabinet in the corner. His thinning hair still clings to his head in carefully spaced strands, but his chin, jaw, and upper lip are shaded dark with end-of-the-day stubble. He looks like a cartoon character—his face shaded darker to show the hard day he's had.

"You, Mr. Foster, have absolutely nothing to smile about."

Pendergrast's intimidation strategies have nothing on Dad's. And no matter what I do now, I'm gonna get suspended. I fold my arms and lean back in my chair. I stay that way, even when my shoulder starts to burn, and stare at his shoes, pretending I can't hear him.

"You think this is funny?" Pendergrast leans in closer. "Do you? Yo, Earth to Mr. Foster."

I'm not looking at him.

Mrs. Danner, the nice secretary, makes this sound, and then I'm looking at her over the counter. It's like in sixth grade, when she caught me daring her son, Jared, to spit out the bus window on the field trip to Gettysburg. She flicks her head, and then I'm looking at Pendergrast, despite my plan to ignore him.

"Your language alone requires a suspension under the nonharassment policy. We do not tolerate that word, as you well know."

"What word?" I was spewing words. I don't even remember what.

Pendergrast plants his hands on his hips. Oh. Shit. I

must have called Pinscher a faggot somewhere in there. Not for the first time, I wonder if Pendergrast takes "that word" a little personally.

"Well?" He waits for me to say something for myself. I don't think he wants to hear what I think.

Whatever. He starts talking. I stop listening. Pendergrast acts like there'd have to be some sort of meeting or vote or something before suspending me if only I hadn't called Pinscher a faggot. Yeah, right. As soon as I had a hold of Pinscher's shirt, I was gone.

"You hear me?" Pendergrast nudges my shoe. I look at him, but I have no idea what he was saying. He throws his hands in the air and shifts to start over. Please let it be the short version. My head is pounding, and my stomach is trying to eat itself.

"Peter is seriously injured. You broke his nose, and you'd better hope nothing else is broken. Tim, Michael, and David got pretty banged up, and Steven's going to need stitches in his arm. And that is all before we get to the display case you're going to pay for."

I feel a little bad about Michael. He's OK, at least compared to a lot of the other jerks Shauna's dated. Stevie's OK, too. I have nothing against either of them except they got in my way. But Pinscher? Pinscher not so much. I actually feel pretty satisfied with breaking Pinscher's face.

"Listen." Pendergrast sags into the chair next to me. "You're lucky you're not down at the police station right now."

He leans so close I can smell his nasty breath. "By rights, you should be. I know Peter and some of the others have been pretty vocal lately. And it's been a rough bunch of months for you. But you're not helping yourself by rising to their bait at every turn."

Every turn? He has no clue how many times a day I have to swallow it all down. Most days it's all I can do just to keep from ripping Pinscher's head off.

"I am sure, if the roles were reversed, you would want to express your views on"—he pauses, afraid to say "war" to me maybe—"political issues without getting the crap kicked out of you. Right?"

There's no point in arguing. No matter what I say, no matter what happens, they'll never get it, not with everyone snowed by Pinscher. They fall all over him, him and his father, the big-deal professor.

". . . learn to roll with it a little more. It may not be fair, but I don't think I have to tell you that life is not fair."

No, he doesn't.

"Seems like you came in this morning spoiling for a fight. At least, that's what I hear." From who? "Want to tell me why?"

No way.

"We can help, Matt. But you've got to talk to us."

I'd be in a world of hurt if Pendergrast said anything to Dad. And besides, the parts not really about Pinscher would sound dumb.

Pendergrast scratches his chin. It sounds like sandpaper, the fine kind Mr. Anders gives me for the edges of woodwork or for going over custom cabinets before I stain them.

"OK. Well, there are about three weeks left. You have a chance to salvage this semester if you buckle down . . ."

Right. I've fallen into quicksand; the harder I try to concentrate, the less I can. I haven't opened a book in months.

Pendergrast taps my chair. "Matthew, whatever troubles you've had in the past, and despite not being the most dedicated student, you've never been a discipline problem until this year. And I get that there are extenuating circumstances, but not even . . . those excuse your behavior today." He waits, maybe for me to pour out my soul. Not gonna happen. "We're running out of options with you. My voicemail's probably full of worried parents and school-board members, wanting me to assure them that you're not a danger to anyone. And right now, I can't do that."

I push my cut-up knuckles against my leg to keep my face blank.

"I know it's been tough. But I'd hate to see you get so far off track that you throw away your chance to graduate with your class. If you can get through these last few weeks without incident, get through finals, you could start fresh next year."

Like that would solve anything. Break my ass? What for? Another year of torture?

". . . I know that this time Peter may have started it."

Bullshit. He waits for me to say something, but it's got to be a trick. Like to get me to start talking. I'm not stupid. No way Pinscher admitted anything.

Pendergrast sighs, shakes his head, and leans back in his chair, moving away from me. Apparently the touchy-feely part of our chat is over.

"Even if Peter instigated it," he continues, "that doesn't make it acceptable to get physical, or to escalate it. You need to figure out how to resolve these kinds of things without violence—walk away or talk it out, anything not to turn to violence. You can't solve things with your fists, Matt, especially when you are bigger and stronger than the other guy."

"Says who?" Dad's voice booms from the doorway.

My ribs and back scream from being jolted to attention, but I hold myself still and straight in the chair. Pendergrast stands up and motions to his office, but Dad's not going anywhere yet. He towers over us, all six two of him, not one regulation salt-and-pepper hair out of place, not one piece of lint on his clothes, not one wrinkle except on his leathered face.

"Seems to me if the other guys started it, and I'm pretty sure you just admitted they did, then it seems to me they just learned the important lesson." Dad's bottom lip juts out for emphasis, like he has just now convinced himself of the truth of the statement. "Don't talk trash to guys who are stronger than you, especially when the trash you're spewing is utter, unadulterated bullshit. Sounds to me like they got what was coming to them."

It'd be nice if Dad stayed on my side, but I know he'll find a way to be pissed at me—like maybe he'll tell me T.J. could have beat them so bad they would have told Pendergrast they kicked their own asses. *You only broke his face? What, Matt, too much of a wuss to break his whole goddamn head? Well, we'll just have to fix that so you learn to hit right.*

Dad shifts his focus from Pendergrast to me. A long, sweat-inducing stare. Then he narrows his eyes and gives me a once-over, his forehead collapsing into wrinkled layers between his hairline and his eyebrows. The look doesn't so much ask if I'm all right as try to assess if anything requires immediate medical attention. Short of a severed limb, there will be no doctors. Stitches are for wimps and pretty boys. We Foster men swear by butterflies, surgical tape, and, for those really stubborn cuts, Super Glue. First time Dad whipped that shit out, T.J. ran for it. But it worked: sealed the cut right up.

I can feel his eyes sliding over me, taking inventory of my wounds. When he looks at my eyes again, I shrug to let him know I'm cool. Not because I am but because I can't let him know just how hurt I let myself get. A shiver races up my spine, and I lock my knees to keep steady. My head can't take another round tonight, not even the openhanded slaps Dad thinks are kidding around.

Pendergrast shifts from foot to foot next to us. He coughs. "Mr. Foster?"

Dad ignores him for one more beat and then stalks into

Pendergrast's office without even looking at him. Pendergrast follows like he's the one in trouble.

Their voices bleed through the closed office door — not enough to hear the actual words, but I can make out the back and forth. More back than forth as Dad gets on a roll, probably with his big "What is wrong with this country?" speech. I can picture Dad: rising out of his seat, slapping the desk, spearing the air with his finger. After a while it becomes clear that Dad's the only one talking. At least he's blowing off some steam. Blowing off steam is good. The longer he rants at Pendergrast, the less he'll have left for me.

Eventually I lean my head back against the wall and close my eyes. Big mistake. With nothing to see but the red-tinged dark of my eyelids, I can't ignore the pain. Everywhere hurts. My right hand, resting on my leg, feels full of wet cement, heavier with every minute. My head pounds in time with my pulse. I open my eyes and shift around until I can see the clock on the far side of the office. Pressing my left thumb against my temple, I watch the second hand on the wall clock.

One minute. Two. The ache in my head pools in my temple, under my thumb. I can't swallow. There's no spit left to swallow. My tongue feels too big, and like it's wrapped in wool.

"Are you thirsty, Matt?" Mrs. Danner asks from behind the counter. "Need some water?"

"Yes, ma'am." I sit up straighter.

"Come over here." She waves me around the counter. I

freeze at the invisible line between the waiting area and the secretaries' desks. "It's OK," she says. "Here, sit down."

After I've folded myself into the chair next to her desk, she hands me a large plastic cup of water. The first tentative sip slides around my mouth. Relief, cold and clean and so good. Maybe the best-tasting water I've ever had. I take small sips, swirling it around my tongue each time before swallowing, just to savor it.

"Thanks, Mrs. Danner," I only think to say when half the water is gone. Her eyes crinkle at the edges. For the first time in hours, my gut relaxes. She's clearly not scared of me or worried I'm gonna lose it again. She doesn't even seem that unnerved by Dad. And when she smiles and rests her chin on her hand, I almost feel like me again—like last-year me, not the guy I've turned into.

"Some more?" She pours me another full cup without waiting for an answer.

I take a really big gulp, holding it in my mouth as long as I can before swallowing. My "Thanks" comes out like a gasp. I need to slow down. No way to know how long Dad'll be in there.

"You're in a lot of pain, aren't you?" Mrs. Danner asks.

"Nah, just some scrapes, a few bruises." I flex my swollen hand out in front of me. "No problem."

"No," she says, "inside, you're in a lot of pain, aren't you?"

The question knocks the air out of me more than any of the hits I took.

I can't breathe. Or speak. She won't let me off the hook, staring into my eyes. The vise around my lungs clamps tighter.

Pendergrast's office door swings open and slams against the wall, jarring me free. Saved from Mrs. Danner by Dad.

He looks at the empty chair where I should be. His eyes go wild, and he swings around. But before I can say anything, he sees me and says, "Let's go."

three

Dad doesn't say anything all the way to the car, not even after we're buckled in and pulling out of the parking space.

At the first red light, we sit in silence. He's not giving me any clue as to how much trouble I'm in.

"Didja shut 'em up?" he finally asks.

"Yes, sir," I reply in the strongest and most assured voice I can muster.

I glance sideways without moving my head—a skill honed by years of gauging my father's moods.

His only response is a slight flexing of the muscle in his jaw.

The light changes, but he doesn't move. I wait for whatever's coming. A car horn sounds behind us. He hits the gas.

Watching him freaks me out. I press my face against the cold glass of the window and watch the houses pass by. He turns out of town, instead of toward home. He doesn't say why, and I don't ask. I don't even care.

Another turn and we're headed to his office. He must have come straight from the site he was inspecting today. He'll want to drop his stuff at the office and check the mail and messages. Can't deviate from his precious routine, even if his kid is dying in the passenger seat.

Outside his building, he turns off the truck, climbs out, and slams the door behind him. No warnings to stay put, no caring "I'll be right back." Not even a look in my direction. He'll take whatever time he wants, and I'll wait, without saying a word.

I close my eyes and roll my forehead against the glass.

Last spring, in the worst of bad timing, Dad's grand plan, his dream—that I would go to State, rise through the ranks of ROTC, and go on to Officer Candidate School—burst the week before T.J. came home for leave. The college counselor practically laughed in Dad's face when he asked about my chances of getting into State. While she stuttered on about my "options," Dad tuned her out. It was amazing he didn't crack a tooth the way he clenched his jaw for the rest of the short meeting.

After, he didn't let me get in the truck, and he wasn't in the house by the time I walked home. I almost pissed myself when he came in late that night. I was ready to bolt until I heard him head upstairs. He didn't say one word to me the entire week, not until an hour after T.J. got home, when it was becoming obvious. Then he tried to put on a good face, but I could tell the stress of trying not to kill me in front of T.J. was grating on his nerves. I think even T.J. could tell. Maybe that's why T.J. came up with the plan to turn our usual day hikes into five days away on our own. That or he couldn't take one more day cooped up in our house, either.

From the moment he got home, T.J. couldn't relax for a minute. That whole first afternoon, he twitched and fidgeted. All week he paced around the house. He didn't sit still for long, jumping up five minutes after he sat down, even during meals. He wasn't goofing around or teasing me, or even really seeing any of his old friends. He wasn't talking much at all. And when he did talk, even his voice was different: deeper, lower. I only saw him relax when we took off on our own.

We'd been hiking together since I was twelve. T.J. came back from his first tour with big plans for us to actually *do* stuff together, at least during the few weeks a year he came home on leave. That first time, the "hikes" were like a stroll for him — he was twenty and combat fit; I was scrawny, even for twelve. But every time he visited, we would drive to some state park for an afternoon, and I'd try not to let on how hard those hikes were for me and he'd pretend not to notice. For my fourteenth birthday, he bought me my first really cool pair of boots and a book on the Appalachian Trail. In the front cover, he wrote we'd hike it together someday and until then, we'd be in training. Every time he's been home, we've tackled bigger trails, longer hikes, getting ready one visit at a time.

When he was home last spring, we started talking for real about the Appalachian Trail. We'd need five or six months, maybe seven, to thru-hike the whole thing — not possible while T.J. was still on active duty. But he said we could start section-hiking it, doing a part every year. My job while he was deployed was to plan the first section hike for the summer after his tour.

That local five-day trip last spring was supposed to be kind of like a trial run. We got a spot at a campground out past Pittsburgh, so we could do a bunch of day hikes on some new, more difficult trails. I thought there was no way that Dad would go for it. But he didn't say anything about the plan, not even when we were packing the truck to leave. Instead, he hovered, staring, making me nervous and T.J. tense.

"Junior." Only Dad called T.J. that. "Run his ass off. Got to start getting him ready for Basic." He was looking at T.J., but he was talking to me. "We're gonna make a man out of him yet. Knock out the pantywaist he's in danger of becoming."

T.J. eyed me, then the truck. But before I could get around and in, Dad cuffed me at the temple, toppling me into the side of the truck.

"Lay off, old man," T.J. said.

"Or what?" Dad stood in the way, keeping T.J. from tossing the last of the bags into the back. "I kicked your ass into gear. Think I'm gonna let this fairy—"

"I said enough." T.J. bumped Dad to the side with his shoulder.

Except for his bleached-out hair, just long enough to curl, T.J. looked more like Dad than ever, with his Dad-like gray-green eyes and his face tanned dark. Dad tensed in combat stance; only the gray in his receding crew cut giving away his age from behind. T.J. barely looked defensive at all. He was two inches shorter than Dad, but rock solid and seemingly relaxed, except for his jaw and the arms bulging across his chest. I left them to their staring and put my still-scrawny pansy ass in the car, well out of their mutual way.

The standoff ended abruptly with a silent truce — maybe Dad remembered that he wanted T.J. on his side in the campaign to make me enlist, or maybe T.J. decided kicking Dad's ass would just lead to more crap. Or maybe they both just decided it was stupid, or I wasn't worth it. Whatever the reason, they both backed off and we were on our way. All cool, except for the sick feeling in the pit of my stomach that whatever just happened wasn't really over.

T.J. and I were stopped at a light fifteen minutes outside of town when T.J. jumped into the conversation we had been avoiding for all of his leave, and probably longer.

"Matt, you're not seriously thinking of enlisting, are you?"

My gut twisted. "Sure. Why not?"

He scratched at his arm, watching for the light to change. "Any chance you could go to college? You know, if you got your grades up?"

"No." There didn't really seem much point in debating the possibility that some shitty school somewhere might take Dad's money despite my grades. I wasn't going.

T.J. grunted, shaking his head and tightening his grip on the steering wheel: so much like Dad, with a lot of the frustration, but with the very important lack of desire to kill me.

The light changed. We drove on. And T.J. chewed on whatever he wanted to say. And whatever it was, I knew I didn't want to hear it.

"Hey," I said, trying for levity, "Basic's gotta be a helluva lot better than four more years of school. It's shorter, and who knows, after life with Dad, I might enjoy the gentle strains of a drill sergeant and the predictability of Basic Training. Not to mention meals cooked by someone else at regular intervals."

"No. You wouldn't," T.J. said. "And Basic isn't what I'm worried about."

I didn't need a lecture.

"Matt." He grabbed my shoulder and squeezed it until I looked at him. "I'm not saying you couldn't get through Basic, though I do think it would kick your ass. But later, the reality of actually being in the Army?" T.J. shook his head, rolling to a stop at the next light. "I'm just saying I don't think you want that, and . . . I don't think I want that for you."

"You think I'm not strong enough? I've got a year to get ready. I'll be so —"

"Whoa, killer. Chill. I'm not saying you couldn't make it. I'm saying you'd be miserable. I'm saying you'd hate it. Every day. And I've seen too many guys . . . hate every minute of it." He stared through me until the light turned green, and then he settled in to drive again. "See, I'm saying you'd be better off doing something else, something that can't get you killed."

It felt like he'd punched me. He might as well have said

to leave the fighting to the men, who could handle it, unlike me. I wanted to climb out of the truck and walk home rather than spend the next five days with someone who thought I wasn't good enough, wasn't strong enough—hell, wasn't man enough—to do what he did, and what lots of other guys he knew did.

"Look," T.J. said. "You don't want to go, right?" I tried to make myself say I wanted it. "Right?" he asked again. The silence stretched until we coasted up to another light. "Then you shouldn't go. Because even when you want it, when you sign on ready for it, it'll kick your ass. But the guys who don't want it? Who sign on 'cause they have to or think they have no other choice? I've seen too many of them crack up in Basic, or worse. The ones who do make it through, well, some of them never really get their feet under them. And by the time they realize what a huge mistake they've made, it's too late, and they're shaking scared the whole fucking time, which makes them dangerous to themselves and to everyone around them." T.J. looked at me for a quick, tense moment before focusing on the road again. "Too many of them end up dead."

I couldn't move.

"Being miserable all the time can really screw with your head, can slow you down. Make you sloppy. Get you killed. Get a whole lot of people killed. So if you want it, go for it. I'll cheer you on. But if you don't, if you're just doing it for him, or me, or whatever, then don't fucking sign up. You can't."

My eyes stung, prickling and blurry.

"Do something else," he added. "Something where you won't get shot if you are so miserable that your mind wanders or you just stop caring."

Having said his piece, T.J. seemed fine with the quiet, with letting it go now that he was done, like we could just push all the you're-not-good-enough behind us and go pretend everything was great. That he hadn't just confirmed exactly what I thought he thought of me.

I couldn't let it go.

"It's not like I'm really gonna have a choice," I said, looking out the window. "I'm not going to college. And he's always said college or—"

"Don't let him bully you into it. Stall. Figure something else out. Junior college or some other kind of school. Or get a job. I'll help you deal with Dad. But you're gonna have to figure out what you're gonna do instead."

"Stall?" My voice cracked like it hadn't in years.

"Jesus, Matt, it's time to grow a pair. You're gonna have to stand up to him sometime. Until you do, he's just gonna keep going at you."

The shame of hiding in the car while he stared Dad down rushed to my face.

"It's your life, Matt. What do you want to do? Dad can drag you down to the enlistment office. But even if he hauled you through the door, they wouldn't accept you unless you willingly signed the papers. So, what do you want?"

"What do I want?" He had to be shitting me. "I want to *not* have you and Dad on my ass all the time." I wanted Dad to go a week without trying to make me flinch or shoving me into a wall. "You left." I wanted T.J. to come home, to want to *be* home. Even when he visited, he wasn't really *here*. "You're never here. You have no idea. Why . . . I mean . . . who the hell are you to, to . . ." I lost steam when my eyes started stinging worse. "What do I want . . ."

At the next intersection, T.J. turned and looked at me. "Do. Not. Enlist." Each word bounced off my brain. "Period."

"Oh, you mean, like you did?" There was so much pressure in my lungs and ears. "And you did OK, right? I mean, you didn't really want to join, at least not at first, but you made it. You're OK, right? I can handle it."

T.J. coasted to the wide shoulder on the side of the road and put the truck in park. He released his seat belt and rubbed his hands over his eyes. He stared out his window for a few seconds before he turned and looked at me again. He crossed his arms over the letters spelling ARMY across his shirt and let out this long sigh.

"Matt," he started, and then trailed off, taking another deep breath and letting it out before continuing, "I chose to go. I talked about it with Dad. I met with the recruiter and decided on my specialization. Me. I chose it."

Scenes flashed through my head. Dad tossing brochures at him across the dinner table. T.J. slamming his door and yelling. All that summer before, the tension between T.J. and

Dad over it. That last morning, T.J. acting like such a jerk and refusing to have breakfast with us and stomping out to the car. He and Dad yelling at each other in the car while Mrs. Gruber held my shoulders to keep me from running after them.

"I knew, deep down, that I needed to get out of here," T.J. said. "I was nothing here, less than nothing. And things with Dad . . . Yeah." T.J. smiled. "I fought Dad. Just enough so he didn't think I was going 'cause he told me to. But deep down, I was relieved. I wanted to go. It was my best chance to actually become something."

But. But he, and Dad . . .

"If I had stayed . . ." T.J. shrugged, his arms moving up and down over the letters across his chest. "I have no idea where I'd be, assuming Dad and I didn't kill each other, or . . ." T.J. swallowed the thought, a sour one by the look on his face. "The point is, this was the right thing for me. For *me*. Then. Now. I'd do it all over again. But, Matt, we're at war. Wars that aren't going to end anytime soon. You enlist now, and you'll be deployed somewhere within a year, maybe sooner."

I swallowed hard, my throat tight and dry.

"Fine if you're ready. They'll train you up, teach you what you need to know. But they can't teach you to want it. So, if you know what you want, and what you want is to serve, then you choose it—eyes open, fully committed, your choice. But if not . . ."

A shudder rolled through me.

"Yeah," he said. "If you let him bully you into it before you're ready, you're gonna be thoroughly screwed."

I was screwed no matter what. But . . .

"And if you're not sure, wait." He nodded and leaned closer to me. "Wait. It'll be there. Do something else for a while; see what you want. And if you decide later to join up, then great. It'll be your decision, and I'll be there to cheer you on. But don't do it for him, or me, or because you don't know what else to do. Do it because you want it, or not at all."

Something had just shifted between T.J. and me, something big. Like five of the eight and a half years between us evaporated.

"I don't want you to get yourself killed because you are trying to make him proud—or make me proud—or because you go before you're ready." My eyes burned. He laughed, shaking me a little. "Then I really would have to kick your ass." He was teasing, but I couldn't look at him.

I rubbed at my eyes. I felt like laughing, but it wouldn't come. All this time . . . all this time I'd been torturing myself, trying to talk myself into it, like I thought he had. Except not, because he'd wanted to go.

"SNAFU, right?" I finally asked. Situation normal: all fucked up. Like always.

With one more squeeze, he released my shoulder. "More like, Embrace the suck."

"Huh?" I didn't know that one.

T.J.'s face shifted into a crooked smile. "Embrace the suck. Yeah, the sitch with Dad and school and all sucks, but deal with it, 'cause you've got no other choice but to deal."

Embrace the suck. Should have been the Foster family motto. For generations. Laughter welled up from nowhere. I jerked with the effort of keeping it in, like holding in a cough. But it bubbled up again, and I just tipped my head back and let it come. I laughed until my eyes streamed, until my sides ached, until T.J. laughed with me, the kind of full-body laugh that makes everything feel good. We laughed until halfhearted hiccups of comfort and familiarity floated between us.

"Matt," he said, his voice so soft I had to lean a little closer to hear. He wouldn't look at me, and from the side I couldn't figure out the look on his face. "I'm a damn good soldier. Damn good." I could see him laughing at himself inside his own head, even though just a bit of smile and a little huff of laughter shook loose. "But I needed orders and discipline. I needed someone to take me apart and put me back together again, the right way, to make me strong, to give me honor." T.J. looked at me long and hard. He smiled again, but it didn't reach his eyes. "Whatever else I am, or whatever else I'm ever gonna be, I needed them to make me strong enough to be that man. But you, you're already smarter than me. And stronger, in your way—you've weathered Dad all by yourself. You have nothing to prove. To Dad. To me. To anyone, except maybe yourself. You'll find your way, a way that uses your smarts, and who you are, and that doesn't involve war."

T.J. put the truck back in gear before I could say anything, and I was glad, because I didn't trust myself to speak.

"Find something else, something that makes *you* happy."

My throat ached, my eyes blurred, but right then, driving down the road with T.J. behind the wheel, I wanted to just head west and keep going, away from Dad, away from T.J. having to report back, away from everything.

I wish we had.

four

"SIT." FIRST THING DAD'S SAID SINCE THE SINGLE QUESTION in the car.

He yanks one of the chairs out from under the kitchen table with his foot. With my ass planted there, Dad'll be between me and both exits from the kitchen. But I have no choice, so I sink into the chair. For the hundredth time since Pendergrast's office, I hope I've read Dad's mood right, and he's not just recharging for round two.

My neck's so stiff, it might break if I turn my head, so I give up trying to read his face. Instead, I track his path around the kitchen by sound.

Refrigerator. Sink. Cabinet. Sink. Freezer. Creak of the ice tray. Ice in a glass. Stray cubes in the sink. Clatter of empty ice tray on the counter. That cabinet opening. Twist of the screw top from the bottle. Whisper of scotch against ice. Long gulp. Silence. Crack-hiss of a can being opened. Silence. Clink of ice on glass. Smaller sip. Smacking lips. Silence. Deep breath. Silence. Movement. Then his feet are directly in front of me. I risk the pain to look up.

"Here." He thrusts a dish towel bundle at my chest and then motions toward my face. "Put it on that eye."

The bundle is clunky but dully cold, filled with some of Dad's precious ice. I hadn't expected that. I also hadn't expected the soda he plunks down in front of me on the table, the can hitting the scarred Formica just a little too hard. He directs me to the can with his chin and waits for me to take a sip before he continues with his drink.

"Thanks." I didn't get enough air behind it, but he doesn't seem to take it as weak, or mocking, or anything.

He settles into the chair next to me, stretches and shifts until he's comfortable. Then he moves to take another sip, but pauses with the glass halfway to his mouth. I brace for it, but he just takes a nice long drink. Then the glass is on the table. He exhales and smacks his lips again. It's a good sound. I can practically hear his muscles relaxing as the scotch does its thing.

"Do I want to know what happened?" Dad asks.

"Didn't Pendergrast—?"

"I want to hear it from you." His eyes don't move. Not even toward his drink.

"Usual crap."

I look down so he can pick up the glass. When he doesn't, I stare at it, watching the light filter through the scotch and ice. His hand flexes on the table. I hold my breath until he picks up the glass. I don't exhale until it's safely on the table again, his hands relaxed beside it.

"If it was usual, why today?"

"Don't know. I guess . . ." Shit. How many times has he said, *Don't guess. Know or shut the hell up?* "It was just too much today."

"And?"

Clink of ice. Smacked lips. Glass on the table.

"And I lost it."

"What did his shirt say?"

Shit.

Dad cracks his neck. "Pendergrast. He said something about if the kid was saying crap, maybe even his usual crap . . . but that this time it was something about his shirt?" The hand wave makes it clear Pendergrast tried to explain, but Dad was beyond caring then.

It'll sound lame. And if I say it wrong, or he thinks I'm messing with him, or even for just saying T.J.'s name, Dad could go ape-shit. But if I lie, and he catches me in it, I'm screwed.

I can see Pinscher's shirt in my head. Not the bloodied and ripped-up version from after the fight. How it looked before, when I closed my hand over the black words and yanked.

Dad's hand flexes.

I close my eyes, trying to breathe and to figure out how to say it.

"Today, please." Only Dad can make "please" sound scary.

"He was just there, like always, in my face." I open my

eyes and look at him. The words won't come. They're here, in my mouth, or throat, maybe even my stomach. I have to force something out. "I hit him. He was saying all this stuff. And, I hit him, and then . . . I just couldn't stop."

"The shirt?" Dad asks again.

"It had . . ." I stumble, catch my tongue, see it in my head: the red words on the front, *OUR Troops,* and on the back, *Pieces,* and then the black words, in my fist. I make myself say, "His name on it."

"So what if the little shit had his name—?"

"Not *his* name."

Dad stares, not getting it. The vein in his temple pulses. He rolls his shoulders. "Then—"

"T.J.'s."

All the air gets sucked out of the room.

"What?" Dad's hands clench into tight fists on the table.

"It was a list, of troops. And . . ." Acid climbs up around the knot in my gut.

"Troops?" His hands unclench and clench again. Tighter. He shifts and leans closer, swelling in his chair. "This kid. His shirt. Had a list of troops—"

"Yes." Stupid. Never get in the way of Dad exploding. "It said, *Support OUR Troops. OUR,* like, from around here. And on the back . . ." I can still see it in my head—and my hand, covering T.J.'s name, like I could make it go away.

His jaw locks like a spring trap. His fists go white-knuckled with rage. I'm not sure how long we sit there, but he doesn't reach for his drink once. My legs fall asleep. I float out the top of my head, wait for the explosion.

"This kid." His voice makes me shiver. "He had your brother's name on his shirt?"

"Yes." Everything's far away, except for Dad's hands.

"And he knew you'd seen it?"

His focus could shift fast. I nod.

"How?" he asks.

"I could see some of it from across the hall, the *Support OUR Troops: Bring Them Home* part, and on the back . . ."

He focuses hard on me.

Burning sour creeps up my throat. *"Not in . . . pieces."* Then all the names on back. And T.J.'s name. I gag.

Dad pushes the soda closer. I take a gulp, then another. I have to say the rest.

"I made him turn around, so I could see the names, and . . . I covered . . . I . . . grabbed . . . it." I swallow. "He knew. Michael told him to put his sweatshirt back on, but . . ."

Dad's eyes go distant. His hands are palm down and calm on the table. I wait.

Finally, he blinks and looks at me again, in a way he hasn't looked at me in forever. His neck relaxes and his head bobs for a few beats. I mimic his nod of recognition. Amazing. We're cool. I press the ice against my eye to hide my relief.

Dad lifts his glass. Two sips. He rolls the glass between his hands, the ice and golden liquid swirling back and forth. Another long sip.

My stomach growls. Dad grunts a laugh. Not a bad sign, all things considered.

He waves the ice away from my eye. It takes everything not to flinch when his hands come near my face. He presses his thumbs along the bones under my eyes and across my jaw, runs his hands over my shoulders, ribs, and finally ruffles through my hair, feeling my skull.

He must be satisfied, because in one fluid move he gets up, grabs his drink, and pushes his chair back under the table with his foot. In the doorway between the kitchen and the living room, he turns and uses his drink to signal for my attention, like I would take my eyes off him until he was out of the room.

"You're out of school until next Tuesday. Pendergrast wanted you to do some bullshit in-school suspension for part of it, but I told him where to go. No one is putting you on display for doing what needed doing."

I nod again, accepting the time.

"So, get some sleep. Take it easy for a few days. But don't think you're gonna laze around the house for the next week. You'll need to work. That display case is gonna cost a chunk."

Great.

"And from what I hear, you've got some serious studying to do." He narrows his eyes. "We talked about this, after the midterm reports."

Yeah, the side of my head still remembers the slap that ended that little chat.

"Hey."

I clench my teeth to stay quiet.

"Failing? Not an option." His eyebrows climb. "You want to piss away any chance at college? I can't really stop you." Another sip, and then the glass is in motion as he waves it for emphasis. "Means no ROTC. No Officer Candidate School. You want to throw all that away? Fine. But if you think you're going to blow finals, flunk out, and that'll be it? Get you out of college *and* enlisting? Think again, boy."

I press my split knuckles against my leg to keep still.

He takes a step back toward me and stops, like something is holding him back from coming all the way over here, something I should be very thankful for.

"If I have to sit on your ass for the entire time it takes you to get your GED, kick it every day until you are enlistment eligible, I'll do it. It'll suck for both of us, but if I have to drag you every step, I'll get you there."

I force myself to stay still. If he comes any closer, I may not be able to keep from running.

He points at me with his nondrink hand. "I am not gonna watch you implode."

It's not like it's my life or anything.

"You hearing me?" He shifts his feet.

"Yes, sir." Reflexive and voice cracking, but enough to keep him where he is.

"Time to get your ass in gear. Or so help me . . ."

He turns fast and leaves the room, the words hanging behind him.

I stay at the table until I hear the groan of his recliner and the hiss-click of the TV turning on. I wait for the garbled sound of twenty-four-hour news and the creaking shifting of Dad's weight settling down. Only then do I let my shoulders relax and release my tired legs. It's safe to find something to eat and head to bed. He's done for the night.

I choke down half a bowl of soggy cereal before my stomach revolts. Leaning into the cold edge of the table, I breathe through my nose, trying to hold off the puke. Sour burn crawls up the back of my throat. And I'm right back there, six months ago.

I was sitting right here, debating between eggs and grilled cheese, chugging the last of the orange juice straight from the carton, when I felt something crawling over the back of my neck. I turned my head toward the door, spilling juice all over my chin and down the front of my gray T-shirt. I was half-way to the door, nearly empty carton still in my hand, when I heard them on the front steps. I opened the door before they even rang the bell. I knew. Before I even saw the uniforms, I knew.

five

THE UNIFORMS ASKED FOR DAD AND THEN DIDN'T SAY another word. I had trouble getting anything out loud enough to carry upstairs, and I couldn't move.

All I could think was *T.J. is dead.*

When I got my voice to work, it took three yells before Dad cursed and stomped down from upstairs. He was ready to rip me a new one for making him come to me, but then he saw me, and then them, and he missed the last step, landing with a lurch. I wanted him to say something, but he just looked at them.

After that moment of flinching, almost stumbling, shock, Dad was stoic: nodding gravely, shaking hands, dead. They said their spiel. I couldn't hear it over the noise in my head.

The woman, who did all the talking, was OK. Older. Calm. Somehow like she was as much a part of this as we were, but not like in our faces or anything. She shook my hand and didn't once look at the juice all over my shirt.

The guy hovered near the door until she gave some kind of signal, and then they left, like they'd never been there.

A different uniform showed up later—our CAO, casualty assistance officer, Cooper. He was younger than the others, and friendly, but all business, with papers and questions, a binder full of stuff to be done. While CAO Cooper was making a call, Dad downed two quick drinks standing at the sink, staring out the back window. Then he brushed his teeth and gargled. When he came back into the living room, Dad acted like everything was fine, like we were just having some kind of visit. I could smell the mint from all the way across the room. I'm sure Cooper could, too, and that he knew exactly why. Before going into the living room, Dad snagged my arm and shot daggers at my shirt, shoving me toward the stairs, like Cooper cared what I was wearing or what I smelled like.

Eventually some neighbors came by, crying, carrying stuff, smiling sad fucking smiles. Dad stared *them* out the door. Then the reporters and the cameras. Cooper got some other uniform to handle them. One short interview and then Dad ran them off, too.

All through the planning, Dad stayed mellow, quiet, slightly buzzed. Just dull enough to handle it, I guess, but it made him slow sometimes. Too slow. Cooper would sometimes look at me when Dad would zone out for a minute, like I could do anything, or even acknowledge that there was anything that needed doing or why. But he'd just wait, like no time had passed, until Dad could handle it again.

I just wanted it all to go away. The people. The plans. The uniforms. Everything. I'd have given anything to have gone to sleep and woken up when it was over. The constant, awful anticipation was choking me.

Everyone had all these questions, but no one could answer the only one I cared about. No one would tell me what happened.

Eight days later, a different uniform, the "escort," arrived with what was left of T.J. He said the least. I don't remember his name, but I remember his face clearly. He was about T.J.'s age and height, but his hair and eyes were dark. There was a scar on his cheek, a rippling, pinkish line from his sideburn to his jaw. He had that hard-body stance like the guys in T.J.'s unit, like a steel rod had been grafted onto his spine. When he shook my hand, he nearly crushed my fingers. But he looked me in the eyes.

The morning of the funeral, he sat Dad and me down in a small office at the back of the funeral home and pulled out a bag with what was left of T.J.'s stuff. One by one, he passed the things to Dad.

T.J.'s dog tags, gleaming on their chain, like they had been scrubbed and polished.

His beat-up sport watch, band fraying a little near the buckle, a patch of some kind of tape on the other side.

The multi-tool I'd bought him for Christmas a few years ago. Scratched but clean, and shiny.

A braided leather bracelet.

A small compass on a chain, the size of a quarter, the arms bright green on the black face.

Some kind of medallion on a cord.

The escort left the room—to give us some privacy, I guess. Or maybe because he could see that Dad wanted him gone.

Dad let me touch everything, but then took each thing back and put it in the bag, bending one of my fingers to the side to get the dog tags out of my hand. He shook his head, sneering at the medallion and tossing it into the bag hard. He pulled the cord tight, sealing the bag. I reached for it, but he slid it into the pocket of his jacket. His hand patted it secure.

Whatever had happened to T.J., it was bad. Bad enough that the casket was gonna stay closed. But before the escort left, he and Dad went down front and the funeral director showed them the inside of the casket. I just got a glimpse before Dad turned away, blocking my view. Enough to see a crisp and perfect uniform draped over something lumpy where legs should have been. The crease in the pants was so sharp, like brand-new. Seemed stupid. No one was gonna see. But Dad liked it—not that he actually said anything.

During the funeral, I kept having this daydream that maybe they got it wrong. Maybe T.J. was still alive, in a hospital even, but didn't remember who he was, and this was some other guy blown so much apart that they couldn't tell who he was, and he'd somehow ended up with T.J.'s dog tags, or he'd been near T.J. and they got confused. Anything to make this make sense.

Some of the guys who had served with T.J. were there, in the back, and I thought about asking them, asking if it was possible. But none of them seemed to question for even a second that it was T.J. in the box, and I figured they would know.

But then, after, Dad pulled out the bag of stuff again. Maybe he was thinking the same thing, rubbing the medallion, and the compass, one in each hand. Because T.J. never wore necklaces or went to church. And I'd never seen that stuff before.

"What is that?" I asked.

"Some saint," Dad said, staring at the medallion.

"Why would—?"

"Hell if I know why your brother does anything."

The conversation was over. Everything was shoved back into the bag, and it disappeared back into Dad's pocket. Later, when Uncle Mac and Aunt Janelle came over, Dad stuck it in the top drawer of the hutch.

After the funeral—after the hellish drive back, with half the town still waving flags on the side of the road—Dad had no need for any of the uniforms or the stuff they offered. Me neither. A few weeks after the funeral, when Dad was out of the room, CAO Cooper gave me a bunch of stuff, pamphlets and sheets, a card with a bunch of numbers on it. I said thanks but threw them away. I didn't want to see another uniform for the rest of my life.

But as much as the uniforms and the neighbors sucked, the strangers were the worst. They would send stuff or call; a couple even showed up at the door, with plants and ribbons. They never came twice.

We ignored Thanksgiving. And Christmas. Somehow New Year's sucked the hardest, knowing T.J. wouldn't see 2007.

The condolence letters slowed after a while but kept coming. And every one Dad dumped unopened in a box in the hall closet. Every single one. Who knows how many.

The first few months were surreal. Some days dragged on like they were eight days long. Others flashed by like blinking in bright light. There were days where Shauna picked me up for school and dropped me off after, and an hour later I couldn't remember a single thing that had happened in between. More than once, a teacher had to say my name to get me to leave a class, because I hadn't noticed the bell. The worst days, though, were the ones where everything was too bright and too loud and I couldn't catch my breath for one fucking minute: those were like a nightmare.

Since T.J. had never really done more than visit since he left for Basic, it was easy at first to imagine that it hadn't happened at all—that I'd dreamed the whole scene with the uniforms and Dad, and the ribbons and neighbors and strangers at the door. But then I would go into the kitchen and see the casseroles. Or later, the box in the hall closet. A condolence letter showed up in the mail, and I was right back there, waiting to breathe.

I didn't go into the living room much, and never past Dad's recliner. But the hutch in the corner seemed to glow, waiting for me. And sometimes when I'd walk through to get to the front door, something would make me look, and then I'd stop walking and stare. More than once, Dad ran into me because I just stopped midstride on my way to the door.

In February I got up the nerve to look at T.J.'s stuff again. I crept through the living room, past Dad's recliner, around the table full of Dad's magazines, and over to the hutch in the corner. But when I opened the top drawer, the bag wasn't there. I waited for a night when I knew Dad would be out, and then I went through every drawer and rifled through the stuff on the shelves.

Over spring break, I searched the whole house — nothing.

No bag, and none of the stuff that was inside. No sign of the flag from T.J.'s coffin, either.

A few weeks ago, the pictures of T.J. that had been scattered around the house disappeared. I came home and they were gone. All of them. Like he'd never even existed. Like after Mom died. And I instantly knew I'd left some clue, something out of place or the dust disturbed. Something to tell Dad that I'd gone looking for the bag. And his removing everything else was a clear message.

For about a week, I stewed and avoided Dad. Then I started searching the whole house, drawer by drawer. I started outside: the storage shed, the garage. Then I worked my way from the kitchen out, searching every drawer and cupboard and box in the downstairs.

Last Friday I decided to check the upstairs again. But before I'd even opened a door, I heard Dad's car. He caught me in the living room near the stairs. He didn't come right out and say he knew I'd been up there, but his look made it pretty clear. And pretty clear that if he ever caught me up there again, I was screwed.

So many times I tried to figure out how to bring it up, how to ask about the bag. Every time, I chickened out. Friday, when he caught me, I actually got half a question out. But he got in my space so fast, warned me off without saying a word. Stared me down. And I wussed out. Like always.

All weekend he'd rocket up to high alert out of nowhere. He'd jolt up out of his chair or stalk into the kitchen, ready, for whatever he thought he'd see. If I was in there, he'd stare for a minute before standing down, fading back into the living room. If I was down in my room, I'd hear him hovering near the door at the top of the stairs or on the landing near the laundry room, listening. I started keeping some music or a movie on, just so he'd have something to hear.

It felt like every time I breathed, he was on me, and I wasn't doing *anything*. Every time he shifted his jaw or came anywhere near me, I thought he might preemptively toss me into a wall. This morning I jetted out the side door early, knowing that if I stayed one more minute, I wouldn't get away.

All the way to school, it all churned and curdled in my stomach.

And then there was Pinscher—one day, one shirt, one asshole move too many.

* * *

I pull the scrap from my pocket.

Army Sgt. Theodore James Foster Jr. Black on white, and now with rusting blood around the edges, where my hand didn't cover it.

T.J. would have ripped that shirt off Pinscher and fed it to him.

That's what I should have done: I should have made him swallow it, name by name.

six

The shower goes a long way to washing away the last of the fight. But everything feels heavy and tired after, like the wet cement has spread from my hand through the rest of me.

The recliner creaks in the living room above. When T.J. left for Basic, we were both still in our old rooms upstairs, across the hall from each other, down the hall from Dad. And for a while, even after it was clear T.J. wasn't moving home anytime soon, I stayed in my old room. But at the start of sophomore year, I moved down here to the basement apartment. Should have done it sooner: with its own bathroom, the kitchen at the top of the stairs, and the side entrance through the laundry room in between, I can go for days without actually seeing Dad.

I flick on my desk lamp. The circle of light spotlights the map hanging on the wall next to my desk—stretching from just above my head to my knees, the entire length of the Appalachian Trail, with different colors for states and parks, rivers and roads.

In my head, so much of that five-day hike last spring is a dying fire and darkness and T.J.'s voice. We talked for hours every night, but we didn't talk about any of the important stuff, nothing that really mattered.

I was so freaking focused on hiking the Appalachian Trail. That's all I wanted to talk about, what would happen when he came home, when we could go, how much fun it would be.

The week after he left, I bought the map.

In the desk lamp's spotlight, I can see the holes where the pushpins used to be, a ghost trail marking a trek we're never going to make.

I push the lamp so the circle of light doesn't land on the map.

My phone plays Shauna's ringtone. Even without her ringtone, I'd have known it was Shauna; she's the only person who really gives a shit if I'm OK. Yeah, things have been weird between us, but she hasn't cut and run yet.

I barely have the phone to my ear before she launches in: "How long did you have to wait for your dad?"

"A while. We haven't been home that long."

"Did he go postal?"

"Naw. Not really."

"Suspended?"

"Yeah. Until next Tuesday."

"But just suspended? Good. Then you can still take finals."

"Yeah, unfortunately."

"Don't suppose anyone thought to get your head checked out?"

I laugh. "Sure. Twice. And then Dad took me for ice cream. Tomorrow we're—"

"That's what I thought, so I looked up some stuff online, and then I called Jenna. She was working, and the ER was hectic, but she talked me through the signs of danger."

To have called her sister, Shauna must really be worried. They drive each other crazy. But at least Jenna's one of the sisters who actually likes me.

"So, here we go. Do you feel . . . ?"

She's relentless. Barking questions until I answer them, rattling off warning signs of imminent coma. On the plus side, having something to do calms her down. When I can't take her fussing another minute, I cut her off.

"Shaun! Seriously, I'll be fine."

"You could have a concussion," she says, like I'm a moron, or like I'm not actually attached to my head. "What am I saying! You absolutely have a concussion. Your head bounced off, like, three different hard surfaces, not including people's fists. How do you know your brain isn't getting all scrambled right now?"

"How would we tell?"

"Matt." Obviously, humor's not gonna work. "Be serious. Jenna said that if you have a concussion, you need to be checked every couple of hours. Who's going to do that? You need to go to the hospital. I can come and get you right now."

Fuck. Dad *will* go postal if she comes over here. "The nurse checked me out at school. If she thought I was in any danger, they'd have taken me to the hospital," I say, hoping she's buying it.

When she doesn't respond, I go for diversion. "And how the hell do you know what my head hit?"

"Michael," she says, her voice saying so much more.

Of course.

"I could come over and keep watch. Or we could call ahead and Jenna could—"

"You can't come over here, and the only place I'm going is to sleep. Call me tomorrow."

I don't hang up fast enough, and she argues some more. She finally gives up, but with a very Shauna-like catch. "OK. Leave your phone on. I'm going to call you every two hours to make sure you haven't slipped into a coma. And if you don't answer—"

"Shaun . . ."

"Matt," she mimics back. "If you don't answer, I'm coming over there. Those are your choices. Hospital now or monitoring by telephone."

"Every two hours? I think I'll chance the coma."

We go four more rounds, and then she hangs up half-way through my turn. The debate's over. She always gets the last word.

★ ★ ★

Our old house on Mulberry Street was two doors down from the house Shauna still lives in. We played in the sprinkler on her front lawn. Rode bikes up and down the block. I never knocked before running in her back door.

When things were good, Mom made us grilled-cheese sandwiches and chocolate milk with bendy straws. Shauna always left her crusts, but she would nibble down to the very outer edge trying to get all the cheese. I would bend my straw back and forth like an accordion, making fart noises, just to make Shauna laugh. The first time I did it, by accident, she spewed milk out her nose.

"That's enough of that," Mom said, confiscating my straw.

I didn't care, because Shauna was still laughing, despite the chocolate milk everywhere.

Mom wiped Shauna's hands and face, pretending to be annoyed but laughing and shaking her head and finally tapping the end of Shauna's nose with her finger.

"Thanks, Mrs. Foster." Mom didn't even hear her, because Shauna talked really softly when we were little, before we started school, at least when anyone else was around.

I heard T.J.'s cleats on the back porch, and so did Shauna. She stared at the door with big eyes, nibbling at her lip, waiting for him. She didn't have any brothers, and she was kind of in awe of T.J., at least when T.J. wasn't being mean.

"Eh! Cleats off," Mom yelled before T.J. could get through the door. "I swear, if you track mud through here again, you're going to be spending the afternoon—"

"Yeah, yeah," T.J. said. He was thirteen and almost as tall as Mom. He leaned against the door frame, kicking his cleats off onto back the porch, grinning the whole time, like it was a game.

He thought he was so cool just because he was on the traveling baseball team with the older kids.

"Time to cut that hair," Mom said, miming with her fingers and catching some of T.J.'s hair. He swatted her hand away, then ducked past her toward the fridge.

"Go wash up first." Mom sighed, waving him down the hall.

On his way past, T.J. slimed my ear with his spit-wet finger.

"Quit it!" I yelled.

"Teddy!" Only Mom got to call him that. Even then, he'd have beat my ass if I called him Teddy. "Act your age, please."

"Mo-om," I whined, rubbing my ear.

"I know, bud," she said, like she couldn't do anything about T.J.'s wet willies.

Shauna rolled her head to her shoulder in sympathy, or maybe to protect her own ear.

T.J. slid into his chair next to me and swiped half my sandwich before I remembered to protect my plate. He took a huge bite while I shrieked. After he put it back, he grabbed my milk and pretended to drink it. I tried to grab it back, but I couldn't reach far enough without jumping off my chair.

"Teddy, cut it out." Mom plucked my favorite red plastic

cup from his hand and put it back next to my plate. I pushed my ruined sandwich half onto the table.

"Mom," I whined, already feeling the heat and tears hit my eyes, but trying not to cry in front of Shauna.

"I'll make you another half," she said, rubbing her hand over my head, trying to calm me down.

It was no fair. He always got away with stuff.

T.J. chugged some milk, then burped really loud. Shauna giggled.

I was so mad. I didn't want her laughing at T.J. She was *my* friend. And he was being a jerk.

He nudged my leg with his foot and did it again — chugging more milk and burping. But this time, it was like we were playing together. I gulped down some milk, tucked my chin, and forced out the smallest burp.

"Nice!" T.J. said, high-fiving me. My hand stung from the too-hard slap.

"Lovely," Mom said, shaking her head but smiling again.

And when Shauna laughed, it was for me.

It was the last good summer, and the last year T.J. played baseball.

That summer we practically lived in the kitchen, Mom and T.J. and me. Dad worked a lot, and sometimes he would go away for a few days if he had sites to inspect too far away to drive back and forth. When he was away, we planned parties just for us, and indoor picnics, or went to the lake until dark.

But even when Dad was around, a lot of the time Mom

would make us our own dinner before Dad got home. We'd have breakfast for dinner, or tacos, hot dogs, or pizzas with faces out of the toppings, things that were more fun than the boring food Dad wanted. And we talked, and made up stories, and laughed. She had a great laugh. When she laughed. When things were good. Before it all went to hell.

Before that summer ended, things were different. Mom was different. Some days she wouldn't even get out of bed.

Mom walked me into preschool that first day, but she started freaking out when it was time to leave, and Mrs. Gruber had to calm her down.

By Halloween Mrs. Gruber was picking me up most days and taking me to her house until Dad got home. Mom rallied around Christmas, but was all weird again by Valentine's Day. In April, I came home one day and she was gone.

A few months after Mom left, we heard she was in Philadelphia, living in the basement of a church or something. An hour away, and it might as well have been the other side of the world.

When the police came to the door to tell Dad she was dead, Dad didn't invite them in. If there was a funeral, no one told me.

Dad moved us to the new house a couple months after Mom died, four blocks from the old one. None of the pictures of Mom or her things came with us, not even the big picture of all four of us that had hung in the hall my whole life.

After we moved, Shauna didn't come over as much, but

we still spent more time together than apart on weekends — at least for a while. Then she found soccer, and a whole bunch of new friends, girl friends. Later, the guys who hung around her girl friends. One day I looked up and she had a boyfriend, and huge tits, and everything about her made me hard. But to her, I was still just her old friend Matt.

It's been getting harder to ignore how hard she is to ignore. Sometimes it's so stupid — she does something with her hand or mouth or laughs at a joke or, hell, sits too close, and I'm scrambling for cover. I have to remind myself not to stare.

She has soccer, and her other friends, her "girls' nights," and sometimes a party. Sometimes she goes on dates, and I sit home and try not to think about what she could be doing.

I have her calls and her texts, car rides to and from school, and a night or two a week when it's just us — not to mention all my fantasy versions of her, who fill in when she's off having a life.

And since November, we have all this new weirdness — mostly mine, I know — getting in the way. She'd been busy all fall, fitting me in, between everything and everyone else. I was pissed at her. Sometimes even at the fantasy versions of her. But when we heard, I couldn't call her, couldn't say it, and I'm not sure she's ever going to forgive me for her having to hear that T.J. was dead from someone else.

Still, after T.J. died, she was right there, whenever I thought I'd lose it. But it got so that I couldn't breathe.

I couldn't tell her what I needed—too close to saying what I wanted, and I felt like shit for wanting anything when he was dead.

She spent one too many nights trying to carry a conversation by herself, then she pushed a little too hard and I said some stuff I can never take back, about how she'll never understand. For a few weeks, we hardly talked at all. Things got better for a while, but not back to where we were. There's only so much of her worried looks I can take, but at least now I bail before I can say something to make her go away for good.

Dad's recliner creaks and groans overhead. I can track his bedtime routine by the sounds. Slow steps to the kitchen. The water runs as he washes his glass. After the water, he checks the back door—open, close, lock. Lights off. Then down the hall and up the stairs, the sound of the creaky second step, and a few minutes later he flushes the toilet and water flows through the pipes. Walking down the hall, into his room, probably dropping his watch and wallet on the bureau, tossing his clothes in the hamper. Then the squeaking bedsprings. Every night—at least the nights when he makes it upstairs—it's the same routine. Once he's snoring away, he's out until morning, barring something really, really loud—like a train through the living room.

I creep up the stairs and stand in the open door to the

kitchen, listening for the bedsprings. Back downstairs, I slide under the covers. Shauna will be calling in less than two hours.

And yet, for ten minutes I lie there awake, thinking.

All that's left of T.J. is in that bag.

No way Dad would just throw away the flag from T.J.'s coffin. Wherever it is, the bag has to be there, too.

I'm not giving up.

I won't give up until I find it. Or until there's nowhere else to look.

Yeah, I've already looked everywhere. Time to look harder. Time to start emptying boxes, moving furniture, banging on walls, and pulling up floorboards.

I can snoop around the downstairs and out back in the shed or garage whenever.

But I'll take a look at Dad's book, see where he's scheduled to be the rest of the week. Whatever day he's farthest away, I'll tackle the upstairs again. Less chance he'll stop home and catch me.

Better wait until Thursday or Friday, at least. Maybe then I'll have healed enough I can outrun him if I get caught.

seven

As threatened, Shauna calls every couple hours for all of Monday night into Tuesday morning, well past the time when it's clear I'm not gonna slip into a coma. Eventually, I threaten to turn off my phone if she keeps it up, and she finally stops.

With Dad gone and my phone silent, I sleep until lunchtime.

But once I'm awake, I start to go stir-crazy. The quiet's making me nuts. I'm climbing out of my skin. Too awake and jittery to sleep. Too achy to move. Kind of hungry, but too pukeish to actually try to make something.

The stupid part is I miss Shauna's calls. They'd be a good distraction. Especially because then we'd hang up and I'd be here, by myself, with time to kill and her voice still in my head.

But she won't call now, and there's no way I can call her, not after making such a scene to get her to stop.

The upstairs is tempting me. But it would be suicide to risk it today. He's local, and no telling when he might decide to stop home. Worse, even if I had a couple hours, it's not enough. I need a whole day so I can search hard but slow, and careful, and have time to put things back together right. One single thing out of place could give it away. Can't risk it. Not today. Besides, I can barely move.

I snuck into Dad's bag last night and looked at his book. He's local all week. But next week he's scheduled to be way up north. Means he'll leave early, be home late, and there'll be no chance of him surprising me. I'll have to find a way — go in late or cut out early, something.

The phone rings, as if he's sensed what I'm planning. The house phone. I don't even have to look at the caller ID: Dad.

"You up?"

"Yes," I say, trying not to shift and make the bedsprings squeak. And good morning to you, too, Dad.

"Good. Enough lazing around. Find something productive to do." The "or else" hangs there between us.

"I already left a message for Mr. Anders to see if he can get me on a crew later this week." It's a lie, but a harmless one. Dad'll never call Anders to check.

Dad says something to someone else, his voice just as irritated as with me. Good to know that not all that pissed off is about me.

"Call Anders again. See if he has anything tomorrow." Tomorrow? "Dominick low-balled his bid on the display case, but he couldn't go below twelve sixty-five." Twelve hundred dollars? "I want this paid and done asap. I told Pendergrast you'd have the first half in by the last day of classes."

Half? No fucking—

"No way he gets to say shit about this family, like he's gonna have to chase us for it."

Shit. Dead set on some insane deadline, just to make this suck that much harder. "I'm not sure—"

"Call him again." Dad hangs up without anything else. No "I'll be home for dinner" or asking how I feel.

I stare at the phone, ready to chuck it against the wall. Everything still hurts like hell, but I've got two weeks to come up with more than six hundred dollars. Even with what I've got saved up, it's gonna be tough.

T.J. worked for Anders & Sons all through high school, and I've worked for Mr. Anders the last three summers. That first summer, he just had me mowing lawns or running errands or doing other odd stuff now and then when I needed money—like picking up supplies at the hardware store or cleaning the paintbrushes at the end of the day. But the last two summers, I've worked my way up to a full-time spot on one of the crews that comes in after the serious renovation work is done. Usually I sand, paint, clean up, or install the final touches, the light-switch covers and doorknobs and cabinet doors and handles. It's not bad—the guys are OK, and I make more than I could doing pretty much anything else.

I return the phone to the cradle and dig for Mr. Anders's cell number. While I listen to the phone ring, I brace for the conversation. He'll find me something. I know he will. But he'll be pissed I got suspended. Maybe so mad he won't let me work during the days I should be in school. It would be just like him to say I should study and not get to make money for getting in trouble.

"You need the money badly?" Mr. Anders asks after I ask if he can give me any work right away.

"Yeah. I have to come up with twelve hundred dollars fast. Any way you can use me this week?"

"*This* week?"

"Yeah, I was hoping Thursday and Friday." Not tomorrow. Probably couldn't hold a hammer or crouch down tomorrow, but I'll have to by Thursday. "Then maybe after school and weekends until school's done?"

"After school, weekends, sure, maybe. But Thursday? What about school? Matt—"

"I got suspended. There was a fight. Display case got busted. That's what I need the money for. I have to pay for it." Freaking Dad. "I really need the money."

Anders blows out a breath across the receiver and then mutters to himself for a minute. I know this is a lot to ask. He'll either be eating the extra cost or shorting someone else, one of his year-rounders, or maybe some guy with a wife and a bunch of kids.

"OK," Anders says. Some papers rustle near the phone. "I have an interior painting job a couple blocks from you. You can work that starting Thursday. The crew I've got you on for the summer doesn't start until the third week of June, but I'll look at the schedules and see if I can use you somewhere else until then."

"Great."

"Might not be painting. Might be some cleanup or hauling stuff."

"Whatever you have. It'll be great. I really appreciate it."

"OK, well, see you Thursday. Get there by eight. On Fenton. You'll see my sign out front."

I leave a voicemail for Dad, telling him about the job. Then make a circuit of the downstairs as best I can. I look everywhere I can without bending over or reaching too high—in every drawer and cabinet, in or under everything on the shelves and in the hutch. Then I knock on all of the panels and walls, looking for any space he could have hidden the bag or T.J.'s things. Nothing.

When I start jumping at every car outside, I spread my algebra notes out on my bed and pop in a movie I know so well I can close my eyes and just drift. Best if Dad finds me down here and zonked out, ignoring my homework, as he expects. Actually doing my homework would be that step too far.

The walk over to the job site on Thursday morning feels weird. The neighborhood is too quiet, with everyone off at work or school except for the old people, the moms, and the little kids. I keep looking over my shoulder, like a cop car or something's gonna come along and ask why I'm not in school. But by the time I get to the house, being out alone feels kind of cool, freeing, and my muscles are loosening up, less stiff with every step. I don't even have to look for the ANDERS & SONS sign, because Mr. Anders is out front, leaning against his black truck sporting the blue Anders & Sons logo on the side. Between all the years T.J. worked for him, and now me, we have a gazillion of his shirts, that logo across the back, splattered with a variety of different color paints.

A second too late to be smooth, I wipe my hand on my jeans and reach out to shake his hand. But when he sees my scabby, messed-up knuckles, his hand stops midair. Instead of shaking, we both pull our hands back and nod hello.

I don't know what to do or say, so I wait for him to start.

Somehow it feels like an interview, or a test: maybe he isn't sure he really wants me working for him anymore.

"Well, you don't look too bad," he finally says. But then he looks at my right hand again and looks away. For the first time I feel a little weird about the fight—maybe not the whole fight, but how bad it got. I pull my hand behind my leg so he can't see my knuckles. "Are you really up for working?"

"Yeah. Not everything, but I can sand, scrape, paint. Maybe not ceilings, because of the ladder, but . . ." I try to stand real straight, like my knee and shoulder aren't throbbing. "Yeah. And, uh, I really need the money."

"So you said." His mouth flattens out into a lipless line. "How much trouble are you in? I mean, other than suspended. Did you have to talk to the police, or . . ."

"No, no, just the suspension — and paying for the display case that got smashed."

"Your dad OK'd you working so soon? Still seem pretty banged up," he says, motioning toward my hand, and then my face.

"He's fine with it. More than fine." I laugh a little. A mistake, because Mr. Anders's eyes narrow. Shit. Dad is cool with Mr. Anders, and not just because Mr. Anders is retired Navy or because he hires a lot of guys from military families. But I'm never sure how cool Mr. Anders is with Dad. "I really need the money," I say again, staring at his boots.

"OK," he says, even though it sounds like anything but "OK." "I just wanted to check on you before you started. So, if you're sure you're well enough to work . . ."

"I'm fine." He fiddles with the edge of the binder, watching me. "Really." I hold my arms out, showing him I'm fine. Too bad I have to drop my shoulder fast.

He steps closer. "Look, Matt, my dad wasn't easy to please. I get it. And I had my fair share of fights. But . . . take it from an old fighter, OK? Just play it cool for a while. Sometimes you've just got to tell people what they want to hear."

Easy for him to say.

He reaches over and pats my back. I shift away, and my backpack slides down my arm.

"And working for me this summer will be good. You'll be around some other guys who understand. Just, until then, keep your head down, and take care of yourself, OK?"

I nod, mainly because I know he means well, even if he has no idea how ridiculous it is to say the right things to Dad or to deal with the shitheads at school who don't know jack.

Mr. Anders hands me a package of blue painter's tape to take in to Jerry, who's overseeing the crew, then waves me toward the house.

"Thanks, Mr. Anders."

He holds out his hand to shake, and I shuffle the tape and my backpack, trying to get my hand free, but it gets caught in between. He just chuckles and pats me on the back again, a little harder this time.

The first time I met Mr. Anders was in a house like this one. I was eight. Dad and I stopped by to drop off T.J.'s lunch. Mr. Anders was holding a ladder while another guy measured something near the ceiling. He reached across his body to shake Dad's hand, without taking his attention or his other hand off the ladder. They pointed me down the hall to find T.J.

I followed the sound of the music, T.J.'s music, dodging materials, tools, and wet paint. Nervous to be walking through the house alone, but I could hear the music and T.J. singing along, his scratchy voice loud over the other voice in the room.

"Wait, wait!" T.J. laughed. "This is the best part."

When I made it to the doorway, T.J. was crouched over the CD player, turning up the sound.

He stood up, playing air guitar as the music squealed out. The other guy, older than T.J., grimaced and shook his head, but he also smiled at T.J.'s elaborate performance. And I watched, all the way to the end of the song, because I couldn't *not* watch T.J. when he was playing air guitar.

"How could you not—?" T.J. started to say to the other guy, dancing toward him, still sort of tuning his air guitar. But then the guy looked at me, and so did T.J. "Matt!" he yelled. "Finally, someone who appreciates my playing. That my lunch?"

"Yup," I said, holding the bag out in front of me with both hands.

"Great, I'm starved. Come on." He was already through the kitchen and near the back door by the time I could catch up.

Every time I step into one of these houses—guys working, music, the smells—it feels a little like I'm gonna turn a corner and find T.J., covered in sweat and paint, singing along to his air guitar.

The long hours of work help clear my head. The rhythmic sanding and scraping is nice to breathe with. And the work is good. After a while, I stop hurting so much. It helps me remember why, all those months, I ignored the crap. I've been ignoring assholes my whole life. I can do it a little longer.

"Matt, you need more stain?" Jerry asks from the doorway of the kitchen. I look down, realizing I've been working on the same cabinet door for a while. Thankfully, it doesn't look all blotchy or too dark next to the others.

"Uh, no, I've still got a couple cans after this one."

I carefully put down my brush and lift the door, moving it to the counter behind me to dry.

Jerry watches me. Not saying anything, just watching, until I've got another unstained cabinet door set up on the sawhorses. I wipe the surface down to get rid of any dust or stuff that could ruin the stain, taking extra care with the grooves. Then I wait, staring back at Jerry, because it feels weird to start staining with him watching. Like maybe he'll say I'm doing it all wrong.

"OK, well, I'm going to run to pick up the paint. If you have any problems, Carl is in the front room, working on the floor. OK?"

"Sure." I pick up the can, but I still wait. Eventually he leaves the kitchen.

Jerry used to be just another one of the guys. Now that Mr. Anders lets him supervise the crew, he's quieter, more serious, less fun.

When T.J. was working for Mr. Anders, Jerry was one

of the new guys: he'd been at the university, but something happened and he dropped out.

He was OK then, but I like him better now, even with the staring.

Jerry's one of the guys who came to T.J.'s funeral. A bunch of them did, all in a group. Mr. Anders came later, on his own.

eight

Everything about the week before the funeral was hell. But it was nothing compared to the funeral itself.

It was so cold. Too cold even to snow. Dad had bought me a new suit and shoes, but he didn't bother with a coat, and none of my regular coats were nice enough. I froze all day.

We got to the funeral home really early. People were already starting to set up on the sides of the road, like there was going to be a parade. Flags everywhere.

After Dad met with the escort, and they'd checked out the inside of the casket, they closed the coffin and Dad went into the office with the funeral home director. He left me with T.J.

It took me forever to make myself inch out of the family-room doorway and walk over to the casket.

The wood gleamed, reflecting all the lights around it. My hand shook where I forced it flat on top of the casket. I held it there until I stopped trembling. But it wasn't enough. I could still feel the shaky terror. I needed to know I wouldn't lose it in front of everyone. Both hands on the wood made me lean forward, and so I went with it until my face was pressed against the smooth, hard top of the casket, cold under my cheek.

No way could Dad come out and find my eyes red. But I could hang on and wait for the room to stop spinning, close my eyes and wait for it to be over.

Shuffled feet. Things moving around. A door somewhere, and some muffled conversation. A door closing. Everything more quiet.

"Son." I couldn't answer, or move. "Son," the man who wasn't Dad said again.

I turned my head, too heavy to lift.

"I'm sorry, but they'll need to open the doors soon. And your father . . ."

He didn't need to say any more.

I pulled myself off the wood, stepped back, and swayed until the man caught my arm and sat me in the nearest chair.

He leaned down, his face distorted, too close.

"Want me to get your father? Or . . ."

"No." I knew he hadn't actually heard me, because he kept looking from me to the door and back. "No," I said again. "Sorry."

"Nothing to be sorry about," he said. "Water?"

I nodded. He jogged to the room off to the side and came back with a bottle of water. My hand shook, but I managed to drink most of it without spilling it all over my suit.

"You gonna be all right?" he asked, moving an easel with pictures of T.J. closer to the casket. "You could go into the family room right there and lie down. We could close the door."

Fat chance Dad would let me hide in there. And he'd skin me alive if he knew I was being a wuss. Time to get it in gear. I chugged the rest of the water and made myself stand up, walk across the room, and throw it in the trash.

The guy continued moving things around the casket: flowers, a low table with some cards on it, a basket for donations to a VA charity.

"You sure you're gonna be OK?" he finally asked after he'd adjusted everything twice and I'd made three laps of the room.

"Yeah," I said, ready.

I walked right up to the casket and touched it, hand fine. As long as I didn't look at the easel, I'd be fine. I stepped back so he could get to the table next to it and stood watch.

"OK, well, you might want to go into the family room. I've got to do something here," he said, motioning toward the casket.

I wasn't going anywhere.

"I mean, I've got to open it for a second. Protocol." He looked ready to freak himself.

"Go ahead," I said, holding my ground.

He took a deep breath and shifted so his broad back would be between me and the casket, then he lifted it open. I moved fast next to him before he could shut it again. I knew not to look to the right, where there weren't any legs. And I was too shitless to look left and risk seeing no head. So, I kept my eyes dead ahead on the arm I could see was there. I reached out and touched the arm. Over the fabric, but hard enough to feel it was solid. I was too chickenshit to do anything else, even to feel for skin, but I touched him.

After, I bolted, so I didn't see any more or hear the guy close the lid for the last time. But I manned up enough to touch him. To say good-bye. Then I puked and dry-heaved until I popped a blood vessel in my eye.

By the time I snuck back through the side room, the casket had been draped with the flag and the main room was packed. I'd thought they'd said it was going to be a private funeral, family and close friends only. My family and close friends could fit in one car, Dad's in maybe four cars, a bus if you count work people. But there were people everywhere. A line out the door. More uniforms. I almost backed out of the room.

Shauna and her parents made their way through the crowd and stayed near me in the doorway to the family room until I could get up the courage to take my place next to Dad.

"Matt," Shauna said, her breath near my cheek, "you don't have to go up there."

"Yeah, I do," I said, steeling myself for the walk.

Her fingers caught mine, and she held me back until I shook them off and stepped out from the safety of the dim side room.

A gazillion pairs of eyes turned on me. Buzzes of sound,

and tears. And none of it mattered. All that mattered was getting up there next to Dad. I took another step. Shauna touched my back.

I don't actually remember the walk. But I remember clearly the moment when I fell in line beside Dad. He didn't move a muscle. I knew he'd seen me come up and that he was pissed I hadn't been there when they opened the doors, but he didn't look my way to say so or stare it at me. I looked back at Shauna, now crying into her father's shoulder, made sure she knew that I knew she was there. Then I matched Dad's stare ahead.

We stood next to the casket forever while people filed past. Most of the time Dad looked like a statue with his hands clasped in front of him, face stone. Only some people got an acknowledgment, a handshake, mostly guys who had served with T.J. or Dad's friends and employees. Most everyone else got a stare, at best. I shook all the hands, said the thank-yous, tried not to breathe my puke breath on anyone. Sometimes Uncle Mac stood between us; sometimes he scurried around, talking to people, making sure things were where they were supposed to be. Aunt Janelle handed out tissues and smiled at people through her free-flowing tears. I didn't look at the casket again. Except when Mr. Anders came in.

A whole group of the guys had come at the beginning, weird and quiet, respectful in their funeral clothes. But Mr. Anders came later. I almost didn't recognize him, in his suit, his hair slicked back. His shoes gleamed. Regulation shine.

Dad broke his pose to shake Mr. Anders's hand and held it a beat longer than I think Mr. Anders wanted. Then Mr. Anders stepped back to shake my hand, reaching over to grab my shoulder, too. My eyes burned, and I stared at his shoes, stared at them all the way to the casket. And then I couldn't help but look as he held his hand over his heart and then laid it over the flag-draped wood. More than anyone else, Mr. Anders felt real. Like it hurt all the way through him, too.

Back at the house, I heard Uncle Mac tell someone they'd only been able to find one of T.J.'s arms. Really stupid, but I hoped it had been his right. I needed it to be his right arm. It seemed really fucked up that after all of that, I might not have touched T.J. at all.

Now I can't care. Even if it was his arm, it hadn't been him, not really, because whatever was in that casket, it wasn't T.J.

nine

THAT NIGHT, EVEN AFTER A LONG-ASS DAY OF PAINTING
and staining, I get home before Dad. Inside, the quiet presses
on me, almost egging me on to take a quick look upstairs.
But Dad could be home any minute. Next week. I can wait
another few days not to tip him off.

I head outside with a soda and some chips.

The long hours of work helped clear my head.

Sun warmed and temporarily less hungry, I wait for Dad.
As soon as he cleans up and heads out again, I'll call Shauna.
I need to see her, and need to be distracted. Next week can't
come soon enough.

Mrs. Russell across the street spends half her day pretending to do stuff in her yard so she can snoop on the
neighborhood. Today that means she spends a long time
pretending not to watch me.

Another reminder that I've been ignoring these people
my whole life: Mrs. Russell in particular, since the day we
moved in and Dad said to stop staring at the old lady sweep-
ing the street.

Dad's truck pulls into the driveway.

The neighbors, the kids at school, everyone. All I have to do is breathe and coast and figure all the other shit out later. People do it all the time. Work. Live. Get by. No need to panic. Except, of course, that *later* is breathing down my neck.

Dad walks across the lawn. "What're you doing?" he asks, looking around like he's afraid people will see me.

"Nothing."

"Nothing?" An edge to that, but more curious than irritated.

"Sitting. Sun felt good."

"And?" Dad asks.

And what? I think, but I know better than to say it.

"Work? Are you going to get enough to pay half what you owe by the last day of classes, as promised?"

As *he* promised. "Mr. Anders has me on a crew next week after school, and he's looking at where he can use me after that until my summer crew starts." Between that and what I had saved up, it'll be close.

"You make sure you take on as many shifts as he can offer from now until summer. I'm not paying a penny for that display case, you hear?"

"Yes, sir."

"OK, then."

Dad looks at Mrs. Russell. "That old bat never misses anything, does she?" Almost a smile — not quite, but almost.

What the hell? He run over a small child on the way home? Maybe a puppy?

"All right, well, enough of this crap."

And mood over.

"I'm heading to your uncle Mac's as soon as I've changed. Might be nice if you tackled that heaping pile of laundry sometime this weekend." It's not a suggestion. "Something's started to fester in there."

I clean up the kitchen, washing out my glass and taking out the trash. Then I head downstairs, so I can avoid any more encounters with Dad.

As soon as his truck clears the corner, I call Shauna, letting her know the coast is clear. Her mother made her promise to be home by ten, but letting her out on a school night shows just how much Mrs. G. likes me. Doubt she'd let her go see Michael on a school night.

In the shower I think about what she might bring me for dinner, hoping for something from home, instead of a pizza or takeout. I can order food with the best of them. And sure, I can live on macaroni, cereal, and microwavables. But I can't cook for shit. Not real food. For the first time since the fight, maybe earlier, I'm starving for something real.

We'll watch a movie down here. Means tomorrow my room might still smell like her. It'll make it easy to close my eyes and pretend she's really there, and we're actually doing all the things I can imagine us doing. Even after I'm trying to think about anything else, my head keeps thinking about her. I run out of hot water and have to rush under the lukewarm spray.

I have just enough time to throw on some clothes and pull up the comforter before I hear her car.

The side door bangs open. "Hello!" she bellows down the stairs.

"Be up in a minute," I yell back.

Her footsteps move up the three steps to the kitchen. One last quick look around the room, which looks OK, and then one last glance in the mirror near the door. I look OK, too.

The microwave dings. My stomach growls in anticipation. At the turn by the laundry room, I smell the heavenly scent of a home-cooked meal, reheated but still home-cooked. My mouth waters. I don't even care what it is.

She's been waiting to see how messed up I am; I know she has. I can't do anything about my face, or hand, or the bruises that show. I planned to take the steps two at a time, shut up some of her worrying by showing her I'm fine. But after the long day bent over baseboards, then later standing over the cabinet doors, the best I can do is try not to limp or show her I can't lift my right arm very far.

Her first look says it all—the forced smile doesn't hide her shock.

"I'm fine," I say.

Her eyebrows climb to the messy hair curling around her forehead.

"Really."

"Yeah, sure, you're just great," she says. It's harsh and kind of angry, but I'm pretty sure she's not angry at me.

As we've done a gazillion times before, without even talking about it, we head to the back porch. She carries the plate and fork. I grab a couple of sodas from the fridge.

She holds the plate, waiting for me to settle down on the top step, facing out toward the woods at the back of the yard. With the sun sliding toward night, and the pinky-purple sky behind her, her hair looks even more golden than usual, streaky and kind of glowy in places. She moves a little and I realize I've been staring.

I trade her one of the sodas for the steaming plate. Before digging in, I wait for her to sit. But she puts her soda down so she can pull her sweatshirt from around her waist and tug it over her head. COUGAR SOCCER blazes across her chest in brand-spanking-new gold letters. I remind myself not to stare. It's new — the sweatshirt, not her chest. Her chest has been tormenting me for years. Last week, all the rising-senior soccer players got their "senior sweatshirts" in one of those very-important-to-them ceremony things. She's been wearing it whenever it's the least bit cool enough and being very careful not to get it dirty. Shauna already has senior fever: excited and going through all the rituals of junior year to be ready.

The way things are going, I may never be a senior. Her team-mates think I'm a loser. They're not the only ones.

I wait until she's seated beside me to start. By then the casserole's cool enough not to blister the roof of my mouth. Sitting side by side, I can't see her face without turning my head, but I don't need to look to know her face right now: tight, pinched, scared and sad and cautious, like she's looked most of the semester, only a little bit worse, because of the fight. Her dark-brown eyes are probably squinted with worry, drowning out the gold flecks.

I grunt my appreciation around a mouthful of chicken casserole. It's warm and creamy and perfect. And pretty soon, there's a growing pile of mushrooms on the edge of the plate and a spreading warmth in my stomach. Shauna must've told her mom she was bringing me dinner, because, despite the mushrooms, it's one of my favorite meals ever.

"Your ribs OK?" At least she let me get mostly done with dinner.

"Never better." I don't really look at her, but I catch the small, mocking smile and shake of her head anyway. "Shauna." My warning voice has never been as good as hers.

"Yeah, right," she says. "Sure."

She *is* pissed, and maybe at me. I can't tell. Unnerving enough that she might be sufficiently pissed to get into it, but after all the months of her constantly studying me, those tense looks, not knowing is torture. I just can't read her anymore.

And now I can't eat anymore, either.

"Let it go." I push the plate toward her on the step between us, knowing she'll pick at the leftovers if she isn't *too* pissed. At least the chicken and broccoli, and with her fingers, not my fork. I try not to smile when she picks up the plate. There's hope for better yet.

"At least clean out your knuckles," she says. "They look kind of red. Are they getting infected?" She wrinkles her face for emphasis.

I look at my hands. They are kind of gross, but I didn't really think about them. I pick at the edge of the scab on my pinky finger until it rips. When I look up, she's stopped eating, obviously disgusted.

"Seriously, Matt, you could get really sick. You should clean them out with some peroxide or alcohol or something, maybe put some antibiotic cream and bandages on them at night."

We don't have any peroxide or ointment or anything. I try to get my pinky to stop bleeding by sucking on it.

"Lovely," Shauna says. "Before the movie, at least wash that off and put a Band-Aid on it."

Back inside, I take the plate and wave her toward the stairs, pretending to crumple in pain when she flicks my chest as she walks past me.

Shauna's already putting in the DVD, but I dig through the drawer in the bathroom until I find a stray Band-Aid in the back. I scrub my knuckles with soap, then put the

Band-Aid on the one that kept bleeding. It doesn't want to stick, but I hold it on with the finger next to it.

When I come back in, she smiles her approval, maybe like the future nurse she wants to be. It kind of makes me want to rip the Band-Aid off for spite. But I don't.

Shauna pulls her sweatshirt over her head. Her T-shirt rides up. I busy myself with the remote. Some of my favorite fantasies start with her shirt pulling up to reveal smooth, pale skin.

Between her being in my room, the weirdness from upstairs, and the general weirdness between us lately, I don't know where to sit. But she sits on the floor, steals my pillow, and leans against my bed. Makes it easy to do the same.

Once the movie starts, one we've seen a dozen times, things get normal between us again, at least what's been passing for normal since November. The crinkling wrappers and flood of grape smell from Shauna's candy feels exactly like a hundred other times we've sat right here, her oblivious, and me trying not to let on what having her here, in my room, does to me.

And it feels good, just us, and little talking except to mock the movie.

After, neither of us moves to put in another right away. But when the quiet gets too heavy, I try to get up fast to change the DVD. Big mistake. My muscles have tightened up and hurt like hell. I can't help wincing and hissing.

"Geez, Matt."

"I'm fine." I smile down at her, trying to convince her. To break the tension, I try for a laugh. "You shoulda seen the other guys."

She doesn't laugh. "I did." She hesitates, then looks away, undoing her messy hair from its band, and then taking her time gathering all the stray hair in again. It's a habit, when she doesn't know what else to do. "The side of Michael's face is turning purple. He had a concussion."

Great, just what I need—Michael using the fight as a way to get back in with Shauna. With my luck, she'll be so impressed with his maturity and concern she'll let him below the equator this time. Just freaking great.

"You really messed Pinscher up." It isn't quite an accusation.

"I know." I close my eyes and shift my weight from one foot to the other. I can't stand her looking at me like that. "Shauna, I . . ." I almost say I'm sorry, but it would be stupid to apologize to her for beating up Pinscher. I try to figure out what she wants to hear.

She takes three steps over to my bed and sits down. "What happened? I mean, why . . . ?"

I can't say it again. If I say it again, I'm gonna go insane.

"OK, not why," she says. "I get *why*."

Great. "Does everyone know?"

"Pretty much." She nods, picking at the edge of the bed-spread with her nail.

Terrific. Every time I think it can't get worse, it does. Screw it. I'm not going back. They can fail me.

"Matt, even the kids who usually suck up to Pinscher and sign his petitions and stuff get that he went too far."

My head's gonna explode. "Went too far?" Pounding in my ears. It's not a fucking matter of degrees. "Went too . . . Is that what *Michael* said, that the asshole *'went too far'*? Do you think that there is any fucking—?"

"Calm down." Her hands fly up in front of her. "I get it. I do. It's just . . ." She trails off, shrugging a little.

Whatever Michael said to her, I know he doesn't get it, so maybe she doesn't, either. "Went too far," like just the shirt would have been OK? Or maybe a shirt with all the names but T.J.'s? It wasn't about "too far." It was about right and wrong. I wasn't wrong.

That first punch, the moment of impact, the crunch and the flood of blood. I feel sick.

"I'm just so tired," I say, "of everything."

"I know," she says, smoothing the spot next to her.

I can't. I can't talk anymore. And I definitely can't sit on the bed with her. Or pretend everything is OK.

Crap. Dad's truck in the driveway.

Shauna's up and in motion, all thoughts of talking forgotten. She's never really felt comfortable around Dad, but it's been worse since the funeral.

I get her out the side door just before Dad comes in the front.

ten

THE NEXT MORNING I WAKE WITH A HEART-CLENCHING jolt. Dad's voice bellows down. All the blood rushes to the top of my head and pounds there, trying to get out. I was in the middle of a dream, a Shauna dream, a good one.

"Did you hear me? Get your ass up here!"

7:27 a.m. Shit. I'm gonna be late for work.

I skip the shower in favor of breakfast. Takes all of ten minutes to brush my teeth, throw on some clothes, and be up in the kitchen wolfing down a bowl of cereal.

Partway through the second bowl, I hear Dad's feet on the stairs. Too late to get my boots on and slip out the side door, I finish my cereal.

Dad looks over his shoulder at me on the way to the coffee.

"Saw your girlfriend's car last night. Didn't hear her leave, though. What, you sneak her out after I went to bed, or was it this morning?"

Dad's leer broadcasts all the things he's thinking: all of them disgusting.

"Just be careful," he says, his chest all puffed out, almost swaggering over to the table, tossing the newspaper open as he yanks out his chair. "Her family can't afford another mouth to feed, and I'll be damned if I finally get your ass in gear just to have you piss it all away."

I should correct him, for her sake, her honor or whatever. But I can't make myself do it, for mine. His thinking we're having sex means maybe he worries a little less that he has to make a man out of me. There's something vomit-inducingly wrong about lusting after your best friend. But letting your fucked-up father think you're screwing her is a million times worse.

"You hear me?"

I snap my chin to chest and up again, like he does.

"I want to hear you say it."

I swallow hard around the guilt. "I hear you."

"OK, then." He beams and cuffs my shoulder as he struts past.

"Working tomorrow?" Dad asks.

I shovel in more cereal, slurping out a "No."

"Good," Dad says. "Don't make plans. Storm windows should've been down a month ago."

Oh, joy. Time for the biannual fun fest of pinched fingers and rusty scrapes, not to mention a whole afternoon of frustrating Dad by failing to follow his orders fast enough.

"Hey."

I wipe my face into a blank mask and nod my understanding.

"Finals in a week and a half?"

He knows they are, but I nod again.

"Better get studying. You fail and we are going to have a serious problem."

Failure equals dead. Sure thing. Got it. Thanks for the pep talk, Dad.

"I looked into it. GED won't cut it for the better assignments, and if you're gonna have any chance at all to advance through the ranks, you'll need to start off right."

Of course. OCS is out, but he's just tweaking the plan. Not giving up the dream. Not Dad. Already thinking beyond enlistment and Basic, like they're a foregone conclusion.

"You hear me?"

I grit my teeth. "Yes, sir."

"Good. Now you better haul ass over to the site. Roger's not paying you to stroll in whenever it suits you." I shovel in one last mouthful. Then one more. "Now," Dad commands, glancing at the clock.

I drop my bowl in the sink and grab my boots, start shoving them on as fast as I can. But he's staring, and I can't find the right feet.

"If you can't get yourself up and—"

The doorbell.

"—to work on time . . ." He trails off into a head-shaking sigh. I struggle to get my right foot into my boot.

Someone knocks on the front door.

Dad glares, pissed, like that helps me get out of here any faster.

Another round of knocks.

Screw the laces. I grab my backpack and head for the side door.

Outside, I go to lock the door, and don't have my keys. Shit. Not in my pockets. Must be on the counter. I debate going without them, but I can't leave it unlocked, and who knows what time he'll be home.

I open the side door as quietly as I can. Skip the squeaky step and inch into the kitchen.

"Mr. Foster."

What the hell is CAO Cooper doing here?

"Come in." Dad's voice is brittle.

I lean until I can see around the door frame.

Dad's staring at whatever Cooper's—

A dolly—with two black footlockers. Cooper turns and grabs another one off the front porch. Three. Army-issue footlockers.

"I'm glad we could finally arrange to deliver your son's effects."

My knees hit the floor.

Dad doesn't talk. Or move. He just stares. Cooper turns

and grabs a box off the porch, holds it for a moment, obviously waiting for my father to say something, and then puts it on top of the footlocker on the floor.

"Why don't we sit down," Cooper says, motioning toward the living room, a large envelope in his hands. "We can go through the inventory, and the report, and then—"

"No," Dad scrapes out. "That—that won't be necessary. I'll just sign the receipt or whatever forms and look at it later." He holds out his hand. Not even going to sit down.

Cooper holds the envelope like a shield. "Of course, that's fine, if that's what you want. But it might help for you, and Matt"—he looks at me until Dad looks—"to have a chance to ask questions or . . ."

Dad just holds out his hand. Cooper knows when he's beat. He opens the envelope. I stare at the footlockers.

I can't move. Or breathe.

"Top of the stairs," Dad says. Sounds like he hasn't spoken in days. "First room on the right."

My arms stop working.

Top of the stairs . . . T.J.'s room.

Cooper picks up the cardboard box. Taps his fingers against the side. "This is the commemorative chest we talked about. I know you were hesitant, but your family is entitled—and later you might want it. If you're not sure, you can unpack it and take a look, try putting some of your son's things in it, his uniform, the flag, his medals. Or you can leave it boxed up until you decide. If in a few weeks you really don't want it, I'll come back and get it. No problem. But you, or someone, might want it later. So, just think about it."

Cooper disappears up the stairs before Dad can balk.

Cooper makes more trips. My eyes follow the footlockers out of sight, and I flinch each time one lands on the floor of T.J.'s room above me.

The third thud shakes me loose. I push myself up, grab the edge of the table to keep from falling over.

"Well," Cooper says, picking up the forms Dad signed, "if you have any questions, any at all, you know how to reach me." He looks my way. "Anytime." He focuses on Dad again. "If I don't hear from you, I'll get in touch in a few weeks to make sure there's nothing else I can assist you with."

Dad stares at the wall. Cooper waits.

Finally, Dad looks Cooper in the eye. "Thank you." And that might as well be good-bye.

Cooper shakes Dad's hand. Nods my way. And he's gone.

I push myself out of the kitchen, pinballing off the wall for support.

Dad hasn't moved—he's still holding the door partway open.

Then he closes it and turns to look up the stairs.

He stands at the bottom of the stairs, hand on the banister, one foot on the first step.

I'm dizzy, and sick, but standing.

He heaves himself onto the first step and up.

I stagger after him, pulled along as if he's towing me up the stairs.

Dad's in front of the open door to T.J.'s room. I want to run past him and lock myself in there until he leaves, but my legs won't work. I push against the wall, force myself up two more steps. It feels like walking against a strong current, sinking ankle deep into the mud with every step.

A soft click. My knees buckle and I land on the step. Dad rests his hands on the worn wood of the closed door. T.J.'s stuff on the other side. Stuff I didn't even think we'd get. Stuff Dad hasn't hidden or gotten rid of yet.

A vise clamps around my ribs; my lungs can't work.

Dad turns, marches away from the door, then leaps, startled when he sees me. He steadies himself against the wall.

The dim hallway hides his face, but his whole body surges up and his hands grip and flex in the air. He stomps down the stairs so fast I stumble backward to get out of his way.

I try to follow, but I can't. I have to go up there, now. If I don't . . . My legs tremble. He closed the door.

I watch each step down the stairs, one foot in front of the other, waiting to wake up or breathe or get my brain to work. I need to figure out what to do. What if I'm still asleep? Downstairs, in my room, asleep, and I wake up and there's nothing upstairs in T.J.'s room?

Dad's standing at the sink, rinsing out his mug, as if nothing happened.

He turns to look at me. I wait for it, hoping that maybe,

maybe this time, he'll get it. He'll let me . . . Even if he said "Later," it would be enough. Something. He hardens his eyes. Warning me off. Warning me off even asking, or letting on that any of this just happened. Unbelievable. I knew it, and still, fucking unbelievable.

He reaches for his keys.

"Dad?" I hate my voice.

"Yes?"

"But . . ."

"What?" Hard. Angry already.

I try to form a question that won't get me thrown through a wall.

Dad does his best to make sure I don't feel like asking any questions. When I start to work my mouth anyway, he turns — full frontal challenge.

"What?" Begging me to say a word

"Dad . . ." I can feel my eyes looking up, like I can see through the ceiling. My throat burns, locked tight. Eyes sting.

He's over me, in my face, so close I have to step back, wedged between him and the wall.

"You mind your own fucking business, you hear me?"

"But . . ."

"No."

Dad holds his ground. I have no choice. No way I can get at them now. And if I stay, if I fight with him . . . he might haul them out right in front of me.

I back down, look at my feet. Shake my head. Act as

whipped as I can. For now. I need time to regroup. I retreat. Grab my backpack and leave, without looking back.

I walk to the site in a daze. All the way there, and for most of the morning, I keep turning it all over in my head. I'm such an idiot. Dad, and Uncle Mac, and Aunt Janelle—everyone—called that bag T.J.'s personal effects. When months went by with nothing else, I thought that's all we were gonna get. But now there's more—three footlockers full—but for how long? How long until Dad moves them, too? Or gets rid of them, if that's what he did with the rest?

I'm pretty sure that bag was in the hutch for weeks, until he moved it, maybe because of how I looked at it sometimes. And the flag—it was up in T.J.'s closet for months. And the pictures. He waited until just a few weeks ago to get rid of the pictures. But he won't wait so long this time. Not now. Not after this morning.

I'll risk the beat-down, if it's what has to happen, to get something of T.J. back. The bag's either hidden somewhere or gone. Either way, I can search for it later. Right now, I've got to get into those footlockers.

eleven

Saturday sucks. Hard. Besides Dad's frustrations and glares, by the time we're done with the storm windows I'm covered in sweat, grime, and stinging scrapes. And my shoulder's throbbing.

I keep up my kicked-puppy act the whole time. Biting my cheek when I have to. The longer he thinks I'm the old, beat-down me, the longer it'll take him to get rid of the trunks. I checked them last night, just for a second, just to be sure. They're still upstairs, for now.

Dad heads back inside while I clean up, hauling the windows back to the storage shed and then winding up the hose. Dad had plans to go out tonight. I hope he still does, that I've acted whipped enough not to tip him off. If I've blown it, I have no idea what I'll do. I can't wait. Not for long.

Dad'll be around Monday — Memorial Day. No way we're "celebrating," but no way he can work, either. No sites to inspect on a national holiday. We'll both be here, pretending nothing's happening. Be like him to get rid of it all tomorrow, if he's leaning that way. And even if he doesn't, after tonight

I'll only have after school, when I'm not working, unless I cut. And if I cut, I'm screwed. Has to be tonight.

I can't stop thinking about what could be in the footlockers—the sweatshirt with the ripped front pocket T.J. wore everywhere. The pictures he took when he was over there, maybe even a couple pics of him. His camera. His CDs and iPods. Please, let his iPods be in there.

I kick off my muddy shoes on the porch and wipe off the worst of the crud before going inside. Dad's standing at the counter, drinking a glass of water.

His white shirt is starched crisp, the pocket sealed to the shirt and the cuffs sharp, and he smells like a sweet cedar closet from a healthy dousing of his favorite cologne. Those aren't poker night or hanging-around-with-Uncle-Mac clothes. Either Dad has an actual date or he's hoping to find one later.

He flashes a grin on his way to the door. Damn near whistling. He might as well have said, "See you tomorrow."

If he does come home tonight, no idea how late he'll be, but I'd bet he'll be gone at least a few hours. And he never brings anyone here, at least not until he's been seeing them for a while. Really no way of knowing if he's got all-night plans or just hopes to have an all-night plan soon.

And he might already have plans to get rid of the footlockers.

What if I wake up tomorrow and he's hauling them out the door?

Or come home sometime next week and they're gone? Like the bag. Like the flag. Like the pictures.

If I don't do it now, tonight, I might never get the chance.

I wait just long enough to be sure Dad's date isn't gonna crap out, text Shauna to blow off our plans, and then start for the upstairs.

Standing at the bottom of the steps, it's like a rush.

Every step is a separate defiance.

Four long strides from the landing to the spot right in front of the door to T.J.'s room.

I spent eight years living in the room behind me, more than two of them staring at this closed door and wanting to be inside. Wondering whether T.J. would let me in if I knocked. Wondering if I could get in and get whatever, look at whatever, before T.J. came home, the fear of being caught clogging my throat. How many times did I sit here in the hallway, reading a comic book or playing a game, waiting for him? Most of those times he stepped over me, walked into that room, and shut the door behind him, without a word.

It takes me three tries to make myself actually touch the doorknob. But once I turn the cold metal, the door swings wide like someone pulled it open from the inside. I stare into the room. T.J.'s old bed. His desk. His dresser.

It looks pretty much the way it did when T.J. left for Basic, only dustier. Same plaid bedspread and nearly flat pillow barely making a lump. Same faded posters and stuff on the walls: Dave Matthews Band between the closet and the door;

some pages cut from magazines, mainly *Rolling Stone*; the huge-ass Bruce Springsteen rocking out over his desk, the *Born in the U.S.A.* album cover blown up and stretched across the far wall, and the *Human Touch* album poster on the wall next to his bed; and smaller pics and ticket stubs and notes and stuff on the corkboard. I can practically hear T.J.'s music radiating from the walls.

Stacks of CDs overflow the rack next to the desk. In the far corner, a few boxes T.J. left before his first tour in Iraq and never bothered to take with him later.

Crossing into the room feels wrong, and not just because I haven't been in here in a few months or because Dad would pummel me if he found out.

No, it feels wrong because it still feels like T.J.'s. Like he's deployed on an extra-long tour and could be home anytime. Or like the times between deployments—he didn't stay here for more than a few weeks at a time, but this was still his room.

The clock in the living room ding-dongs its quarter time. I don't know quarter after or to what, but it's enough to make me step over the dividing line of competing carpets and into the room.

The cardboard box—Cooper said that's the commemorative chest. Waiting to be filled, meaning there's nothing in there now. It can wait.

The three footlockers sitting in the middle of the floor are made of heavy black plastic. New, not scarred. These haven't been anywhere but wherever they packed his stuff up and here. Inside could be anything, could be everything.

An itchy anticipation crawls over me.

I can't stop hoping for all kinds of things.

Then cold dread sweeps it away. There are zip ties locking the footlockers shut. I try pulling at them, to see if they can be opened or something. But there's no way in except to cut them.

I stand there, staring at them. If I cut them, and he comes in here, even just to check, he'll see what I've done right away. I was hoping to take just enough so that he'd never really know. Now he'll know whatever I do. Shit. No choice. Whatever happens, I can't walk away, not again.

I race down the stairs, through the house, and into the kitchen. Dig around until I find the scissors and some tape.

I examine the zip tie loop through the latch of the first footlocker again, just to make sure there isn't some way to pull or stretch it open. There's not. No way in except to cut them. I'm wasting time.

The scissors are awkward in my hand. It takes me three tries to get them positioned just right to cut the zip tie up near the top of the latch where the cut won't show unless Dad looks closely. My hand shakes. The first cut feels like it takes forever, almost vibrating through my fingers, ending with a whisper of sound.

I pull the loop free and test the plastic, lining up the ends.

It'll be easy to tape the ends back together enough to hide the cut some, at least from across the room.

The first bit of excitement cuts through the fear. I'm actually doing this.

The latch snaps up with an audible pop, slapping back at my fingers. I open the lid a little too hard, and it falls back with a loud bang. For a split second, I wait for the sound of Dad's feet or an alarm. But the pounding fear fades fast as I look inside.

On top is a heavy coat and a set of sheets, smelling like some probably supposed-to-be-odorless laundry detergent. The sheets look pretty new, even though T.J. had been in Iraq this last time for almost six months and on base before that. Was this just his stuff from the last tour? He had to have left some stuff in storage or something, right? Maybe that stuff comes later. Or maybe they don't even know where it is. Who knows.

I lift out the sheets and the coat and lay them aside. The coat slips, unfolding in my hands, too fluffy and slick. I try to refold it, but without something to hold it down, it doesn't want to be folded. I dump it beside the sheets. A flat, faded-out pillow is next, nearly as flat as the one on the bed behind me. At least it still smells a little familiar. I put it on the opposite side of the footlocker.

Next are some clothes—a couple of sweaters, jeans, thermal shirts, and sweats. Nothing all that interesting or special, and all of it smelling like strangers. No sign of the T-shirt or sweatshirt I want the most. Got to keep moving.

Next down are bags of socks and underwear, and then shoes — sneakers, loafers, flip-flops. A pair of low hiking boots I think he loved more than any other shoes he'd ever owned. I pull them out. New laces, not even creased or worn, still tight and clean. The boots are too big for me; stupid to take them. I put them back in.

An old pair of slippers — worn and beat-up, and duct taped at the bottom. I didn't even know he wore slippers.

Other shoes and clothes. Nothing worth taking. I pack everything but the pillow back in as best I can and shut the lid and slip the zip tie back in place. Takes me four tries to get the edges lined up and the tape in place to hold them together without looking wrong or having a bunch of tape sticking off the side. But once I get it right, you can't even see the cut without looking real close. Perfect.

The second footlocker opens just as easily. But as soon as the lid hits the floor, I forget how to breathe.

T.J.'s uniform is laid out on top, still in plastic, fresh from the dry cleaner's, waiting for him to put it on. My gut clenches, and for once I'm glad I didn't have dinner. My hands recoil. I can't touch it. But having come this far, there's no turning back. And I can't live without knowing what else is in there.

I make my shaking fingers approach the thin plastic again. I lift it up by the plastic and swing it over to the bed, and then smooth it out flat so it won't get wrinkled. My eyes won't look away. I stand there, staring, hands cold and head dizzy. A car horn outside jars me loose. I need to move on.

As far as I can see, the footlocker is full of more folded clothes. Mostly his everyday uniforms, but other clothes and some small bags of stuff, too.

I'd been expecting something more. That I would open them up and immediately understand something more. I'd see something that had been T.J.'s and get what he had been thinking or doing right before. Or I'd see something meant just for me. Some piece of T.J. that would be all mine.

But I didn't count on everything being handled and reorganized, sanitized, and not by his buddies or anyone who even knew him. I didn't think about some stranger packing everything up in secure plastic bags, with no clear answers for me.

Kneeling down, I start to sort the stuff. The first bags hold nothing interesting. I sift through things, glancing and moving on until there's a pile of the everyday crap of T.J.'s life, none of which is going to answer any questions.

The next layer isn't any more enlightening: some more clothes, washed clean of all traces of T.J.; a striped towel; a fleece jacket with some kind of logo; and finally, together under the rest of the clothes, the T-shirt he wore the day we left on our hike, the one with the crack in the word ARMY, and his favorite sweatshirt, with the ripped pocket. I put them both to the side, pumped to at least have those.

More plastic bags. A few books. A handheld game player and a bag of games. A bunch of CDs, mostly by groups and singers I've never heard of. Some aren't even in English. I pull out a couple of the CDs that look interesting and put the rest in the pile to go back in.

I practically dive into the footlocker for the next bag—T.J.'s laptop, his battered case empty next to it. But when I lift it, the bag's too light, and when I open the bag, there's a gaping space where the hard drive should be. A letter in the bag says it was damaged beyond repair. Losing that hurts. I guess down deep this is what I wanted the most, so much so I didn't even have the guts to wish for it. I drop it onto the pile of stuff. No point in taking it without the hard drive. Disappointment seeps up inside me. What if there isn't anything here that can tell me anything important?

A Discman. A few more plastic bags of CDs, and one holding some papers. I shuffle the papers around. Statements and forms. Some pamphlets with other soldiers' names. Memorials. Other dead guys T.J. had known. No thanks.

I repack the footlocker, with, I hope, something at least close to the care used to pack it originally. I lay everything back in neatly, stacking some things to make it look full even without the small pile of stuff that's coming with me, until all I have left is the uniform on the bed. I force myself to once again pick it up by the plastic edges and, as gently as possible, lay it in on top. I smooth out a couple of ripples. Someone who didn't even know T.J. made it look perfect. The least I can do is try to keep it that way. I slip the zip tie back through the closed lid, wrap tape around the cut, and slide it so the tape doesn't show as much.

In the third footlocker, there's more clothes, and then a portable DVD player and several bags of DVDs. I look them over one by one, wondering which was his favorite, which ones he watched over and over, which ones he would tell me to watch, if he were here.

I have to take a deep breath and make myself keep going. If I stop to dwell on the stuff I wish I knew, on all the ways I wish I had known T.J. better, I'll lose it. The DVDs go into the pile to go downstairs, but I put the player aside to put back in. The DVDs, Dad will never notice around my room, but the player, covered in stickers and so obviously T.J.'s, will make him ask questions.

The next layer down, I hit pay dirt. T.J.'s iPods—three of them, all different sizes. They're beat all to hell and scratched and are probably the things he loved the most out of everything here. Most people don't need more than one. T.J. took all three with him on deployment. He probably had some reason—something about their uses, or time, or convenience. Hell, maybe even types of music. He bought the Shuffle the last time he was home—he couldn't resist its tiny size. But I guess he just couldn't bring himself to get rid of his first true-blue one, even with the others.

T.J. always fell asleep to music. Ran to it, too. He did pretty much everything to music. I can't wait to hook them up and try to figure out what he listened to the most, what he fell asleep to in the middle of a war zone, and what he listened to last. God, to scroll through the songs, see his history in music—maybe even some of my own. Probably a lot of songs I first heard through the closed door of this room, my ear pressed against the other side. I put the iPods in my keep pile and move on.

His camera's a mess—scratched and cracked and held together with some kind of tape. I can't get it to turn on. No memory cards. I put the camera back in, at least for now.

A few more books, some falling apart, like they might disintegrate if I handle them too much. T.J. didn't read much when he was home—a book or a magazine by his bed, maybe, but he didn't just sit around and read. But these, all beat up and creased, he read these a lot. One in particular is held together by a rubber band, with the front and back cover gone, and the pages crinkled and fluttering like it's been wet and dried out at least once. Another says *Stories from the Appalachian Trail,* a scrap of paper sticking out, marking a page. I choke, hold my breath, push on my eyes. I'm not ready to see what's on that page, how far he read before . . . I put the four books with the pile to go downstairs.

The next layer's a blanket I've never seen before. Then a box, black-and-white and glossy, with some kind of shiny stones or shells in an intricate pattern on top. I pull it out of its plastic bag. The inside smells like wood, but it's nearly as glossy as the outside. It's beautiful, and I have no idea why T.J. had it. It doesn't look like something he'd carry around with him, and I can't see him giving it to me or Dad. But there's something about it. I want it. But no way could I pass it off if Dad saw it in my room. Too much to risk.

More plastic bags with nothing interesting. At the bottom are a couple pairs of jeans. Kind of a letdown, and I feel sick to my stomach. I was sure I'd find some answers, but I'm leaving with just some stuff. Some cool stuff, but still.

I reach in to roll up the jeans so they'll take up more room. My hand hits something more, something underneath them. I yank the jeans out and toss them aside.

At the bottom, like afterthoughts, are more plastic bags.

Something crackles in the air around me, shoots through me.

I drag the first one out with shaking hands. Pictures. Stacks and stacks of pictures. I open up the bag and grab some at random, their slick surfaces sliding around.

The first picture's all light and dark. But after turning it, a window and side of a building, and some sign in a foreign language, becomes clear.

I dump all the pics back in their bag. The other three bags are full of envelopes, loose letters, and cards, even a couple of drawings.

Shit.

The things people sent him. I grab all four bags. No doubt they're coming with me.

I glance at the clock in the kitchen on my first trip downstairs. Shit. Later than I thought.

If I can get it all downstairs, hide it, then even if Dad finds out, maybe he won't be able to find it all.

I'll hide my stuff better than he ever could. But I know, even if he finds out, I'll deal with it. No way he's taking anything back.

I repack the footlocker as fast as I can, one layer at a time, but not nearly as carefully as before. Too much to lose now. And still, so many times I have to resist the urge to add to my sizable pile, knowing there's every chance I'll never get another look. It hurts to put the black-and-white box back in, but of all the stuff, it's the thing Dad would know, on sight, was wrong. I just can't be that stupid.

It takes three more trips to get everything down to my room, and on each trip, things fall and my spastic hands scrabble to gather them up again. I toss stuff onto my bed and run back for more. When it's all downstairs, I stare into T.J.'s room again.

From the doorway, everything is exactly in the places I found them. The footlockers are exactly where I found them, and I rubbed my shoes all over the carpet so there are no obvious dents or roughed-up places to give me away. From the hallway, you can't even see that the footlockers have been opened. Dad would have to go all the way in and crouch down to see that the zip ties have been cut.

Back down in my room, I start to panic for real. A bunch of T.J.'s things sitting around in piles will beg questions. There's no telling when Dad might get home, or when he might get it in his head to come down and check up on me.

I dump the stuff from my lowest desk drawer into a trash bag and then put most of the smaller stuff in there. The T-shirts and sweatshirt I hide in my bureau, underneath my other sweatshirts. The books and DVDs get stacked under the desk, in the back, behind the comic books I haven't read in a while. Then I push my desk chair in as far as it will go.

In the bottom of my closet is my box full of hiking stuff. I dump it all out, and then shove the bags of letters and pictures into it and slide it under my bed. Close enough to grab in an emergency, but still out of sight.

Then I wait for Dad to come home.

twelve

Dad's truck doesn't pull into the driveway until after midnight. I hold my breath, listening as he moves through the house.

Instead of going right upstairs, he walks around the kitchen. I hear the cabinet. He gets a drink. If he comes down the stairs, I might shit my pants. If he heads to the recliner, I'm gonna have to sweat it out some more.

Then I hear it: the open, close, lock of the back door. The steps pause near my stairs. I dive for the bed, ready to pretend I fell asleep listening to the music. But the door doesn't open, and his footsteps head through the living room and upstairs.

I wait for the water through the pipes, the sounds of him walking around his room, and count to one hundred. Wait some more, and there's nothing but silence. He has to be out. Then, moving as quietly as I can, wincing on every step, I grab my backpack. I drop it next to my nightstand, in case I still need to hide the letters and pictures, quick and portable-like, or make a run for it.

Just before climbing back onto the bed, I slide the box out from underneath it and turn on the bedside lamp. I pull out the bag of pictures. The first few I grab are of buildings and people, looking like every pic I've ever seen of Iraq. One of two little boys holding thumbs-up at the camera, the smaller boy holding a candy bar clutched in his hand. A couple of some kind of market, with colorful stalls. Some kind of water. A sunset over a city.

Next are three of guys from T.J.'s unit, or maybe another unit, but Army guys, recognizable even in jeans and tees. They're standing in front of a restaurant or a bar. A couple of pics of the same guys at some kind of party, but this time all looking a little wasted. One of T.J. leaning over with some little kids — he was blowing up balloons. His face, so happy. I stare at it for a long time, then slip it into my backpack, in the small pocket at top.

One of a woman in uniform, dark skin and hair, serious, except for her eyes: her eyes seem to be laughing, maybe at T.J. taking the picture? Maybe she's in T.J.'s unit? Another picture of her, more relaxed, sitting at a table under an umbrella, with T.J. and two other guys. She's the only one in the sun, and her dark skin is glowing, shiny and kind of coppery. Her hair's pulled back from her face, cool sunglasses on top of her head. She's beautiful, smiling into the camera. The other people around the table, including T.J., smile, too. A couple more of them, in different places, but the same clothes. More pics of kids.

Some soldiers in full uniform talking to a classroom full of kids. Another of the woman with T.J., arms around each other. He's grinning his shit-eating grin, and she's laughing, her feet dangling like he had just lifted her off the ground.

Lots more of Iraq. Buildings. People. Streets. Lots of other soldiers. Even more pics of kids.

Another of T.J. and some guys around a picnic table. These guys don't look like Army, but I have no clue where it was taken, or who they are. Were they friends? A woman leaning against a fence. A whole bunch of a lake, houses on the other side. Some people windsurfing. A cat on a chair. Still so many in the bag. So many people I don't even know. Who are they?

And letters. Cards. Three bags. The sheer number of letters is overwhelming. Dizzying.

I push the pictures to the end of the bed and reach into the box. The first bag's about three-quarters full. I tug it open and grab a handful of letters. Shuffling them into a neat pile, I get all the return addresses aligned. Someone in North Carolina. T.J.'s friend Dan. Mitch, from work. Florida. Texas. Wisconsin. I grab some more, scan the names as they slide across my lap. There are so many. Some don't even have envelopes. Some classes sent pictures and handmade cards, with little-kid signatures.

About two dozen in, I find the first one from me. No envelope. Before his birthday, probably in with the package we sent. Written fast and stupid. It's even pretty sloppy. Lame. Idiot.

One with Dad's business labels. Another from Dan. Mr. Anders. I stop and start to read that one, then feel weird, like if I read his letter, it'll be hard to look at Mr. Anders next time I see him. I put it back.

A few more from strangers. A girl T.J. went to high school with. Some with return addresses of classes, schools. A card from Dad and a letter from Denver, from one of T.J.'s buddies I've actually met, from his first tour.

I work my way through the whole bag, reading a few at random.

Whenever I wrote T.J., I never knew what to say. Reading some of the letters other people sent him, they all sound a lot alike — how proud they are; how thankful — but at least they had something to say. Nice stuff, but nothing interesting, really.

I don't know a lot of the people, but some of them had to be his friends. People who wanted T.J. to come home soon. Talking about what good times they'd have when he came home and news of other people I don't know. He hadn't really lived at our house in years, so I guess I always knew he had to have friends all over. Maybe some were guys who got out. Or maybe people he met near base: North Carolina, Georgia, and Wisconsin. A lot of the letters are from Wisconsin. Makes sense — that's where T.J. had been posted before this deployment. But seeing the letters, from so many different strangers, drives it home, how little I really knew what he did when he wasn't here.

Dad's letters are short. To the point. How proud he is of T.J. How he hopes T.J.'s staying focused. Asking if T.J. needs anything. Mine are all lame.

Through the first bag, and all I feel is guilty, and kind of sad. It's embarrassing how few letters I sent. We sent e-mails back and forth all the time, and T.J. sent me postcards sometimes, but we just didn't write each other letters. I really only wrote a letter when we were sending a package. But I still feel like a total jerk. Even Dad wrote more than I thought he had. I guess I just never saw him do it. But Dad's and mine together aren't nearly as many as some of the others. Dan wrote more letters than I did.

I grab the next bag out of the box. Almost as full as the last one. The first three I grab are all from Madison, Wisconsin. The fourth and fifth, too. C. CARSON, on the first label, and second, and then CELIA CARSON, but the same address. Tingles start in my hands and ears and shiver through me. I feel like I'm floating off the bed.

Another handful: the same. I dump the bag and fan them out. All of them from C. or Celia Carson, 754 River Road, Madison, Wisconsin 53703. The whole bag, all of them are from her. Fuck. My mouth goes dry. Hands shaking, I open one at random.

Theo,

Theo? Who the hell is Theo? I scramble for the envelope: T.J.'s name and address. A shudder crawls down my back. Since when was T.J. "Theo"?

Dad, Theodore Sr., was "Ted." Dad always called T.J. "Junior" or, when introducing him to people, "Ted Jr." Mom called him "Teddy." To everyone else, T.J. had always been "T.J." He didn't even like it when I said it like "Teej." More than a few guys ended up in stitches for calling him "Theodore." But . . . "Theo"?

> *It's just after midnight here and this is the first*
> *chance I've had today to write. I read your letter last*
> *night and actually started a letter back, but I didn't get*
> *it finished, and decided to start fresh tonight instead*
> *(last night I was missing you just that much too much).*

Whoa.

> *I'm working on another package — the magazines*
> *and supplies you asked for, some more of the tees and*
> *socks, two CDs that came in the mail (bet you miss eBay*
> *almost as much as you miss me), a few other things*
> *(and tell Tito I found more of the cookies he's been*
> *nagging you about) — but it won't get sent until at least*
> *next week because there's something special I'm waiting*
> *for. You'll like it. Wink.*

Holy shit.

Your letter sounded tired—and yes, I can hear that in the letter. Trouble sleeping again? Me, too.

In case I haven't made it clear, I really miss you. It's turned suddenly cold here, and it makes me miss you even more, if only for the warmth at night—just kidding. . . .

Holy fucking shit!

I grab the pictures. Dig through the bag. Knowing what I'm gonna find but still needing to see. The one of her in uniform. Has to be her. I squint at the uniform. Is her name there? Could be Carson, but I can't see it clear enough to be sure. I dig for more of her. The one at the table, with T.J. and the guys, all of them toasting the camera. Another of her with some people near a swing set. Another of her, but her hair's longer.

In the meantime, know I love you, I think of you day and night, and I hope you are being safe. All my best to the guys. Lol. Xoxo.

Love you, C.

I look at the picture of her in uniform, then at the letter, and then back at the picture of her at the table, sunglasses on top of her head, back to her in uniform. Celia—in uniform and in regular clothes. The one of T.J. lifting her off the ground. Has to be her. One of a bunch of people near water, the sun glinting off the surface behind them: Celia and T.J. and their friends?

My heart pounds so hard it might crack a rib, and still I feel like no blood is reaching my brain.

T.J. had a girlfriend. I scan the letter again. T.J. had a girl-friend, and he never told me. And she called him Theo. And she sent him sexy letters, and packages, and . . . Fuck. I start reading as fast as I can.

thirteen

My head's been spinning since Saturday night. Every time I think I've wrapped my brain around what I found, it hits me all over again.

I read all night Saturday, slept for a few hours, and then started over again.

By Sunday night I'd read all of her letters twice, sifted through all of the pictures to find the ones of her.

I was already dreading Monday, but the lack of sleep and all the stuff whirling around my head made it a soul-sucking hell.

As if I'm not rattled enough, Tuesday starts with a nice long session with Mr. Lee in Guidance. And I have to play nice.

When I came in this morning, they made me sign some paper that said if I don't cooperate in the guidance sessions and be a good boy, I'm gone for the rest of the year, I'll miss finals, and I'll have to do summer school to be a senior next year. And they're putting a hold on my grades until I pay for the display case. Not sure how I'll even know if I have to do summer school if they won't release my grades, but I decide I don't care enough to ask.

I'm supposed to be reading some article about the stages of grief or something, but my head is pounding and my mind keeps wandering.

After some Googling around yesterday, I have a little more than a name and address. The online phone book showed a bunch of addresses for C. Carson and Celia Carson, but it looks like she's still at the River Road address. I also found a listing in a staff directory at the university. And from there, I found a picture. A group shot at some kind of event, small and hard to see, and I think from a few years ago, but clear enough to see that one of the women in that picture sure looks a lot like the woman in T.J.'s pictures.

"Matt." Mr. Lee sighs. "Are you here? I mean, really here?" He rubs his eyes.

It's only 8:42 a.m. and already this day sucks. I sit up in the chair. Focus.

"Yeah," I say, so he knows I'm paying attention. "Sorry."

I'm not sure I can take much more. Mr. Lee shuffles through the file in front of him, then picks up his clipboard again.

"Your brother's death isn't the first loss you've suffered, Matt. How did your family cope when your mother died?"

It takes everything in me not to walk out the door.

"Take a few minutes. Think about it. You have to have done something," Lee says, reaching for his coffee.

I've been dreaming about her a lot. Just fractured images mostly, but sometimes in full-out Technicolor replays. Sometimes I can even smell her, or more how our house smelled when she lived there. I don't dream much about the good stuff. Mostly of Mom right before she left, her wild, fast talk, eyes all shiny and weird. Crazy or silent, somewhere else in her head. Lost before she even left.

That last fight, T.J. threw me in the closet and then tried to get between them. Dad yelling: *It isn't worth it. None of it's worth it. After everything I do for you . . .* Her screeching and tearing the house apart. Wild.

T.J. was only thirteen, and no match for Dad, but Mom was the one throwing things, and he could usually get her under control if Dad let him. T.J. ended up with a split lip. She took off three days later.

It's worse when I dream about the nicer times. Her hands, soft and gentle, even when she could barely hold herself up. She used to make me butterscotch pudding with chocolate-chip faces on top.

How do you grieve for someone who kissed you good-bye one morning when you were five years old and then left while you were at preschool, so that you came home to an empty house and never saw her again? *Do* you even grieve when you spend the next year and a half confused and scared and sometimes worried that she might come back?

I can see Mom's face behind my eyes: twisted like in every fucked-up memory. The smell of her: sour-sweet breath and sweat, or, when she was doing OK, that perfume she loved. T.J. trying to get her out of the car. Dad yelling while counting pills and trying to clean up the mess. Breaking glass. Like I'm still cowering in the corner, listening through hands fisted over my ears. Choking on the sudden sour burn in my throat.

"Matt."

Shudder. Head rush. My throat burns. Lee's half out of his seat. I've never seen his face like that.

"Are you OK?" he asks.

"Yeah." I rub my sweaty palms over my knees to dry them. "Fine." I pull the paper closer to me. *Stages of Grief.*

Mr. Lee pushes the paper aside right out from under my fingers. "OK, let's try a different tack." He settles back into his chair. "Yesterday was Memorial Day. What did you do to honor your brother's memory?"

Worse than Mom.

Dad got up, got dressed, and left, like it was any other Monday. No idea if he actually went to the office or what, but he left around the usual time and he came home around the usual time, and then he spent the rest of the night in his recliner, as if there were nothing at all unusual about the day.

I tried not to lose my fucking mind. I had no idea when Dad might come home, and in what kind of mood. I sat in my room, wishing time would move faster, doing some research and looking at the letters, but with my shoes on and backpack at the ready, just in case he came home and decided to look at

T.J.'s stuff. If he'd even paused outside the door to T.J.'s room, I'd have been out of there.

"Come on. You and your dad, you have to have done something to honor him." He motions with his glasses. "Or be planning on doing something?"

Mr. Lee taps his pen against his clipboard. When I look up, he glances down at my lap. My hands are clenched. I force them to relax, wipe them on my jeans. He clears his throat, raises an eyebrow, the message clear: I'm gonna have to say something.

I just sit there, picking at the inner seam of my jeans. The rhythmic flick of my nail over the edge is nicely distracting. Mr. Lee's clipboard clatters onto the desk. Other papers shoved aside.

"Come on, Matt. One thing. Cooperate. Talk to me. So I can tell Mr. Pendergrast you're complying."

I shift, rub my temple, try to make a show of thinking about it. Dad's honoring T.J. by pretending he isn't dead and ignoring every bit of evidence that proves him wrong. But me? What am I doing? Well, aside from kicking the crap out of losers who call his death a waste? And breaking into his personal effects? And wondering why he never told me about Celia?

But there is something I can do. And I already know what. But doing it, actually doing it, will be hard. A little crazy.

"This is it, Matt," Lee says. "Last chance time. Talk to me. Convince me that you're ready."

I bite the inside of my cheek. Because I'm not ready. For school, yeah, fine. I'll lie low. Whatever. But for what I really need to do? I'm nowhere near ready. And I'm running out of time. Finals next week. Then my regular work crew starting the week after. Can't miss work. Can't let Mr. Anders down, or make him think he can't trust me.

"There's something, isn't there?" Lee asks.

I swallow hard. Nod. But that's it. That's all I can do.

"You're not going to tell me what, though, are you?"

I shake my head. "Can't," I say. Bite down to hold it in. Take a deep breath. "Sorry."

"Well, something is progress, so long as it's something good. Something productive, positive. Something worthy of your memory of him. Something that isn't beating up your classmates," Mr. Lee says. And despite everything, I smile.

Mr. Lee's face flashes some new emotion and then resettles into his bland nonjudgmental mask. He grabs the clipboard again.

"Well, then that's your homework for next week. I want to know three things you did to honor your brother's memory, and three things you want to do in the future. They can be small things, even personal things, like looking at a photo album or writing down a memory—even talking to someone about your brother. But three things you actually did, and another three you want to do. Take the time to put some real thought into this, Matt. I think you might surprise yourself." Mr. Lee grins at me. I want to wipe the smile off his face, but

I can't bring myself to say anything that might. Not with this little gnawing feeling inside that he's right.

Time to step up.

I reach for my backpack, but Lee waves me back down.

"Now," he says, like we're best buds, "let's talk about some strategies for dealing with anger in a more productive way, OK?"

Sure. Whatever. Talk away, Guidance Man. I'll be over here plotting.

I nod in the right places. Offer a suggestion or two. Watch the clock. Finally, he's satisfied.

"I think we're making some progress, Matt. Good work."

Good work. What a crock. Yeah, I'm gonna do something for T.J. Something big. Biggest thing anyone could do for T.J. now. But somehow I don't think Lee will approve.

I take my time leaving Guidance, hoping the halls'll be clear before I have to stop at my locker. Instead, Shauna's there, frantically looking at her watch, waiting for me. When she looks up and sees me, she relaxes for a second, then tenses up again with a whole new kind of anxiety.

We haven't talked since I blew off our plans on Saturday night. She's left three messages and sent a bunch of texts since Sunday. I didn't call her back. Not even yesterday. Unreturned calls and texts are pretty much the worst thing I can do to her—she always assumes the worst, every version of the worst in turn. The last time she worried herself into a fit, I promised never to completely ignore her calls again. I'm an asshole.

From the look on her face, now that she knows I'm alive, she's heading past worried and sliding into pissed off. I know it's up to me to fix things. And I'll need her help. But there's no way I can explain in thirty seconds in the middle of the hallway.

"Hi," she says, but it sounds like "Fuck you." Definitely pissed.

"Hey."

"Everything OK?" Not too pissed, if she can bring herself to ask.

"Yeah." I wave my pass at her. "Another soothing encounter with Guidance."

"Mr. Lee?" Small flicker of something there. Maybe not *too* too angry.

"Yup, Mr. How-Does-That-Make-You-Feel? himself."

"And how do you feel?"

"Now that I can't smell his particular blend of coffee, smoke, and aftershave anymore? Fine. A little tired, but . . ." I try my best grin, and get only a small pink smile in return.

"So, things are . . . OK?" There are so many questions wrapped into that, and I don't think any of them are about Guidance.

"Yeah. I still have a ton of crap to make up by next week. And finals." I make a gun with my hand and shoot myself in the head. She doesn't laugh. "Yeah," I say, "fine."

"I meant . . . yesterday?"

Fuck. I thought she'd let it go. "Just another Monday," I say, ducking into my locker.

She blows out a breath, loud near my ear. "OK," she says. "Look, are we . . . ? Did I . . . ? Are you mad at *me*?"

"What?" Buzzing, in my ears. "No. No, I'm not mad at you."

"Because you've been acting really weird, and you blew me off on Saturday night, and I waited for you to call Sunday, or yesterday, but . . ." She throws one of my own shrugs back at me. "Look, I know I was a bitch when you blew me off on Saturday, but . . ." She blows her hair out of her eyes. "When you didn't call me back, not even yesterday, I got worried, and . . ."

"I've just been breaking my ass trying to get all this stuff done. And I had to do the storm windows on Saturday, and then—"

"If it's your dad, you know you can—"

"There's nothing—"

"Matt." She tucks her chin to her chest. "This is *me*."

Well, there's no arguing with that. I'm gonna tell her anyway. But not here.

"It's not Dad." Her eyebrows arch. "Well, not any more than usual."

"But there is something." She steps a little closer, uses all her skills at intimidating me with her eyes. "I know there is. So talk."

The bell rings, jolting me, even with pass in hand. Not so much her.

"The bell." I cringe at stating the obvious. She couldn't care less. "I've got to get to the library, Shaun."

She doesn't react. Or move. She's not going anywhere. She sets her jaw and holds on to my locker door. Great. Her line in the sand. Terrific. The second bell sounds and she doesn't even flinch. Shit.

"Go. Meet me here after school."

"And?" she asks, already shifting her bag to run to class.

"And we'll go somewhere." Not enough. "We'll go somewhere and I'll tell you." I look her in the eyes. "I'll tell you everything."

That gets me a real smile and a quick squeeze of my arm. Then she's gone in a blur, her curly hair bouncing around.

The morning limps by in a kind of fuzzy-around-the-edges haze. I do Spanish and Ritzler's class, but then retreat to the library to work on a makeup English paper.

In the bend past the cafeteria, I run into Pinscher, literally, as I am rounding the corner. He's got a couple of guys with him, like they're on guard, on alert, for me. Pinscher steps back and out of my way before he can stop himself. I hold my ground.

In the stalemate, I can't help but stare at his face, still kind of puffy or something. Like he's wearing a floppy mask of his own face. I almost feel sorry for him, almost, but then

I remember all the shit he said, and that shirt. My hand clenches into a fist.

Pinscher swallows hard, his Adam's apple bobbing. I force my hand to relax, and I walk sideways, my open hand up in front of me, hoping to make it clear I have no intention of jumping him—at least not without provocation.

"Be cool," Michael says, one hand on Pinscher's shoulder, the other palm up to me. "Everyone's cool."

We move around each other, rotating so that we each edge toward where we were heading before we ran into each other.

"We OK?" Pinscher asks.

"No." We've never been OK. "Pull some shit like that again . . ." I trail off. Jake steps past Pinscher toward me. Stevie grabs his arm to stop him. "But stay away from me and I'll stay away from you. All of you."

Pinscher nods and I nod back. I make my arms fall limp. After a beat, Pinscher holds out his hand to shake. I ignore it, keep staring at his face.

"Come on, Matt," Michael says.

No way will I shake that asshole's hand. "Just stay away from me."

I force myself to turn around and walk away, but I don't relax until I hear their footsteps moving in the other direction.

There are only a couple of other losers in the library trying to catch up on end-of-the-semester stuff. Ms. Roberts keeps squinting at me if I even dare breathe too loud. But

I can't concentrate. All I can think about is Celia. T.J. and Celia.

Images from T.J.'s pictures keep flashing in my head between sentences from Celia's letters, almost like a slide show, but one that's been edited out of order or messed up. I can close my eyes and see them against the red-black of my eyelids.

> *The ice is melting, making these little rivers that trickle along the edges of the street. Spring's almost here. . . .*

One of the smaller pictures: Celia and some guy dressed for skiing. Both of them falling over, laughing, their dark skin vivid against the snowy background and ski clothes.

> *. . . laughing while Aiden wiped milk . . .*
> *. . . harder when it's cold, and dark and . . .*

Picture of a house, white and gray. And trees, near a river.

> *. . . all the kids with ice cream and dressed in the most ridiculous costumes . . .*

Two little boys, holding plastic guns. A mosaic, scarred and battered.

> *You left only yesterday, and already I can hardly stand it. . . . Sometimes I dream you're still here, and your leaving was the dream . . . When I wake up, it's like you just left. . . .*

I thought he had redeployed right after he left us. But he went to visit her, without telling me.

> *Jordan and Shay took me out tonight, sweet in their*
> *attempts to distract me. I smiled a lot for their sakes.*
> *Even danced some. Made it ache even more, how much*
> *I miss you.*

So many of the letters talked about people I don't know, have never even heard of. She wrote about a party they had for him before he left on the last deployment. It made me dizzy to think about all these people who knew him and to wonder who told them he was gone, if they even know.

> *Dinner with Missy and Will tonight. They're not*
> *letting me hibernate. I promised Zoe she could pick the*
> *ice cream for dessert.*

After the first fast read, I'd read through her letters more slowly, more carefully, tucking each back in its envelope before moving on, keeping them in order. I've read them so many times that parts of them are burned on my brain. When I close my eyes, I can see her signature branded on the inside of my eyelids; always signed the same, *Love you, C.* Her flowy script and a loop to the single letter, so that it looked like more. Always telling him she loved him, she missed him, she said *they all* did, whoever "they" were.

Her mushy stuff and *missing him*s were hard enough to read, but a lot of them were full of details and stories that made me feel like I was reading about a stranger in a magazine or newspaper. Like this "Theo" wasn't my brother at all.

She sent cards: for Christmas, T.J.'s birthday, Valentine's Day, others, some for no reason at all, obviously sent with packages, because there were no envelopes. One birthday card had had something taped to the inside of its cover, gone. I wish I knew what.

> . . . I couldn't really find Halloween masks this early,
> so I bought whatever other stuff I could find —funny
> glasses and noses, makeup . . . Have fun! (But not too
> much fun.) . . . Miss you. . . .

I didn't even know T.J. would want Halloween stuff. Did he tell her, or did she just know? Dad and I sent T.J. food and news and magazines, and things he needed. I know we did. And yet I wonder how much better her packages were, how much more special. If she knew to send things we didn't. Maybe she sent him sexy things.

> . . . I miss waking up with your hand on my
> stomach . . . rubbing slow, lazy circles . . . your soft
> snoring into my neck . . . your bristled chin rubbing
> against my shoulder. . . .

I keep trying to picture T.J. with the people in the pictures, and in the letters, but the words are all wrong, the images all strange. I can't even make sense of some of the words. Not like I can't read them, but that none of it seems real. So, in my head, the words all jumble together in weird combinations, like the Mad Libs we played as kids.

"Matt?" I jump. Ms. Roberts twists her mouth to the side. "Are you in need of assistance?"

"No. Thanks." I pull myself up in my chair.

"Then I suggest you get to work."

I try to work on the paper. But I can't. There are more important things to think about, to plan.

fourteen

After last period, Shauna's waiting at my locker, like I knew she would be. She probably left class early and ran all the way, just to be sure I couldn't sneak out.

"I heard about the hall," she says. "You OK?"

News travels fast, unless Michael took it upon himself to run right to her. "I'm fine."

"Yeah, you're great." She laughs, but nothing's funny.

We walk in silence out to the parking lot.

"Is there going to be trouble?" she asks, resigned to it.

"No." I turn so she can see my face. She bites the inside of her lower lip. She isn't sure whether to believe me. "At least not today," I add. "Probably not even this week. So, no, I don't think so."

She studies my face until she's satisfied that I'm telling the truth, then hands me the keys. I drive when she's really excited or trying to say she's sorry. Today, probably a bit of both. She bounces toward the car, all nervous energy and excitement.

"Where to?" she asks once we're buckled in.

"The river?" I suggest.

She looks at me for a beat, blinking, clearly understanding that something really is up if I don't want to go to her house, where her mom will feed me.

We drive through for some snackage and then park in the small gravel lot near the bend in the river where it's shallow. A picnic table in the shade is perfect and quiet.

I take my time eating, trying to work out how to start or what to say. Shauna's done and waiting for me before I've eaten much at all, which pretty much never happens. When the waiting gets to be too much, she makes a frustrated yelp and smacks my arm.

"I can't take this anymore! What's going on?"

I push the rest of my burger away and wipe my hands on my jeans. I reach for my shake, hit the cup, and scramble to right the cup before it spills all over. Then I move it away from me, so I can't knock it over again.

"Matt, just tell me." She takes a deep breath and then lets it out with a shaky sigh.

I work my throat to get it out, the words crammed in and jumbled. "We got T.J.'s stuff." I suck in some air. "His personal effects."

Shauna's eyes go wide. "But I thought . . . that bag . . . from—"

"So did I. But Cooper showed up Friday with three footlockers."

She grabs my hand and squeezes it. "Did your dad go crazy, or . . . ? Wait, he did let you see them, right? I mean—"

"He, uh, didn't. He just put them away, in T.J.'s room. But—"

"You have to go through them!" She jumps up, then sits down again to grab her backpack, preparing to jump again. "I'll help you, or be your lookout, or . . . we could wait for poker night, and—"

"Shaun, I already did." She drops her bag and flops back onto the bench. "I went through everything Saturday night."

She settles in, eyes huge. "Oh, my God. Does he know?"

"No. I snuck in while he was out."

"Shit." She looks impressed. And all's forgiven.

"Yeah, well . . . I figured I'd better look through it all, and fast, just in case."

"Yeah." She reaches for my hand again. "And?"

I shake her off—too distracting. "And . . . his uniform, clothes, iPods, books, photographs, games, CDs . . . all kinds of stuff. The letters people wrote him." I reach into my backpack and pull out the heavy plastic bag. "Including these."

Her eyes dart back and forth between the letters and my face. "From?"

"T.J.'s girlfriend."

"Get out!" she yells, slapping my arm again. "Who . . . I mean . . . Where? Girlfriend?"

"Yup."

"And she wrote him letters? You have letters from her?"

I pick at the edge of the table. "Yeah." I look back up at

her. "Some of them are, um, kinda . . ." I can't say it, even if I can't scour the sexy parts from my brain.

Her cheeks go suddenly pink. She gets it.

"Want to read some of them?" I ask quietly, pushing a bag with some of Celia's letters—sort of a best-of-Celia selection—toward Shauna.

"Seriously?" She reaches for the bag between us, but pauses when her fingers touch the plastic. "I mean, it's OK?"

"Yeah." I need her to read them, to see her reactions.

She starts pulling them out of the bag.

"They're in order by postmark, so . . ." I sit on my hands to keep from reaching for them, to protect them.

She smiles. "Keep them in order. Check."

I turn my face away, hot at her teasing. But while I sort through a few of the pics she should see, I watch her carefully pull them out in small groups, keeping them in order.

When I was reading them the first time, words kept ricocheting off my brain and bouncing around the inside of my skull. Words like *love* and *bed* and *kisses. Hands. Sheets. Sweet. Sexy. Touching. Missing. Worry. Sad.* Phrases like *be careful* and *come home* and *love you.*

It's easy to see the letters that are extra worn, with creases and marks and edges frayed from careful, but repeated, handling. T.J. read those letters over and over. They were always the really sexy ones. Which was weird, like spying on him, on them.

There were just so many. She had to have written him a couple times a week. And so many didn't have envelopes, and others were stuck into cards, meaning she had to have sent more packages, too. As many letters from Celia as everyone else combined. I skimmed some of the other letters, but compared to Celia's, they're pretty boring. I left them in the box under my bed.

Shauna unfolds the first one, postmarked right after T.J.'s unit deployed. The last one's postmarked a few weeks before T.J. was killed. I keep hoping that Celia didn't find out he was gone by her letters coming back.

"Holy shit." Shauna looks up from the letter, her eyes blinking rapidly. *"Theo?"*

It's kind of fun, watching her. "I know. Keep reading."

She clears her throat and starts to read aloud, which feels weird, but I can't tell her to stop. I want to hear her read them.

"I just this morning answered your latest e-mail, so it feels stupid to write again already, but this is a letter day. And I never miss a letter day. Even though these take so long to get to you, I can't help it. There's something NOT ordinary about writing you a letter. Picking out the paper, touching it, tucking in a treat, an article or a picture. Giving you some part of me to hold. To feel. [Insert deep sigh here.]

"I miss your hands, holding me, touching me. Don't

*get me wrong, I love your e-mails (and don't stop sending
them), but I love the letters more, for having something
from you to hold.*

*"So when you get this letter, and all the news is
not really newsworthy anymore, just think about how
I picked out the paper and paused over the words and
signed it, knowing you would be able to feel me . . ."*

Shauna trails off, waving the letter at me. "When you said
he had a girlfriend, I thought, I guess, like"— she leans a little
ways back from the table —"some kind of . . . fling, but . . ."

I nod.

"Matt! I thought, like . . . Holy shit!" She laughs, hits the
letter with her hand. "This . . . She . . . Matt!"

The laughter ripples through my chest, too, because of all
her possible reactions, this one is the best, the most fun. This
one is pure Shauna. My Shauna. It's strangely calming, like
pretty much nothing else has been.

"Now you understand why I've been weird?" I ask.

"No shit. But, Matt, she loved him."

"I know."

"And if she was writing this, then T.J . . . ."

"Loves, or, uh, loved her? Yeah," I say. "I've figured that
part out. Keep going. There's more."

"More?"

She dives back in. Reading me bits from time to time.
Other times curling in on herself and reading with her

fingers pressed to her lips. She hands me a candy to unwrap, too engrossed even to deal with the wrapper. After I hand her the candy, I chew the bits of sticky grape off my fingers and continue looking through the pictures.

"Are any of those of her? Do you know?"

I hand her the one of Celia in her uniform. "I'm pretty sure this is her. I Googled around, found a picture of her on a website for a university — I think she works there."

"Wow."

"There's a bunch of pictures of her, at different times. Not a lot of anyone else. And I just . . . I don't know, but I instantly knew it was her. And then the picture I found online confirmed it." I stare at the picture of her at the picnic table. "I've been thinking that maybe that's why he didn't tell us."

"Huh?"

My face gets hot in a different way.

"Oh," Shauna says. "Because she's black? You really think he would think that would matter to you?"

"No. Maybe. I don't know. Maybe Dad, but . . . T.J. didn't tell me, either, so . . ." I hand her the next couple of pictures so I can stop talking. "I found those, too."

"Do you know any of the guys?"

"No. But these two," I say, pointing to the guys outside the restaurant with her, "I think they're Army, too. Probably all from his, her — I don't know, maybe their — unit."

"What about them?" she asks, pointing at the two guys at the umbrella table with them.

I look at their faces again—could be more of the unit, I guess, but on leave. Or friends. The guy on the other side of T.J. could be Army. He has that look: short hair, strong, something about the way he's sitting, too. His skin is almost as dark as hers, but not all suntanned like she is. Can't tell if that means he doesn't spend a lot of time outside or just never really tans. But the guy on the other side of Celia doesn't look Army. And his skin's light enough that it's even kind of sunburned, especially his nose, so he doesn't spend much time outside. And his hair is way longer than regulation. No, I'd guess not military.

I blow out my breath. "No idea."

She goes back to the letters. I wait. She'll come to it soon—maybe three or four letters down.

The closer she gets, the harder it is not to jump ahead and just force her to read that letter, to ask outright. But I need to see her find it, figure it out for herself.

When the small square flutters out of a letter and falls face up on the table in front of her, I brace for it. She turns the photo around. Her brow creases. Then her face smoothes out and rounds with her smile. I know what the picture looks like—I've stared at it for hours. Celia—softer and more relaxed than the other pics, but definitely her—holding a little girl.

"Matt?"

"Read the letter."

T.J. read this letter many times. He opened and refolded

it again and again, the edges fuzzy from his hands, each time tucking it safely back in its envelope, picture and all.

I can tell she just wants me to tell her, but she hands me the small square picture and prepares to read.

"Theo," she begins.

Already I pretty much know this one by heart, but I close my eyes and listen anyway.

"It's Friday morning, just after 8am. It's been an oh-so-long week, so I took the day off. Mom picked up Zoe an hour ago for a day with Grammy and Pops. So Missy stopped up for coffee before work, bringing fresh cherry scones, still warm. Wonderful! Especially because we could just have a relaxing morning, and talk, really talk, without Zoe's little ears to worry about. Love the girl, but sometimes I just need some time with Missy, alone, to talk.

"Now, a fresh cup of coffee, just on the good side of too sweet, a blissfully quiet house, and a fresh sheet of paper. So, where to start?

"Sunday, Thomas stopped by with a few pictures he took on Dad's birthday—the best one of the bunch is enclosed. Zoe looks like an angel (as you can see, it's pre-chocolate cake and ice cream). I framed a bigger copy, but Thomas thought you'd like a smaller one—easier to have with you, to hold on to.

"Yesterday was one of those crazy unseasonably

warm days where everyone forgets their troubles for a while. I was done early, so I called Missy and Mom and told them I'd pick up Zoe from day care, and we went to the park. You would not believe how much she's grown—and how much she's talking—can hardly shut the child up! And it's all, 'I do it by my sef' (no L as far as I can tell). Baby Girl is turning into Little Miss Independent. Made me smile and wish you were here.

"She misses you. She keeps asking when you'll be home from work. She must think you're always at the office, like Missy, or Will, work being where the adults go when they're not home. Yesterday she got that puzzled expression midslide, and when I caught her at the bottom, she looked around like you were just there, and she asked again. I didn't have that talk in me yesterday, so I distracted her with ice cream. I'm sure you, of all people, could get behind that. She wanted 'los and los and los of prinkles' on hers—and her idea of 'los' is definitely in line with yours when you order lots and lots and lots. She even waved her hand for another spoonful like you do. We all thank you ever so much for teaching her that.

"I miss you, too. But that's no secret. And, I should say that everyone misses you.

"I think yesterday was the last gasp of summer. It's supposed to get steadily colder this week. I dread the first really cold night. I just know I'll be huddled under the

covers, probably even wearing socks, but wishing for your perpetual warmth. I miss waking up with you in the morning, and going to bed with you at night, and it will only be worse when it's cold.

"I promised myself I'd wait to write until I snapped out of this mood, but apparently it's back. So, let's try for some levity, shall we?

"Missy and Will are having a little dinner tomorrow night. (Can't really call it a party, can we?) Zoe's excited. She keeps babbling about it, about how Missy said she could help. Not sure what she thinks she'll be helping with, but tonight she was packing her little backpack with crayons and stuffies. And she's insisting on wearing her pink camo overalls. Missy and I both tried to talk her into something else. No luck.

"I know I should go, but I just got the special edition DVD set of West Side Story *in the mail. So, I'm thinking instead I'll make a pot of cocoa (or a pitcher of sangria) and watch it all. I might even turn it off before Tony dies and pretend that Maria and Tony ride off into the sunset together (or at least across town — the neighborhood be damned). And just think, if I watch it enough times (over and over and over again) before you come home, maybe you'll only have to watch it once or twice with me. (Stop making that face. You'll love it. And if not, I'll make it up to you. The way you like.)*

"And a little more good news: the house—our
house—is back on the market. Maybe I'll just have to
have a look inside one of these days. (I know, I know,
but I can dream.)

"Well, I guess I should finish this up and get it in the
mail. I know saying 'Be safe' annoys you, because you are
always Mister As-Safe-As-Possible-Given-the-Fight, but
saying it, for me, is like a prayer, or a wish. So—be safe!
(Please, for me.)

Love you, C."

I can see Shauna feeling it, that buzz, under her skin or
in the air. She reads it again, more slowly. To herself. At the
first mention of "Zoe" she stops.

I hand her the picture again. The little girl waving her
small pudgy hand. Her eyes and skin lighter than Celia's, but
with Celia's hair, Celia's nose. Celia and Zoe.

Shauna takes a gulp of air. Squints. Her mouth moves,
but she doesn't say anything. She tilts her head, reads a bit of
the letter again, then looks at me.

"You think?"

And there it is.

"I don't know," I say, my voice cracking.

"Zoe. You think . . . Shit. Not just a girlfriend. You think
Zoe is T.J.'s kid?"

I turn it all over again in my head. "Maybe." She stares,

making me commit. "Yes, I think Zoe could be his kid. But I'm not sure."

Shauna flails on the bench, gargling, sputtering, practically vibrating. "Matt! What else could it mean? I mean, the picture, and Zoe asks about him, and . . ."

I rub at my neck, trying to chase away the doubt. "Yeah, and I thought, maybe, but read it again. It's like . . . she doesn't come right out and say it, and wouldn't she? Wouldn't she say something, like, I don't know, she misses her daddy or something?"

"No, not if . . . I mean, he knows who she is, right? What about the other letters? Do any of them say for sure?"

I shake my head. "I've read them all, more than once. She talks about Zoe a lot, but never actually says *daughter* or *daddy* or anything."

She looks at the picture again. Runs her finger along the edge. It's not perfect, like the other sides, and there's a little sliver of blue along Celia's arm, like someone else's shirt. I stared at it for like an hour last night. Someone cut it.

Shauna's finger traces the blue line. "Celia cut out herself and Zoe from a bigger picture and sent them to T.J. Why? Why would she do that unless it was so he could have this picture with just them?" Her smile keeps growing.

I take the picture and look at it again.

Shauna grabs my arm until I look at her. "I mean, if this wasn't . . . if she was just Celia's kid, why would Celia bother?

And if she wasn't Celia's kid at all . . . I mean, Celia talks about Zoe a lot, and about day care, and . . . Why wouldn't she just send him the whole picture, unless she wanted him to have one of just them, just the two of them?"

"Maybe whoever else was in it, maybe T.J. didn't like them or something. Or maybe there were a lot of other people in it. Maybe—"

"No," Shauna says. "No way. She sent T.J. this picture of just the two of them. Her and Zoe. Alone. She had to have done that on purpose. She was sending him a picture of his family, like she said, for T.J. to 'hold on to.'"

I stare at the picture. Zoe's skin *is* a lot lighter than Celia's, and she does sort of look like she *could* be T.J.'s kid, maybe. And this picture, you can tell just by looking at it, Celia's definitely her mom. They way they are, and how much Zoe looks like Celia. And if Zoe is Celia's, then Shauna's right, she has to be T.J.'s. There's nothing else that makes sense. But the rock in my stomach won't let me totally believe.

"Who's Missy?" Shauna asks. Shauna points to the letter. "Celia talks about Missy coming over. Missy not needing to pick Zoe up from day care. So, who is she? Do the other letters say?"

"A friend, I think. Maybe a neighbor. She babysits Zoe sometimes. Some of the other letters talk about Missy stopping by or picking Zoe up."

I try to order the bits from the letters jumping around my head.

"Celia talks about Missy and Will in some of the other letters, about having dinner with them, and about them getting her out of the house. And both Missy and Will sent T.J. letters, too. Not a lot, but some. They mention Zoe, too. But—"

"Oooh," Shauna yelps. "Do *they* say anything about Zoe? About, like, 'your daughter' or . . ."

"No. Nothing like that. They don't call her T.J.'s daughter or anything. But they both say things about Zoe missing T.J., and talking about him. And there's one letter from Missy where she wrote about putting Zoe to bed, and that Will fell asleep, but she waited up. So, I think they were watching Zoe, and she waited up for Celia to come home."

Talking about it, thinking about all the bits and pieces, it starts to sink in. I start letting myself believe. "Celia talks about Zoe, about Zoe and T.J. . . . like . . . she's his." . . . *los and los of prinkles* . . . "Celia talks about Zoe missing T.J., asking about him, about things he taught Zoe." . . . *her little fingers, pointing to your picture on the fridge . . . making you a picture . . .* "She talks about T.J. tucking her in, cuddling Zoe. She talks about Zoe missing T.J. almost as much as Celia does. It just doesn't sound like stuff you'd say about someone else's kid. And Celia's letter says 'Mom' picked Zoe up, not someone else's mom. I think she's Celia's. I just do." She has to be.

"And if she's Celia's," Shauna says, "then she's T.J.'s, right?" She grins at me.

She has to be. "Yeah."

"Yeah," Shauna says, nodding, like she won.

I hand Shauna another picture, the one of T.J. picking Celia up, both of them laughing. She studies the picture, then looks at the letter again. Her cheeks climb with her smile. Her eyes shine.

"Makes *total* sense." Shauna laughs.

My muscles relax. Yeah. It does make sense. I know she's Celia's. I *know* it. And if she's Celia's, then she's T.J.'s. T.J. has a kid.

"And he never . . ."

I shake my head. "Not a word." The picture in her hand, their smiles. Does Celia know he's gone? "Got to hand it to him. He sure knew how to keep a secret." I point to the letters she hasn't read yet. "Keep reading. Tell me what you think after. Maybe there's something I missed."

I go back to sorting through the pictures. He only had a few of Celia and Zoe. Too few. He took a lot of pictures of other people's kids, but he only had a couple of his own.

Watching Shauna read the letters is almost more intense, or emotional, than when I read them myself. Or maybe it just feels that way because I've read them so many times. But Shauna, whose face has always shown everything she feels, shows me now what *I* should feel. Especially now that she knows about Zoe. The more she smiles, cries, frowns, the more I trust it. When she bites her lip, blushes, my face gets hot. She blushes a lot. She looks at me, now and then, sometimes even stopping for a few seconds, looking off somewhere, and then continuing again. I gave her the best of the bunch to read, but maybe I'll let her read the rest of Celia's letters sometime.

When she reaches the last letter in this stack, she tucks it back into its envelope, then lays it gently on the table in front of her, facedown with the rest. Then she looks at me. She nods.

"There's one more thing," I tell her.

"More?" She seems to have trouble wrapping her brain around that. I know the feeling.

"Just one," I say. "One more letter."

"From Celia?"

I pull it out of my backpack, still segregated in its plastic bag. I hand it to her.

She turns it over, and then right-side up, and her eyes water as she reads the address.

"*To* Celia," I say. "T.J. never got to send it."

"Oh. My. God." She gasps. Tears pool in her eyes. She seems to ask a million questions without saying a word.

"I know." I barely get the words out past the rock in my throat. I have to clear it twice to go on. "It was in its own bag, with that label sealing it shut, just like that. I almost missed it because it was kind of stuck to one of the other bags. Obviously he meant to send it to her. It had to have been in the envelope and ready to go, because they slit the envelope open at the top, then sealed it in its own bag."

She runs her finger over the label that seals the plastic

bag shut where the opening folds over at an angle. Maybe an accident, because none of the other bags were like that. But no way to open it without breaking the seal. Then she runs her finger over the C. CARSON and the address, already on the envelope, ready to go. Then she touches the seal again. Testing it, like I did. A bunch of times.

"You didn't?"

I shake my head. "I couldn't. It . . . didn't seem right."

She glances down at the letters around us. There's that flutter of nerves in my stomach again.

"I didn't really think about it when I started reading them," I say, "that it could be wrong to read his letters or that there would be anything, you know, personal in them. I just wanted to know what people said. And then I found Celia's, and pretty much didn't care about the others. But by the time I found that one, I had already read a lot of hers. And . . ."

"You kind of knew her?"

"No, but . . . well, it seemed . . ." Wrong. "Not really like it even belonged to T.J. anymore. It was already her letter, you know? If he had dropped it in the mail slot before the patrol . . . and with the seal . . ."

Shauna nods and strokes the seal again. "I'd feel the same way," she says, like she's proud of me. "This one is different."

"Soooo," I say, drawing it out until she looks up. "I've been thinking about it." I take the letter from her hands. "Can I borrow your car?"

fifteen

THE NEXT COUPLE OF DAYS ARE NUTS. BESIDES CRAMMING for finals, I have the stupid English paper and three Spanish conversationals to make up. Oh, and less than a week to plan my great escape.

Mrs. D. gets me out of all my nonfinal classes on Wednesday and Thursday so I can go to the library and try to throw together enough of a term paper to pass English. Yesterday I actually did some research for the paper, but today I'm spending most of the day researching the trip. I've got to figure it all out before next Thursday. As soon as my last final is done, I'll take off.

Plus I've been trying to be home whenever Dad is, hanging around in the kitchen, like I'm studying really hard. I don't think he'll go into T.J.'s room if I'm around. If he does, I want to know it, as soon as it happens, so I can get the hell out of town. I keep Celia's letters, T.J.'s letter, and the photos in my backpack, along with all the money I have. Just in case. It's not enough money, not yet. But it's all I have.

Today I had a makeup lab, meaning Dad could be home any minute, and I'm still at school, waiting for Shauna to pick me up, with no way to know if I'll be walking into an ambush.

I leave her another voice mail.

I sit down on the steps and pull out my notebook. I've got a running list of what I'll need. Top of that list, I need to figure out how much the trip to Wisconsin will cost. Mr. Anders'll pay me part of what he owes me tomorrow, but he's not paying me the rest until next Friday. With what I've got saved up, it might be enough to get me to Wisconsin, maybe. But not enough, not yet, for someplace to stay while I'm there, or the gas back. I'll have to come up with some way to get the rest.

Dad made a big deal about how I'd turn in the first half of the display case money next Friday. Apparently Pendergrast didn't bow down low enough in gratitude when Dad called him. Now Dad wants to be there when I deliver it. He probably has a whole speech planned, or just some serious glaring. If I take off Thursday right after my exams, I can be long gone before Dad has a clue, and before he can take the money or march me down to the school to hand it over. But he's gonna be supernova pissed—like I'm doing it on purpose just to shame him. He's gonna—

Car horn. Shauna's harried face stares at me through the car window. She starts talking before I've even got the seat belt fastened. I wave my hand to get her to drive, pointing at the clock. She keeps talking but puts the car in drive.

The drive across town is a nightmare: we hit every red light; Shauna jabbers non-stop about a fight with one of her sisters. I have no idea which one. I stare at the clock on the dash.

I'm still trying to figure out what I'm gonna do if it's an ambush when she screeches to a stop in front of my house and throws the car into park.

Dad's truck is in the driveway.

I've already got my seat belt off and the door open.

"Call me," she yells after me.

Through the window in the back door, I can see Dad sitting at the kitchen table sifting through the mail. Shit. He glances back when I open the door.

Playing it cool is a fierce act of will.

Dad looks at the clock and back at me.

"Where you been?"

He's sneering. Not good, but I can't tell how bad yet. I regrip the strap of my backpack. Ready to run. "Makeup lab. Then Shauna was late."

"Your legs broken?"

"She was on her way, so I thought . . . it was . . ." He loses interest, so I stop talking, which is good because I'm still scrambling for a foothold and flying blind.

"Bullshit." He flicks two envelopes into the trash bin next to him, then slaps a couple on the table, bills by the looks of them. "What a waste on all this bullshit." Three more in the trash.

He pauses over the next letter before placing it on the kitchen table away from the piles of bills and magazines.

Even from across the room, I see the loopy handwritten address and the preprinted red-white-and-blue return label, the kind with an eagle—a condolence letter. We haven't received one in a while, at least not that I've seen.

He works through the last of the pile. I wait for some hint of whether I'm standing in quicksand or on dry land. Well, and for permission to leave the kitchen.

"Whoa-ho," he shouts. "Mail for the pretty boy."

The sharp edge of an envelope catches me in the chest. It lands faceup on the floor in front of me. Great, another recruiting letter. Don't even have to open it to know what it says. He has to have signed me up with every branch, in hopes that one will send me a shiny-enough brochure to convince me. Or maybe he just likes getting them himself.

Dad cuffs my shoulder on his way to put the trash can back under the sink. "Nine months."

I bite the inside of my cheek to keep from correcting him. It's only been a little over six months since T.J. died: 195 days to be exact. The look on his face is hopeful, happy, confusing. Then I realize he means the months until my eighteenth birthday, in March. My mouth goes dry.

I stand there, shaking under my skin, waiting to be dismissed.

Dad shuffles the bills and the magazines, and then hesitates before picking up the condolence letter. He walks over to the hall closet, just beyond the kitchen. He pauses again, just looking at the letter, runs his finger along the edge, and then lets it fall into the box of similar letters he's been collecting since November. He never opens them, and he never throws them away. He closes the closet door with the faintest click.

"Anyway, I'm heading to your uncle Mac's. He needs some help with the truck." Really? Or does Dad have another date? "You need money for dinner? For a pizza?"

"I'll make something." Just leave. Now.

"OK, well, just in case." Dad tosses a twenty on the table. "And while we're talking 'just in case' . . ."

For the second time in ten minutes he flips something at my head. This time, the small box connects with my chin and lands on the floor. And just like before, I don't have to pick it up to know what it is. The brand name screams up in big block letters. Side view of a warrior with his mohawk helmet. *Lubricated*. Oh, fuck me.

"I meant what I said."

His grin is disgusting.

"I'm not telling you not to have a good time."

I'm gonna puke.

"I'm just saying, you gotta take care of yourself, because you can't trust her to. You wear one every time. Every single time. You got it?"

Shit. What, they have a two-for-one deal?

"I bought this box. But when they're gone, you buy your own. If you're man enough to have sex, you're man enough to take responsibility for it. You got it?"

God, if he only knew how much of an über-virgin I really am. And to not defend her, to let him talk about her, like—

"Hey. You got it?"

"Yes, sir."

I totally suck.

"Good."

His meaty fingers dig into my shoulder, until I look up into his leering joy. It's so fucked up. The only thing about me that makes Dad proud is complete and utter crap.

Still gripping my shoulder, his face gets serious again. "I called Pendergrast. Told him we'd be by with the first payment first thing Thursday morning."

"Thursday? But—"

"Yeah, I've got to be up near Lewisburg on Friday."

Thursday.

"What, you're gonna have it by Thursday, right?"

"Not all of it." Shit. "I—I don't get paid again until next Friday and—"

"So, you'll give him what you have and then deliver the rest the following Monday."

Thursday.

Dad's fingers knead a little too hard. His eyes narrow, and he takes a breath like he's gonna say something else. My heart skips. Maybe . . . but then he just gives one more bruising squeeze and lets go. "See you later."

I kick the condoms all the way down the stairs, and then into my closet. Not gonna need them anytime soon.

Thursday. Shit. Algebra and Spanish are on Thursday. I might still pass algebra, even with a zero on the final. But not Spanish. I skip the final in Spanish, I fail.

But if I stay, and Dad makes me give Pendergrast the money, I won't have enough to go. Fuck.

I grab my phone, flop down on my bed, and dial Shauna.

"Did you get ambushed?" she asks.

"Sort of." I try to wipe my brain clean of Dad's leering pride and the Trojans in my closet.

"What happen—?"

"Dad's scheduled a command performance to deliver the money to Pendergrast."

"Yeah? So, you knew—"

"Thursday morning."

"Shit."

"Yeah." I bang my head against the wall.

"What are you going to do?"

No choice.

"Leave on Wednesday."

sixteen

BY SATURDAY I'M A MESS. I'VE BARELY SLEPT. I'M SCREWING up, acting like a spaz. Enough that Dad's giving me looks. Leaving Dad at home alone on Saturday night, slouched in the recliner, glaring when I walk by, seriously wigs me out. But I can't plan the trip at home. Or without Shauna.

Still, staring up the walk at Shauna's sister's house, I'm not sure I want to go in. The last time Stacy came home and found me in her house, she acted like she was gonna have to fumigate. And Shauna's been acting strange — stranger than usual. The last couple of days, Michael's been circling. Hanging by her locker, sitting near us at lunch, hovering near her car after school. I'm sure they're texting. Maybe there've been some calls, or more, even if Shauna hasn't let on. She clearly hasn't green-lighted him yet — or he'd be doing more than staying close. And it's weird for Shauna to pretend not to notice. Even weirder for her not to let me in on whatever's going on. 'Course, I usually ask, but right now I can't deal with knowing one more thing that might make my head explode.

"What are you doing?" Shauna asks from the open front door.

"Nothing," I say. Too late to turn back now.

"Well, get in here. I ordered already."

She fidgets, pulling at the bottom of her shirt. Nice shirt, tight across her chest, making her tits seem even bigger than usual. She tugs at it, trying to make it longer. Her jeans are tighter, too. And her hair's all poofy. She looks like she's going out, not babysitting.

Each step closer, she looks less like herself—stuff on her eyes, her lips redder, like she had stuff on them, too, but wiped it off. Like after a dance or party—when I see her, in her regular clothes, but there are pieces of dressed-up her still hanging on.

"Oh," she says, tugging at the shirt again. "Went to the mall. With Kerry and Anna. Got back late."

Kerry and Anna. Mall. And a shirt that's gonna test the physics on my jeans? Sure. Bet Michael was at the mall, too. Up close I can see her face in the light, see the makeup, the sparkles. She's looking anywhere but at me. Is it all official again? Or are we gonna keep playing this game? And what do I care? Might as well be Michael. Whatever.

"You sure Stacy's OK with me being here?"

"She's thrilled," Shauna says.

"Yeah, that was believable."

"Stacy's working until tomorrow morning. She'll never even know." She's practically bouncing. Devilish smile, all the more with the makeup and everything. Must have been a fan-fucking-tastic afternoon. Have to ignore it. All of it. I need her help.

"The kids won't tell her?" I look up the stairs, waiting for the rug rats to peek around the wall.

"Not now that they're in bed. They both sleep like the dead, and besides, their bedrooms are up in the loft at the back of the house. I even bribed Jess with my iPod; she'll be too busy blowing out her eardrums to hear us." She swipes her hair out of her eyes, tucks it behind her ears, and then untucks it. "And if Stacy wants me to keep sitting for her, she'll deal."

I kick off my shoes and toss my backpack on the couch.

"Whatcha get me?" I ask.

She bats her eyes like she's not gonna tell me, and then laughs. The knot in my stomach loosens, but everything else tightens in a little more.

"Pork fried rice, dumplings, and egg drop." All of my faves.

"No wontons?"

"Of course, but they're mine. You'll have to be nice if you want me to share." She twirls and looks out the window again. "Find us something to watch?"

I turn to find the remote, and stop. Shauna's set the coffee table with plates and silverware and place mats and everything, and next to the plates are two already-open bottles of beer.

"Beer?" I ask.

"I thought, maybe, well, why not?" Her fingers play with the hair hanging in her face. Makes it hard to see her eyes.

She reaches for her beer and hesitates just a second before taking a sip. She lowers the bottle. I can't stop watching her swallow. My mouth's suddenly dry.

"Food should be here soon," she says, sort of pushing me toward the couch, but weak-like, not like I know she can shove.

She moves back to stare out the window, leaving a whiff of something perfumey in her wake. Spicy. Different from her usual herbally grape smell, but not the perfume she usually wears for Michael. Her reflection in the window watches me, her fingers teasing at the label on the bottle. I can't stop watching her. Not even when it starts to get to me.

"Here they come," window-her says, breaking the connection.

I take a gulp of beer and try to clear my head. Hold out Dad's twenty toward the food.

After paying, Shauna puts the paper bag on the table and takes another long sip of her beer, head tilted back with the effort, but eyes on me. It's definitely a challenge. My mouth waters with the smell of the food, and the thought of the beer. We've drunk beer before. Lots of times. We've even been buzzed a few times. No big deal. But this feels thrilling, like the first time when we had one warm beer between us.

The bottle's slick and sweating under my fingers. The

cold liquid coats my tongue and slides down my throat. It should've cooled me down, but instead all the heat in the room rushes to my face. I drink long and hard to chase it away, nearly downing the bottle.

"Should I go ahead and grab us another?" she asks.

I close my eyes and nod, finishing it off in loud gulps. When I put the empty down, my hands are shaking. Need to slow down. But it feels nice and cold in my stomach.

The second bottle is ice-cold. Her fingers brush mine before she lets go, and I almost drop it. She's so close I can smell the beer on her breath, under that perfume. I take another long, cold swig.

Watching Shauna eat is kind of overwhelming, even when she's acting normal. She makes these approving little sounds when she gets an especially good bite, keeping her plate full by adding more food as soon as she has a clear spot. Tonight she's so distracting I give up on the food and sip at my beer, watching her.

"What?" she mumbles around a mouthful of my last dumpling.

"Nothing." Her face is flushed from the beer and the food. Maybe from her mall-date day. Whatever it is, her eyes are bright, kind of glittery. Her cheeks pink. I like it.

She swallows, motioning at me with her fork. "You're smiling at me weird."

"Sorry." I drain the rest of the bottle.

"If you want another beer, help yourself."

I'm tempted. Very. But I'm feeling the two I've already had. Starting to stare when I shouldn't. Forgetting none of this is for me.

"There's also soda, but if you want another, it's OK. I had Nate pick up a six-pack for us. And they have to be gone, one way or another, before Stacy gets home."

"Your brother-in-law is providing you beer now?" I ask. "For while you babysit his kids?"

"I said it was for this weekend."

"Still . . ."

"Let's review," she says, crumbling a wonton over her rice. "Me. Babysit. For an adults-only anniversary weekend in AC. Nate would have bought me crack if I asked him to."

"Glad you showed some restraint." My Shauna's back, underneath the hair and perfume and shirt and all. My Shauna, but not. Wish she'd put her sweatshirt on. I really want that third beer. "So, another?" I ask, already heading to the kitchen.

"Yeah. I think I'll take one more."

I place the bottle next to her and drop back into the corner of the couch. She peeks out from under her hair. The look's like a pause button. I freeze.

"What?" she squawks.

"Nothing." But it isn't nothing. It's something. Everything's tense, and how she's all weird, like maybe she's waiting to tell me something. And before that look, or the look from the window, maybe I'd have thought it was Michael.

Like she was just waiting to spring it on me — make it official. Would make sense. I cheered pretty hard when they broke up last time. And I've been making a point of ignoring all the signs, hoping he'd go away. But . . . something's going on . . . and whatever it is, she has me all wound up, even more than usual.

And the looks. Like now. Up through her hair, waiting. But . . . not like when she's trying to work up the nerve to say something. She's not trying; she's just watching. My brain's getting stupid. Beer isn't helping. I push the bottle away and grab a fortune cookie from the pile.

You are the master of every situation.

Great. Now even cookies are mocking me. I crumple the fortune and throw it in the empty rice carton.

Mood gone, Shauna's totally focused on her food again. She tears apart her egg roll, dumping out the insides and dipping the shell in the mess of duck sauce and mustard. Means she's almost done. She takes one last bite of egg-roll shell and then pushes her plate to the far side of the table, wiping her greasy hands on the napkins.

"Any problem getting the rest of the money?" she asks.

"No. Anders said if I come by the site on Tuesday afternoon, he'll give me the rest early." Her eyebrows climb. Guilt flutters up again. "I told him I had to make the payment on Wednesday."

She doesn't judge me *too* hard for the lie.

Instead, she carefully selects her fortune cookie from the three left, breaks it into a gazillion pieces, and reads her fortune. She smiles at the little slip of paper, tilts her head, smiles bigger, and then folds it in half and pushes it into her pocket. Oh, great—one more thing for me to obsess over.

"So, you're really going to blow off your finals?" she asks.

"Yeah," I say. "I am."

"What about seeing if you can take them early?"

"And say what? 'Principal Pendergrast, can I pretty please take my Thursday finals on Wednesday, so that I can skip town immediately after, with the money I'm supposed to pay you, and break that agreement I signed, promising—'?"

"OK," she says. "I get it."

"I can't risk it. I'm not even going to bother showing for the history final on Wednesday. Can't risk that they'll haul me into Guidance or insist I go to the Spanish or algebra reviews that afternoon." She nods, knowing I'm right. "Mr. Lee's been all over me. If he decides we need a chat, I could be stuck in Guidance for hours. I need a good head start on Dad. At least four or five hours, even better if he doesn't know I'm gone until I'm out of Pennsylvania. If I leave early on Wednesday, as soon as Dad leaves for the day, I'll have a shot. If I don't, if I get stuck at school until sometime in the afternoon . . ."

She looks at the stack of stuff in front of her, plays with the edge of the folder.

"Shaun." She looks up. "Only way to make sure I get

out with the money is to leave early Wednesday." I need her full attention on planning, not on trying to find another way. "Please?"

"OK," she says, finally convinced.

While the laptop's booting up, she leans across me to look at my map. She presses close, her tits soft and squishy against my arm. All the blood rushes to my face and neck, and then plunges away, leaving me dizzy. I swallow hard. Her breath hits my neck, and my stomach jumps. Everything pretty much jumps. Including me, back into the corner of the couch.

"Shauna, I think you could just focus on when I get there. I'll handle the drive. It's hard with you looking over my shoulder." Nice. Moron.

"Oh, OK." She moves behind the computer again. But she's still close enough to smell, and her leg touches mine every time one of us moves. I can't concentrate. I also can't ask her to move over any more without explaining.

"Mind if I turn this off?" she asks, reaching across the table for the remote.

Her knee digs into the outside of my thigh, pushing my legs together. The added pressure feels good. And bad. The warning buzz that things are getting out of control rushes past the good. Her hair touches my shoulder, making the hair on my arms stands on end. And not just my hair. My brain fights for control.

The alarms sound a higher warning, but I can't move.

And then she's gone, curling into the opposite corner of the couch, facing me, pulling the computer onto her lap.

I concentrate on shutting down the sirens, breathe out, testing if I can move. After a few careful breaths and a stealthy tug at my jeans, I chance a look her way. She has no clue what she does to me.

We work on our parts of the planning and only talk to ask or answer a question. She works on stuff about Madison. I focus on nailing down the route and double-checking the costs: gas getting there and back, some kind of place to stay, food. Math calms everything the rest of the way down.

We've already printed out everything we could find on Celia. Not much. I had Shauna trace Celia herself, to make sure I didn't miss anything. Loads of Celia Carsons in the world, but no other hits for a Celia Carson in Madison, Wisconsin, anywhere else online. So, it's her home, work, and the few places I could pull out of the letters. That's where I'll look.

Shauna nudges my leg with her foot, then leaves it there on my thigh. "Matt?"

"Yeah?" Her toes wiggle. I stare at them.

"How many nights?"

"I don't know yet. I . . ." I can't remember the question. Her shirt is pulled tight and low by the computer on her lap. I can see the outline of her bra through the shirt. Just above the screen, I can see the shadowy space between her tits. They felt so good squashed into my arm. I make myself look at her face, but she isn't paying attention, so I let myself look down again. So good. Love that shadow.

"So . . ." She sits back suddenly, shadow gone. "Still thinking you'll get there on Wednesday night?"

"Yeah."

She's looking at the screen. She hasn't caught me staring. I focus back on the map and the gas costs. But I keep getting really stupid-wrong answers and losing my place, making me start over again and again.

Crackling plastic. Without even looking I know what she's doing—I've heard the sound a gazillion times. But still, I look. Absorbed in the research, she unwraps the candy, stopping every so often to scroll down the screen with her pinky finger, while the other fingers continue to peel the plastic away from the sticky candy.

She slides the purple rectangle into her mouth, curls her tongue around it, sucks it hard before pushing it around her mouth. The whole world has gone supernova. My wrists sweat. Heat climbs from my toes to paint every part of me red with humiliation, extra swipes at my neck and ears. Twitching pressure builds.

I hunch over the map in front of me for cover, but it's no use. I can hear her sucking anyway, and it's almost worse not watching, because my brain makes all these pictures to go with the sounds.

I can't *not* watch her.

Her tongue sweeps the candy around her mouth. She

examines the end of her finger, nibbles away some candy at the tip. Then she licks the side of another finger, her tongue tinged purple just a bit on the edges, but darker in the middle, like tie-dye. She shifts the candy again, rolling her tongue along the side of her cheek.

I need to look away. Now. But all the blood that usually makes my brain work is AWOL. And the voice that usually talks me down is panting.

She looks up. "Want one?" She reaches for the candy on the table, tugging her shirt tight and down again. Fuck. Less shadow, more skin where her tits squish together. She leans back, less skin, more shadow. Fucking hell.

"No, thanks." Didn't even sound like my voice, but she doesn't seem to notice.

I push my legs together and try reasoning.

But it's not like she's helping.

She pushes her candy against the roof of her mouth. Her cheeks cave in a little. My pulse pounds all the way through me.

"You sure?"

Shit. She has no clue. Except . . . she's not looking away. She's staring right at me. Playing with that candy. But she can't *know* . . . she'd be totally grossed out.

I pull the road atlas onto my lap. Study the roads. This is about to get monumentally embarrassing. Every time she sucks on that candy hard enough to make a noise, the sound vibrates down my spine and pushes me closer to the edge.

All the voices in my head tell me to run, except for the one telling me she'd taste like grape and that her mouth would be wet and warm.

I try conjugating Spanish verbs, the few I can remember. Sing the alphabet song in my head.

The couch creaks and dips and then she's moving closer. I beg for anything to get me out of this without her knowing.

I try to think about disgusting things—open sores, roadkill, what my puke would look like if I threw up right now. If she figures it out . . . if she sees . . . God, I'd never be able to look at her again if she knew how often . . .

"OK, I think I've found somewhere to stay." She moves even closer, putting the computer right in front of me and leaning over my arm. "They have a youth hostel. The one in Madison . . ."

I try to pretend everything's OK, but when I look at her, I can see down her shirt all the way to her bra. Light blue and shiny. Alarms bounce off my skull.

I bolt.

Leaning against the back of the closed bathroom door, I try everything. But none of the usual things are working. Cold water: handfuls in my face, and then over my wrists. Holding my breath. Usually making my lungs fight for air will work, but even when I'm seeing spots and ready to pass out, no dice. I dig my thumbnail into the skin between my thumb and finger for as long as I can stand it. Still at attention.

Then Shauna's phone in the next room plays the theme song for the Wicked Witch of the West: Stacy's calling. And just the thought of Stacy, calling now, how she'd look if she came home and found me here — if she knew right now I was in her bathroom with a raging hard-on for her sister — does it.

Still uncomfortable, but good enough for now, I walk back into the living room. Shauna's still on the phone.

"Sure. No problem." She rolls her eyes and uses her free hand to make a talking head. "Stacy, it's fine. They love cookies and ice cream for breakfast. Take your time."

The table's been cleared. My map and her computer are there, but everything else is gone. Like it was never here.

"Stacy, I'm kidding." Didn't sound like Shauna was kidding. "Really. We'll be fine."

Shauna put the TV on again, but on mute. I flip channels without sound, looking for something decidedly not sexy. C-SPAN. Sharks. Professional bowling. I finally settle on competitive fishing, without sound. Perfect.

"OK, good night." Shauna snaps her phone shut. "Man, she is such a pain."

I've heard Shauna brawl with Stacy before. This one sounded like nothing. And Shauna doesn't really look all that pissed.

"Checking in?" I ask, testing her mood, and how much she got of what just happened.

"More like checking up. She thinks she knows everything about everything." Shauna rolls her eyes. She's fine. "You OK?" She gathers up her hair, then seems to remember she doesn't have a hair band and just lets it all fall again.

No. "Uh, yeah."

"You sure?" Shauna plays with her phone, snapping it open and shut, not looking at me.

"Yeah, just, uh, maybe that third beer was too much, or uh . . ." Maybe she'll think I got the runs, or puked or something; anything's less embarrassing than the truth.

"Want a ginger ale?" She won't look at me. Shit. Maybe she did get it?

"Yeah, that'd be great."

Normalness, even faking it, is good. I move her computer in front of me and look at what she's found.

"Here you go." She plunks a glass down to my right and then curls herself back into the far corner of the couch.

"Oh, sorry, I was just looking at what you found," I say, moving away from the computer, and from her.

"No, feel free. Go ahead." She sips her soda. Watches. But doesn't make eye contact. Feels like I'm in some dream, like this is a dream version of Shauna, a dream where I don't know the rules and things can change on a dime.

I look at the pages on the hostel. It's perfect. Cheap. Looks better than the other places we found that didn't require a credit card. Shauna's cousin is hooking me up with a community college ID anyway, so an ID to register is no big deal. But no credit card required, and probably lots of kids stay there. "This looks great. Thanks for finding it."

She buffs her nails on her shirt and then blows on them. "Yes. My Google-fu is strong."

I click over to one of the other pages, showing a map of Madison. Then another, a link to somewhere at the university: the library where Celia works. Shauna's been busy.

I couldn't have found half this stuff without her—I'd probably still be sitting on my ass, trying to figure out where to start looking. I owe her big-time, even before the car. And the car is what is really making this possible. Whatever the hell is going on, she's still got my back. Like she always does. Saving my ass.

"Shaun." I look at her and again forget what I was gonna say. Because she's watching me over the rim of her glass. I have no idea what the hell she's thinking, but the look scares the shit out of me. Too intense. And all of it coming at me. Like heat.

She takes a sip. Then another. Her cheeks flush darker and she looks up, staring straight at me. Grins. And I feel myself smiling back—I can't help it.

She bites the edge of her lip. I can't figure out what the hell it all means. Nothing makes sense, least of all that look. But it feels important, like by smiling wider I'm agreeing to something. But I have no idea what.

She's all mischief again. I can't help but keep smiling—it's been a long time since I've seen her like this. Maybe never like this, exactly. But . . .

I've *never* seen her like this, not with *me*.

It's like getting sucker punched. Everything goes loose and lost, and for a second I can't breathe.

The shirt. The makeup. The beer. The perfume. Not for Michael. Or anyone else.

Holy fuck.

She stares at me. Her eyes narrow to dark slits. She puts the glass on the table and begins to move closer.

I stare at the map.

The couch creaks, cushions shift.

Pulse pounds in my ears and dick.

Fuck, she's right there. Still smells good, too good, 'cause now I can smell the grape, too. And I can't think. I can't breathe. I'm dizzy and so fucking hard.

I turn my head. Her mouth is right there. All I'd have to do is lean.

Her fingers squeeze my arm.

I can't move.

What if I'm wrong? What if this isn't really happening? What if . . .

"Matt . . ."

"Yeah," I whisper.

"It'd be fun. You. Me. Road trip?"

"Huh?"

"I'll come with you," she says, her breath warm on my cheek. "I don't have any finals after Tuesday, just take-homes. I'll get them done early and then I can come with you."

Her fingers squeeze my arm. My dick throbs.

"We'd be away from here . . . together . . ."

Fuck.

"Shaun . . ." As soon as I say her name, she knows. Her face changes, confused, pale. And she leans a little away.

I swallow hard, shift away from her until she lets go of my arm. Can't think. Can't talk. My mouth flaps like a guppy.

She shakes her head. "I want to help—"

"No." I cringe at her flinch. "I mean, I know you want to help. And I really appreciate it. But I really want to do this alone."

She stares. Shudders. Turns so she's not facing me, hugs herself and nods, like it's no big deal.

"I need to do this by myself. This, it's sort of . . . the last thing I can do for T.J. And it doesn't feel right to bring a friend along to—"

"Fine." She jumps up. Her bottom lip quivers and she won't look at me. "Sure." She nods again. Tugs at the shirt. All of the teasing gone. "I just thought . . . but . . . if you don't want . . ."

"Shaun . . ."

The bathroom door slams behind her. Kid feet scurry across the floor upstairs.

"Aunt Shauna?" Jessica whispers down. I don't answer, not sure whether to hide or just stay still. But before I can decide, the footsteps retreat back across the upstairs.

I stand in the middle of the living room, not sure what I'm supposed to do.

When I asked if I could borrow her car—like, asking to take it, not asking her to bring it—I thought she understood. I thought she got that I needed to do this alone.

But shit. She's pissed. No, worse. Hurt? Any other time, a road trip with Shauna, especially . . . fuck, I'd give choice body parts for that. But this is about T.J.—for T.J. Can't she see that I couldn't say yes?

But this was real, right? She dressed up. In date clothes. For me.

I spin in a circle. Trying like hell to make the last few hours make sense.

I could have totally kissed her, right? When she leaned close? Before she said that stuff about coming with me? I could have . . . then . . . she . . .

Shit, if I had just moved in then, I'd be on that couch making out with her, right now.

The room tilts. She . . . likes me. Or liked me. Maybe that was it—my chance. I could have totally kissed her.

A drawer slams, loud even behind the closed door. Then another.

A noise upstairs.

Footsteps in the hall near the steps. I move to the kitchen, out of view from the stairs. Footsteps on the top steps.

"Aunt Shauna?"

They're not going back to bed.

I know I shouldn't take off until she comes back out here. But if Stacy finds out I was here, or about the beer . . . Shit, I can't be here if they come down here.

I grab my shoes and backpack and make a run for it.

Standing in my socks on the front walk, I don't know what to do.

Should I wait and go back in?

Call? I could try to explain, and . . .

Shit. No. No way she wants to talk to me right now. Maybe not for a few days.

And what if she changes her mind? Without her car . . . What if she says I can't have it? Or I can't have it unless she can come, too?

Or, fuck, forget the car. What if this is it? Not just no to more . . . what if this is it for anything, for us, like . . . we're not even friends anymore?

"Fuuuck!" I groan, clenching my hands in frustration.

I've seen Shauna pissed at guys before. I've seen her eradicate them from the face of the earth, at least as far as she's concerned. Invisible. And now she's pissed at me.

seventeen

SHAUNA'S ANGRIER THAN I'VE EVER SEEN HER. AT ANYONE.

I tried calling her when I got home Saturday night. She said she didn't want to talk about it. Ever. When I tried to apologize, she hung up on me.

She wouldn't talk to me at all on Sunday.

Monday, I pretended nothing had happened. For a while that worked, but when I tried to get her to laugh, she seemed to get even more pissed at me—like being able to pretend everything was fine somehow made me a bigger jerk than she already thought I was, even though it's what she said she wanted. But I didn't try to point that out.

By yesterday after school, we were back to her not talking, at all, but she took me to get my money from Mr. Anders anyway, like she promised. She didn't say a word the whole way there, at least not to me—she seemed to be arguing with someone in her head. The whole time I was in with Mr. Anders, I kept wondering if I'd come back out to find she'd left me there, stranded across town, just out of spite. When I got back into the car, she was looking at the map again.

I waved my pay envelope at her.

"So, you're all ready to go?"

Took me a few seconds to answer, because it sounded more like an accusation than a question. "Yeah. Pretty much."

She traced my route across the map. Her finger followed the orange highlighter across the spiderwebs of roads and ghostly state lines, past landmarks and cities, over rivers and mountains, snaking along the bottom of two huge patches of lake blue before pressing down over Madison, Wisconsin, like she could make me forget by hiding the destination.

"What if your dad decides you have to turn it in tomorrow instead of Thursday?"

"He won't. Early day at a site out by Johnstown. He'll be gone early and home late. Hopefully."

Her hand was still on the map, hiding Madison and its star. "You know this sucks, right?"

I didn't try to answer. I knew many things sucked right now, but I wasn't gonna try to figure out exactly which one *she* meant, especially since I was starting to get a little pissed off myself. Why couldn't she see that I needed to do this alone? But I just let her fume and kept my mouth shut—I'd had enough practice at that with Dad. I needed the car.

Eventually, she slid the map closed and turned in the seat to face me. She held it to her chest and we had a staring contest, but eventually she handed it over.

When she dropped me off, I thought she was gonna say something else. But she didn't. When I reached for the handle to open the door, she laughed, but it was a bitter, awful sound. Made me panic.

I left her two messages last night, but she didn't call back. Until I got her text this morning—*I said id be there*—I wasn't sure she was gonna show up. I'm still not entirely sure.

It's actually kind of amazing she's still letting me borrow her car. Assuming, of course, that she is, that she shows up this morning and then hands over the keys.

I'm ready to go—as soon as Dad leaves. He should have been long gone by now.

I read Shauna's last text again, for the tenth time, just to be sure. Still pissed.

I hear Dad's footsteps on the stairs from the second floor. Panic burns up my throat. If he calls me upstairs, I could bolt out the side door. But if he comes charging down here, there's nowhere to go.

His feet around the kitchen. The refrigerator door.

I'm a sitting duck.

When I hear his steps near my door, I grab the strap of my backpack, ready to run. But he keeps going. I don't breathe until the front door slams shut. Then I race to get my stuff together.

I wait for the sound of his truck pulling out of the driveway. Picture him turning toward the center of town. Past the gas station. Each likely turn until I'm sure he has to be near the highway. Then I text Shauna.

When she picks me up, we don't even talk. Her eyes are red and puffy, and there's nothing left for me to say.

A block from school, she pulls onto a side street, just as we planned. But instead of turning the car off or unbuckling her seat belt or making any move to get out, she just sits there, her hands gripping the steering wheel so tightly that they look melded to the gray vinyl. Each second she just sits there, I'm more sure she's changed her mind, or that she's already confessed everything to her mom. Something.

"I hate this." She hurtles out of the car.

At least she said "this" and not "you." Unless she really means me.

Outside the car, she hesitates just a few seconds before dropping the keys into my hand. Then she reaches into her backpack and pulls out an envelope. She thrusts is at me, hitting me in the chest.

"Here."

"Huh?"

"Take it."

It's too thick to be a letter. I squeeze it and start shaking my head. Don't need to open it to know it's full of money.

She holds her hands behind her back. "It's only what I had on hand from my birthday and babysitting, so not that much, but there's no way you'd make it back with what you have."

"I'm not taking your money." But even with the words out of my mouth, I know I will. I need it way too much.

"You can pay me back. Later." She looks into my eyes. "You'll pay me back. After you come home."

"I will." I cradle it close. "Thanks. For everything. I mean it. I —"

"You'd better go."

She tries to leave but I grab her arm. "Shauna . . ." I don't know what to say. But I don't want to leave like this.

She shakes free and wraps her arm around her middle. "Look, whatever happens, or . . . whatever you decide to do, just call me, OK? Every day? Because I'm going to worry, and probably be grounded, and it's going to suck and . . ." Her hard eyes scare me. "Just promise, OK?"

"Yeah." I barely gasp the word out. My chest feels tight.

"Every day."

I cover my heart with my hand.

She lets out a long, shaky breath and then moves away from the car, not even looking at me.

"Shaun."

When she turns back, her eyes are already filling up. "Just go."

And then she's gone. Walking away. I turn to get in the car, but she grabs me from the side in a quick, awkward hug, too quick for me to even get my arms around her to hug back. She makes this sound in the back of her throat. Then she's gone again. This time I watch her until she rounds the corner out of sight. She never looks back.

★　★　★

Flying up the Pennsylvania Turnpike, I swallow over and over, trying not to puke. Acid churns around the rocks in my gut.

Every dark truck in the rearview mirror is Dad, racing after me. Every state trooper, a trap waiting to grab me. I'm driving like a maniac, practically begging to get caught.

The panic evaporates as soon as I hit I-80 and actually start heading west. My shoulders and arms lose the steel tension that made me cling to the steering wheel. I pull my fingers off the sweat-slick wheel, and shake and flex them in turn until they work again. Even the burning in my gut starts to cool. When I finally sink back into the seat, my shirt is soaked, but I can relax and just drive.

Crossing over the Susquehanna River feels like the last drop on the big coaster at Dorney Park. I've never been this far away by myself. I give the Williamsburg exit my very best one-fingered salute and pick up speed.

Just outside DuBois, I take my first break, mainly because I've got to piss so bad my eyeballs are floating.

The wall-size map next to the bathroom shows I'm already more than halfway to Ohio. I-80 stretches out to the left until it runs out of Pennsylvania and off the map. Long day ahead, but just a couple more hours and Pennsylvania will be behind me.

Before heading back to the car, I splurge on provisions: a huge-ass soda, two kinds of chips, a couple of candy bars, and two hot dogs. There's been no call yet from Dad, not surprising since Pendergrast probably doesn't even know yet that

I'm not gonna show. About another twenty minutes, at most, and Ms. Tine will send a note to the office. Toss up of whether Pendergrast will call Dad right away or wait. But eventually someone will ask Shauna. She'll withstand Pendergrast, but she'll crack wide open in a wave of guilt with just one long look from her mom.

I chow down, leaning against the car. Driving through mountains, as opposed to over or around them, always amazes me, ever since I was little. And I always wonder the same thing: Exactly when did people start thinking of going *through* mountains? Did the first guy to suggest it get laughed at? Did they give him any credit at all when they finally tried it?

As soon as the second hot dog is gone, I push the question aside and climb back into the car. It's a long way to go before Madison. Time to gas up and drive on.

Back on I-80 and safely coasting in the center lane, I picture the road stretching out in front of me, like on the map. I lean back and drive.

The next time I stop, I switch iPods. Had to get one of those wall chargers. Couldn't figure out how to sync it with my computer without messing it up, at least not yet. T.J.'s trusty blue was playing on shuffle, and it was fun at first to have a little bit of surprise with every new song, but too many of them were weird, or songs I couldn't even recognize.

Just from scrolling through the playlists, I know the bigger one has more songs I already know, some I can already hear in my head. I pick "Top 25 Most Played," knowing this is pretty much my only chance to hear what T.J. listened to the most, before my replays and skips start messing with it.

I can't kid myself, even for one moment, into feeling like T.J. is here with me. But with his music playing, I pull back onto I-80, feeling better than when I pulled into the stop.

Dave Matthews Band's "Ants Marching" pours out of Shauna's crappy speakers as I merge back into the flow of traffic. The summer I was seven was pretty much Dave Matthews 24/7, until Dad threatened to toss the stereo out the window if T.J. didn't give it a rest. Before that summer, T.J. had been all about Bruce Springsteen, and even after that summer, he played a lot of Bruce and the posters stayed on the wall. But that summer was Dave Matthews all the time.

Three more DMB songs, and then Bruce wails about the need to run. It feels like a good omen, and I can't help but smile. I can almost hear T.J.'s scratchy voice in my head.

The song pulls me back to lying on the floor of my room, elbows on the floor, face braced on my palms, listening to T.J. and his best friend, Dan, and the music drifting across the hall. I would close my eyes and pretend I was a part of it. All I wanted was to be in there with them.

The songs flow past like old friends. The sounds of the year before T.J. left for Basic, and many of the times he'd been home since. And all those long nights when Dad was MIA, the music floating across the hall, or through my open bedroom window from the garage or the back porch or, later, Dan's beat-up truck in the driveway.

I'm slapping out the beat on the steering wheel with my fingers, and in an instant it's like last spring, like being back in the truck with T.J., driving west toward Raccoon Creek State Park, all the way on the other side of Pittsburgh.

After all of T.J.'s revelations on the side of the road, we were both pretty quiet. I was nervous to drive—I'd only had my permit for a few weeks—but T.J. insisted. With everything T.J. had said swirling around my head, and needing to concentrate on what I was doing, I didn't really feel like talking. Seemed to suit T.J. just fine. He turned the music up and started singing along. Everything melted away until it was just us and the music and the road.

That first afternoon, we hiked an easy warm-up trail. The ball of dread inside me loosened with every step. And as the days wore on, I started to believe that anything was possible. I started to trust that when T.J. came home for good, we'd have a real life. Together. Maybe start a business. I pictured us, someday, like Dad and Uncle Mac, poker nights and fixing the trucks and being together, like friends. Picnics with our wives and kids. Fishing out at the lake. I thought we'd have time for all kinds of stuff.

All that week, even when he had to take it easy on me or when I puked twice the first full day of hiking, I'd never felt stronger or better than standing there next to him after each hard climb. He laughed when I puked, and when I lost my footing or tripped or stepped in the creek, but every time he was laughing, his smile was so big, his laughter so easy, I didn't care. I finally felt like T.J.'s brother, instead of a lesser human who happened to share his last name.

Sometimes he moved us at a vicious pace. But other times, when we stopped for a break, it was like he went somewhere else entirely for however long we stayed still. Most of the time he would come out of it fast and jump up ready to hike on, but a few times he came back slowly, quietly, and his eyes focused in on me for a long, charged moment before he moved.

In the dark of the tent, T.J. talked about towns and buildings and mosques, about the kids he saw and the landscape, about mountains and deserts. He talked about some of the guys in his unit. He talked about sand. And about thirst. But he didn't talk at all about what it was really like, what he did over there. When I tried to ask about war stuff— about suicide bombers, IEDs and ambushes, about what he'd seen and what he'd done—he shut down, with just a look in the fading light of the fire. And in the pitch-dark of the tent, just the angle of his face and his rough-drawn breath was enough to tell me I'd gone too far.

I had never spent that many days in a row alone with T.J., but even for him, he seemed quiet and tense. That last night in the tent, the quiet stretched between us, and I think I talked for hours just to chase it away.

★ ★ ★

When my cell plays Shauna's ringtone, I jump and swerve, and realize I was barely paying attention. I scramble for my phone on the passenger seat while trying to stay in my lane.

"Hey." I brace for her mood after the scene this morning.

"Hey, where are you?" Tight, but no tears.

"About thirty miles from Ohio." I can't help but be a little proud at that. Like I had something to do with making Ohio appear in front of the car, as if I'm about to conquer Cleveland or something.

"Wow," she says, and I can hear her moving around. "You're moving fast."

"Yeah. I'm making good time." Dad's said that a hundred times; makes me grin.

"Well, that's good, because I just got out of Pendergrast's office. He knows you didn't show. He wanted me to tell him where you are so that he could try to avoid, as he put it, 'getting you into a world of hurt.'" I can hear Shauna's air quotes. "He suggested that I call you, using the cell phone I'm not supposed to use at school, I might add, and try to convince you to get your butt here and to his office, pronto." Her imitation of Pendergrast is right on. "He said if you don't get here fast, he'll be left with no choice but to call your dad. So, here I am, calling. I think he really doesn't want to have to call your dad."

Probably doesn't. "Thanks, Shaun."

"I'll hold off on giving any of it away as long as possible, but we both know Mom'll notice the car gone tonight, and then I'm done."

"Wait," she says to someone else. Then I can't really hear anything, muffled sounds. Did she cover the phone? "Great."

"Gotta go," she says to me. All bright and chipper.

"What's up?"

"What do you care?" And there's the edge again. "Look, they're waiting. And since it'll probably be my last social outing for a few weeks, you know, with the impending grounding and all . . ."

"Yeah. No. Sure."

"So, just drive safe, and call when you get there."

She cuts the call. And I'm left wondering who "they" are. If "they" were Trish or Kara or whatever, she'd have said so and not bothered to cover the phone. Terrific.

I toss my phone back onto the seat. My stomach roils with all the junk I've eaten.

I wish she would've talked to me — more than just grunt the bare minimum — sometime in the last three days. I've replayed Saturday night over in my head, over and over. There was no way it was gonna go well. Sure, I could have not wimped out and kissed her, and then I think there would have been a whole lot of kissing, and maybe more. But eventually she would have asked to come with me, and I would have said no. And somehow I think it would've been even worse if we made out and then I said no. But maybe now she's come to her senses. Remembered I'm not really boyfriend material. Maybe all I've done is shove her faster and harder toward Michael. Maybe he'll round the bases while I'm gone. Shit. Fine. Whatever.

I grip the steering wheel and try to just focus on the road. But I keep hearing that muffled part of the call, trying to decipher the muffles. Maybe it was just Trish or the team, and she's just trying to get back at me? Would be like her, when she's in proving-someone-wrong mode.

And Pendergrast . . . she said he didn't want to call Dad. I don't blame him. I wish I could call and explain, but he probably wouldn't care anyway. I skipped my finals and broke the contract thing they made me sign to stay out of trouble. And even if he would understand, it's too much to risk. Dad won't call the cops, but Pendergrast just might.

Better to just turn up the music and drive.

There's a rhythm to the driving: the sound of the road and passing cars adding to the music. Rivers and cities, bridges, houses, animals, all give me something to look out at, when the thinking gets to be too much. I pass farms and stores and schools, and wonder what it's like to live there.

Mostly, and despite every effort not to, I think about T.J., and the fact that he didn't trust me enough to tell me any of the important stuff.

I pass a sign for 79 South. My foot hits the brake and the car slows, swerves. I recover and look in the mirror. Everyone slowing. My bad. I pass the actual exit. Just another reminder that T.J.'s gone. When he got home, we were gonna spend a few days at McConnells Mill State Park, about a half hour south down 79 — wicked hikes, rafting, good fishing. No overnight camping, but enough places nearby to make it work. A great warm-up to some serious climbs. He was gonna teach me to climb. Now we'll never do it. Any of it.

For most of Ohio, I think about all the things T.J.'ll never get to do. And I can't stop seeing Zoe's face in my head. I've stared at the pictures of her for hours, reread all the letters. She has to be his. I'm sure of it. Well, as sure as I can be with the what-ifs that keep creeping in.

Shauna went through the rest of the letters last week, pointing out all the places where Celia talked about Zoe like she was theirs. And I reread Missy's, just to be sure. Nothing. At least nothing that says she's not T.J. and Celia's. But there's this little voice in the back of my head, reminding me of the obvious — that she never actually said daughter, or father, or anything like that. Shauna had a point, that if they know Zoe's their kid, then they don't have to say it. And the picture — the picture he had of just them, just Celia and Zoe. Cut so that it showed just Celia and Zoe. Why would she send him that unless they were T.J.'s family? With that picture, nothing makes sense except for her being his daughter. She has to be his.

When I see her, will I know? Just know for sure? Will she look even more like him in person? Or do something just like T.J.? Like in this one picture of them, the way she made her mouth just like his — and the one with the ice cream, her head tilted, both hands on the cone. In both she looked just like T.J., like the way he would do those things. I just have to believe. Believe that she's his. And when I know for sure, I'll tell Zoe about him. She'll never know him, not really, but I'll tell her stories, the good ones, not the crappy times.

A groaning truck horn jolts me. My car is straddling the line, half in the left lane. Cars and trucks are passing blurs to the right. The truck horn blares again, closer behind me, and then the grinding brakes kick in. I swing the car to the right and barely miss a minivan shifting into the center lane to pass a clunker crawling along in the right. The truck driver glares as he accelerates past. Time for more caffeine.

I pull to a careful stop in the parking spot closest to the rest-area building. My hands are shaking. Well across Ohio, spitting distance from Indiana. Got to keep going.

Splashing cold water on my face wakes me all the way up. Not taking any chances on running out, I get a huge coffee and a bottle of soda, though the kid who sold it to me called it pop. I stretch my back against the car and sip at the coffee, waiting for it to cool enough to gulp.

And as if on cue, my cell plays Dad's ringtone. For a second it's like he's here, and I have to clutch the cup to keep from dropping it. But once I've caught the panic, I climb into the car and open the phone.

"Hi, Dad."

"Where the fuck are you?"

Sounds like he's in the truck. "Uh, where are you?"

"What?"

My head jerks away from the phone.

"What do you mean, where am I? I asked you a question. I got a message from Pendergrast that you didn't show for your final today. Where are you?"

"There was, uh . . . there was something I had to do."

"Wh-what do you m-mean?" He's probably spitting all over the phone. "You get your ass home now."

"I can't."

"What?"

How long has it been since I openly disobeyed him? "I, uh, can't come home right now. Listen, Dad—"

"No, you listen. If you don't get your ass home right now, you're gonna wish—"

"Dad, I left you a note. On the table. Read it, but, uh, I needed to, uh, take a trip. But don't worry. I'll be home in a few days, a week at most."

"You w-what? Trip? What the hell do you mean you had to . . . ?"

Car horns. He swears. I can hear his blinker. He's probably getting to the side of the road.

"Where the hell are you?" I can hear it, the second it hits him. "And where's the goddamn money?"

"I needed to do something, for T.J. I . . . I went through his stuff."

Gulping breaths and I can practically hear the sound of his veins popping out all over. His jaw working against the phone as he grinds his teeth. "I told you—"

"Dad, he's gone. He's not coming back. And there's this one thing I can do for him. So I'm doing it."

He sucks in air, furious and harsh. "You get your ass home!"

"No." There's a calm in it. One I don't feel, yet, but one I can see, in front of me. I've rehearsed this call in my head, over and over, and while it went a dozen different ways in my rehearsals, I knew we'd get to this part. "I have to do this. Just . . . if you just let me do this, for T.J., I'll come home and you can yell or whatever then."

I can hear the battle on the other end of the phone. I close my eyes and swallow the fear.

"What is it you think you're doing?"

"I'll tell you when I get back."

His grinding teeth chill me. Despite the slick of sweat all over me and the heat of the sun broiling through the windshield, I'm shivering.

He could probably stop me. I'm only seventeen, and he could call the police and make them find me. There's no way he could figure out where I'm going, unless the police can trace my cell, like on TV, or Shauna cracks wide open. But I'm banking on his ego to make him wait until I'm home, to deal with me then, himself. No witnesses.

"Dad, I have to do this." I hate how I sound, like I'm begging. I owe it to T.J. to do this right. I clear my throat. "Read my note. But right now, I have to go. I'll call you. I promise. A week at most, but . . . I need to do this. For T.J."

I wait a few seconds to see if he'll respond, and then I close my phone. I haven't even pulled out of the space yet when it rings again. I ignore it. He calls two more times before he gives up. I don't think he'll send anyone after me or call the cops or anything, but I can only shudder at what he'll be like when I get home.

Crossing into Indiana, and then for all the miles dancing along the Michigan border, I think about all the places T.J. will never get to go, and all the places he went I'll never know about. And I think about what would have happened if I had chickened out and not gone through his stuff.

Just before the Illinois border, I stop for gas—hopefully, my last refill before Madison.

In the gas station, I get another soda and some chips and, on impulse, a pack of gum from a bin by the counter. The price tag on the side is bright pink, slapped on by one of those handheld roller things, one edge still sticking up. There's a place at home that still does the price stickers by hand, too. Even the gum and candy. I thought they were the last people on earth who did that. I smooth the sticker down so it wraps over the edge of the pack while I wait in line. Almost there.

Back in the car, I fold the map open on the seat so I can look at it if I get confused.

Just as I cross into Wisconsin, my phone beeps at me. Text. Has to be Shauna. *Busted but ok — call when u get there.*

Almost there. By this time tomorrow, I'll know everything.

eighteen

WHEN I CALLED FOR DIRECTIONS, THE GIRL ON THE PHONE said, "Look for the palm trees." In Wisconsin? I should have asked more questions, but she didn't really give me a chance, and I didn't want to call back.

I circle around again, and once again face a one-way street heading in the wrong direction. I've been round and round these streets and still have no idea where I am, or where I should be.

Some more lefts, another right, and I'm thinking of sleeping in the car. But there, twinkling lights, and lo and behold: palm trees. Green, plastic, twinkling-green-light-outlined *fake* palm trees. An illegal U-turn and I'm here, and wondering how I could have missed it the first eighty-seven times around this block.

At first I don't see anyone inside, but when I open the door, a bell jingles and a woman pops up from behind the counter.

"Hey. You made it! Assuming you're Matt. Are you Matt?"

The woman is out of some kind of time warp, or maybe one of those trippy movies. Tall and thin, long neck, pale-pale skin, and no makeup, save the blue glittery teardrop painted on her cheek, just below her right eye. Ring through her left eyebrow, and a speck of diamond in her nose. Flowy white blouse with flowers and butterflies along the neck. And a necklace that hugs her throat in a ripple of tiny, shiny beads. The overall effect is pretty, and earthy, and almost childish. But then there's the hair: long, clumped, and deadened dreads, tangled and tied to hang down the center of her back in a dirty-blond bunch. Just weird enough for me to know I am so not in Kansas anymore—or Pennsylvania, for that matter.

"I'm Maya." The accent, flat and nasal, is almost comical, and just all wrong.

"Uh, hi, yeah. Sorry about the calls and being late and all."

"No prob. You made it, didn't you?" Definitely weird. "But listen, can I get you checked in and show you where to go? Because I do need to close up for the night."

"Oh, yeah, sure." You betcha. I drop my stuff next to the desk and dig through my backpack for my stash of cash.

I find out during the surprisingly quick check-in that she's a grad student and has lived in Madison "for-ever," so I should feel free to ask about places to go, restaurants, cooperatives, community involvement opportunities, if I want to "give back" while I'm here. That last bit, the giving back, she punctuates with a huge, hopeful smile. I nod and smile and mumble something I hope sounds positive and uninterested all at the same time. I am here on a mission, with no time for anything else.

She barely looks at my ID. I count out the money for my room, relieved they still had my single left even with my almost-too-late arrival. I'm not sure I could sleep in a room with a bunch of strangers.

When she's done with the check-in, she sort of dances out from behind the counter. I pick up my stuff and start to follow, but Maya twirls to a stop just past the desk. I shift my stuff, waiting, but she just stands there with a stupid look on her face—kinda like a smile, but without her top lip showing. Is this some kind of joke? What the hell?

She just stands there, smiling that odd, annoying sorta smile.

"What?" I ask.

She tips her head toward a sign on the wall just before the hallway. WE ARE A SAFE AND SHOELESS ENVIRONMENT . . . WTF? "Huh?"

"We are a shoeless environment. So . . ." She looks down at my feet, her face comical and expectant.

"Oh, uh, right." I toe off my shoes, then shuffle everything so I can pick them up. "Socks OK?"

"Yup. Good, then," she says, turning on her heel and heading off. I have to race to catch up. "We'll get you all settled, and then I have to skee-daddle."

She is skipping. Down a long hallway, around a corner, and through an open area.

"Common area, communal kitchen, TV and computer room there. There's Internet service, but it's su-low."

Another short hall. I look around, try to take in as much as I can without dropping everything I'm carrying. She's still talking, now about food. My stomach growls.

". . . from the place next door. But they have veggie entrées, too, and they're actually really good. And there's plenty of vegan and even raw-foods places around, if you prefer. Oh, and the co-op has the best vegan peanut-butter cookies."

Except for the peanut-butter cookies, it doesn't sound too good. And how good could vegan cookies be?

"Coed dorms, divided dorms, a few other singles and doubles, bathroom." She points out spaces and places in a blurring cadence timed to her skippy-trippy feet. "If you change your mind about the single, we can switch you to a dorm room tomorrow," she says, like it would be a good thing. Would save me some money, but I don't think so.

Through a door and down a short three-step jump. I miss the last step and shuffle myself and my stuff to keep my balance.

Maya calls out some greetings and introductions as we go. A guy named Lyle, with no hair and at least three rings through his lip, says, "Was-sup," and then goes back to strumming a guitar. It's missing a string. A guy I think she calls Kack merely grunts as he slides past us on his way out. A young couple with gross-smelling takeout containers smile and bob in unison and slip back into their room. I'm *so* not hungry anymore. A couple of pretty blond girls, not from around here either, I'd guess, but on their way out and dressed to party. An old couple, wearing identical sweatshirts from some state park. Huh.

"We're almost full, but a lot of people are out. You'll see more people around tomorrow. We're almost there. Your room is actually on the main floor. You just can't get to it from the front area."

That is not at all surprising.

We pass another dorm room, and I decide no amount of savings will tempt me to sleep there. No freaking way. Too full of strangers. And strangers who are too strange. And who reek. Three guys and a girl. Smile. Wave. Seem nice, but . . . man. I hold my breath for a couple of doors.

In the last room at the end of the hall, a girl is leaning against the door frame, laughing into the room, where music is playing. She sips from a bottle of something in her hand and turns to smile over the lip at us when she sees us coming.

"Hi, Maya," she says, all the while watching me.

"Hey, Harley, this is Matt. He's in town to . . ." Maya turns to me, head tilted, forcing me to get another whiff of her very smelly hair. "I didn't get around to asking what you were here in town for, did I?"

"Uh, no," I stumble, caught unprepared for questions. "Just, uh, visiting."

"U-Dub? Friends?" Harley asks, but her eyes twinkle, and I think she's mocking me.

I have no idea what the first part means, but "friends" I'll take. Good cover. "Yeah. Friends," I answer, not bothering to be more specific.

Her mouth turns up in a heart-shaped smile. She narrows her eyes, like she's trying to figure me out, and runs the tip of her tongue around the edge of the bottle. I have the sudden urge to tug at the collar of my sweatshirt. It's choking me. But with the backpack and duffel and shoes and all, I can only crane my neck, trying to get it loose.

"Well, nice to meet you, Matt. If you need anyone to show you around, or . . . anything, let me know. I'll be here," she says with a wave of her hand. Then a wink.

Before I can respond, Maya pushes me on, but I can totally feel Harley watching me all the way down the hall. I look back. She tilts her head. Smiles. I stumble, hit the wall, and drop all my stuff. Harley's laughter is definitely at me, and not nice, and yet I can't help but look back again. She pivots back into the room with a toss of her hair.

At the bottom of the stairs leading down to my room, Maya turns unexpectedly and I almost run into her. She waves me into the room.

"Bathroom just at the top of the stairs. Let me see — what else do I need to tell you . . . ?"

She dives back into the spiel she's been running through in between distractions and introductions. Too much information all at once, about house rules and community space and safe environments and lockout times, and eventually she just hands me a bunch of papers.

"You'll be fine. Stu will be here in the morning. He's been around for-ev-er."

Guess that's longer than Maya.

"He'll be able to answer any other questions, and whatever. You got what you need for tonight? Great."

Maya disappears in a swirl of skirts, leaving me alone in the spartan room. Door closed and locked, I sit down on the unmade bed and swallow the sudden realization that I am actually here, with no more than a few days to find Celia and Zoe, and deliver T.J.'s letter.

nineteen

A WHOLE DAY AND NOTHING TO SHOW FOR IT. TECHNICALLY
more, if you count the drive and last night.

In my head—at home, all the way here, even last night,
before I fell asleep—I had it all worked out.

Get up early, go to the address on the envelopes, look
around. Wait. Celia would come out and go to work, maybe
with Zoe in tow. I know from the letters that she takes the
bus. I figured I'd catch a good look in the morning. Follow the
bus to see where Zoe goes to day care, then on to the library
where Celia works. Maybe hang around, see her go to lunch
or run errands, then maybe on to some of the other places,
like the playground or the ice-cream place. All in plenty of
time to position myself back on their block to see them come
home again. I thought maybe I'd even be able to hear Celia
talk to a neighbor, maybe watch Zoe play on the front lawn.
Piece of cake. Just watch and wait.

I hoped, maybe, I'd get lucky. Maybe Celia would come
home early, like she said in some of her letters, take Zoe to
the park. In some of my better fantasies of how this could go,
I imagined that Celia would recognize me and she'd know

who I was. And I wouldn't have to tell her anything. She'd just know.

Instead, I spent all day stalking them without a single sighting.

It sure doesn't help that I can't drive within two blocks of their house. The whole damn street's torn up, equipment everywhere, piles of pavement and dirt. This morning there were men there working, but this afternoon they're gone, leaving all the piles and equipment vacant. I parked the car three blocks over, near the lake—close as I could get—and walked down.

There's a river that flows parallel to the street, emptying into, or maybe flowing from, the lake. I'm not sure which. I parked myself there, across from their house, next to a big tree, and I watched until pretty much everyone else on the block had come home. Still no Celia or Zoe.

One of the neighbors kept coming outside to sweep her front walk. I leaned against a tree, trying to blend in, staring at the big dirt-mover thing next to me, anything to hide what I was really doing there. But she was obviously watching me watch the house. I left before she could call the cops or something. Back in the car I had to admit—my plan sucked.

I drop my backpack and shoes and fall back onto the bed in my room. I owe Shauna a call, but I just lie there for a few minutes, gathering my courage.

She's in the middle of something when she answers. I

can hear her moving around, and she's only tossing me half-hearted responses. Finally, there's the soft click of a door closing and I have her full attention.

The frustration of the day lets loose. When I come up for air, she laughs, but not like she thinks it's at all funny.

"So it's not as easy as you thought." There's more than a little I-told-you-so there. "To be honest, I always thought it was insane to basically stalk the woman and then think she'd invite you in."

Shuffling paper. Sounds. But she's not talking. She should be giving me a hard time, reminding me I should have brought her with me. But all I'm getting is her you're-so-stupid sighs. I've seen her do this over and over—it's just not usually directed at me.

"You still opposed to calling her on the phone?" she asks.

"No way." I suck on the phone. Obviously.

"Okaaayyy. So, if stalking her isn't working, and the phone is out, then it's probably time to go to the library where she works. Right?"

I push my chin into my chest, bite the inside of my lip.

"Come on, Matt." She laughs, at me. "You know that's what you're going to have to do, unless you're going to just mail T.J.'s letter to her. This isn't rocket science."

I guess I deserve the attitude. But it's not helping me want to go to that library, where I don't belong.

"Well?"

"I'm not sure I can get in if I'm not a student." Visions

of being detained by university cops for trespassing play through my head.

"Won't know if you don't try." She sounds tired of me. Not even pissed anymore. Pissed would take more effort. More interest. "And that's probably your best bet."

I know she's right. I knew even before I called her I would have to go there tomorrow. I guess I just needed to hear her say it. But the thought of actually going into the library really freaks me out.

"Hold on," she whispers. There are muffled sounds. Then voices. Then I can hear her saying good night to her mom. Then her door closes again. She picks up the phone, but she doesn't say anything for a too-long-for-normal pause. Maybe she's in more trouble than she told me.

"Listen, I've got to go." Her voice is strained. "The battery's dying and Mom will kill me if she finds out I'm on the phone."

"On the phone at all? Or just with me?"

"I'm definitely grounded for a yet-to-be-determined time. I don't know exactly what level of groundedness I'm in yet."

"How—?"

"She won't say."

Shit. If her mom won't even . . . "And your dad?"

A puff of her breath—I can practically hear her thinking. I used to have this uncle-y thing with Shauna's dad. It was sort of fake, with lame teases and little pats on my shoulder, but it was better than hate. If he hates—

"Honestly? I think he's most pissed about the car, something about the insurance. But he keeps hugging me. He even took me out for ice cream after Mom left for bingo, and then he stumbled through this totally bizarre conversation, with a whole lot of sports metaphors about responsibility and trust and other stuff I have scoured from my brain. It was a little too A Very Special Episode of *The Grubers* for me."

"Like he's happy it's only me on the lam?"

"Yeah," she says softly.

I close my eyes. Hit my head back against the wall. Yeah, part of me wishes she were here right now. Hell, yeah. But I know I made the right decision. Even if she hates me for it.

"Shit," she says. "Battery. Bye."

"Shaun?" Shit.

"Yeah?"

"Thanks."

She sighs, and I think she's hung up, when she says, "Call me as soon as you meet her. 'Night."

Not exactly still in hate with me. But not a whole lot better. I'd do anything if we could just talk like we used to, if we could just go back to how things used to be. Well, almost anything. And the *almost* is pretty much the problem. So, maybe this is just the way it is.

I pull the lists and directions she made me out of my backpack. I open the red folder to see her handwriting, small and sharp, in numbered rows, and on the tab of the folder.

I'd know her handwriting anywhere. It's neater than when we were ten, but the same, sort of slanted and way more legible than mine. If someone put a hundred pieces of paper in front of me, I could totally pick out the one Shauna wrote. If she was writing me letters, I'd know her letters from how she wrote my name on the envelope, before I even looked at the return address.

Maybe T.J. saw Celia's handwriting on his letters and felt the thrill of knowing it was from her before he even opened it. Maybe he rubbed his finger over the words to have some kind of connection to her. They wrote letters, even with e-mail and all, to have something to touch, to feel. Celia said as much, but did T.J. feel it, too? Did he smell her on the paper?

I keep thinking about Saturday night at Stacy's. I imagine I didn't wuss out—that when Shauna asked if I wanted a candy, I said, "Yeah," and stole hers right out of her mouth. That I got to taste her mouth, and put my hand under her shirt. That we made out all night and she never asked to come here with me. I can imagine what her mouth would have tasted like, would have felt like, her hands . . .

When I'm done, and the buzz has faded, I sink back into reality. I can't go back. I missed my chance. She'll never let me back there again. She never does—when a guy screws up this bad, he's done. Not always dead to her, but might as well be. She never gives them more than a nod or a look again. They never get a second chance.

Well, except for Michael. Michael's got some kind of

do-over card. But, then again, he's never screwed up. She just always gets annoyed and cuts him loose.

Maybe now she'll take him back and go for the goal.

And if she did, nothing I could ever say about it.

The best I can hope for is maybe she won't punish me forever. Maybe someday we'll be us again, even if we'll never be *us*.

twenty

I'm USED TO COLLEGES LOOKING LIKE COLLEGES, SEPARATE
and distinct from the towns around them, so that you know
when you've crossed the border. Like Sucks U. back home,
with its red brick and columns and green areas, all tree-
lined, like a private park. You have to pass through a gate on
either side, each marked by a spotlit sign, announcing the
school's borders. You can't drive twenty minutes in eastern
Pennsylvania without seeing a college or university, but
they're usually clearly marked, so you know when you've
crossed into la-la land.

This is all city. But I must be "on campus" now, because
there's a parade of kids being led down the street by a clip-
boarded guide in a red shirt. And the buildings have names
like people. Definitely college turf.

After parking in the cheapest place I could find, I hit the
street. One of Shauna's printed maps shows College Library,
so I head that way, cutting through a shady area between
buildings, past food carts and stalls selling stuff. Past
students. Past a guy in orange coveralls playing a tiny flute.

Past crazy guys arguing and two girls hanging up a banner. Past a couple kissing hard, right there on the sidewalk.

I emerge into bright sun and a big open grassy-green area, with a fountain in the middle. The library should be on the other side of the street.

Groups of people, not even all of them kids, are scattered in clumps all over the place, sprawled on the grass, slumped on benches, sitting on the steps of the buildings. Some talking and eating lunch, others sunbathing or hanging out.

Past the fountain and down to the corner, where three streets intersect. A little glimpse of water between the cement. A different lake from the one near Celia's house, I think. Sailboats bob and sway in the breeze. So blue and so far across.

Turning away from the water, I see the glass doors and busy students and a sign that says, COLLEGE LIBRARY. I grab a seat on a big cement planter thing off to the side and watch the door. It's almost all glass around the entrance, making it easy to see the people inside. No one stops anyone when they walk in, but a lot of them walk over to the main desk. Are they showing ID or something? I can't tell. I move closer.

Sometimes the people behind the main desk look up or smile or something. Are they waving in students they recognize? I move to the side, against a wall, to get a better look. It doesn't look like anyone is showing ID or checking in or anything. Fifteen more minutes and I'm sure of it: everyone's just walking in.

But once I get in, where do I go? Near the front door, to the right of the main desk, there are some tables and chairs where I could sit, and maybe no one would even notice me. I could totally wait for Celia, and then maybe watch her for a while, find a way to go ask a question or something. A few more people go in.

Then I see her. Celia. I think. She walks behind the big main desk in front, talking to a guy. She disappears behind the desk and comes up with a book, does something I can't see, and then hands it to him. He smiles and walks away. She stands there, talking to the woman behind the counter with her. She laughs. Another woman comes up, and the three talk, laugh some more. I think it's her, but I'm not sure. It'd be pretty embarrassing to go up to the wrong woman. The other two leave, and she's standing there behind the desk alone.

It's now or never.

But I can't make myself go in. I argue with myself, but I can't move.

And then the easy answer appears: one of those tours heading this way. With a deep breath for courage, I wait until the end of the long line of people is at the door, and then I hoist my backpack over my shoulder, smooth down my shirt, and walk toward the door. I stay with the tour until we're inside, giving me cover. Even so, just inside the door, I panic.

Celia is standing there, alone, behind the desk, with nobody else around. I could walk up and just ask a question, or maybe I should just go ahead and introduce myself. *Hi, we haven't met, but I'm Matt Foster, T.J.'s brother . . . Celia? Hi, I'm Matt Foster. T.J.'s brother?* Or, no, *Theo's brother.* She called him Theo. *Celia Carson? Could we talk for a few minutes? I promise I'm not a stalker.*

Someone drops a book. My head snaps up. I'm still standing just inside the door, facing the counter. Celia is staring at me, head tilted to the side. I open my mouth to say something, anything, and then realize I'm too far away to really talk to her. But my feet aren't working, or my legs. I'm stuck.

"Excuse me," an annoyed voice says behind me. I'm shouldered out of the way.

"Oh, sorry, sorry." I struggle not to fall over, what with the bumping and the nonfunctioning legs. My heart is pounding. Sweat breaks along my collar and hairline.

By the time I look back at the desk, she's busy. I walk over and sit down at the table to the right of the door. There are some magazines on a shelf behind me. I grab one at random, look just enough to make sure I'm holding it right-side up, and position it so I can see over the top of the page while I pretend to read.

The guys walk away, and she leans over the counter, writing something. Up close, I'm still not totally sure it's her. Her hair is way longer than in the picture, and in lots of small braids. Her face is different, too—rounder or softer, less soldier-like. Her skin is less glowy than in the vacation pictures. She seems smaller, too, not as tall, or maybe just not as tough. But I'm pretty sure it's her.

She smiles at one of her coworkers, and then I'm totally sure. It's the face in the pictures: familiar, pretty, transformed by the bright, open smile, dimple on her cheek. Just like in the picture of her and Zoe in my pocket. My fingers itch to pull it out and look at it, even though I don't need to look at it to see it.

I look up over my magazine again, and she's looking at me. But now her eyes are wider, so big they seem to pop forward out of her face. I feel the magazine drop down in front of me. I can't look away. I smile, hoping to convey the *I-come-in-peace* line that keeps running through my head. I push my chair back, ready to go over to her. But she's gone. I wait, wondering if she's just ducked behind the counter. I didn't see her go anywhere, but she disappeared in the time it took me to reach for my backpack. I guess I should sit again, wait some more. Maybe she went on break?

I stare at the magazine in front of me. It's been almost ten minutes. Some guy came out and took up a post behind the counter, and he keeps looking this way. I think maybe I screwed up this plan, too. But I can't think of another, so I wait, hoping I'm just being paranoid and she'll come back out behind the desk soon. Or maybe she'll just leave for the day. Would she leave by another door?

"Can I help you?"

Whoa. Tall woman. Between me and the door. Guy at the

counter, standing at the end closest to us. OK, so not para-noid. This plan sucks.

"Is there something I can help you find?" Her voice is too calm. She knows I don't belong here.

"Uh, no?"

"Do you need help finding something for a class?"

"N-no?"

She smiles down at me, hands clasped in front of her, like I'm mental. She's clearly waiting for me to say something, or else stalling while someone calls security.

"I — I promise, I'm not, uh, crazy or anything."

"Well," she says too nicely, "I didn't think you were."

"Oh."

"But it looks like you're looking for something. So, can I help you find it?"

"Um, actually, I was looking for Celia? Celia Carson?"

Her eyes sort of blink, or flinch, on Celia's name, both times, but otherwise she doesn't really react. Like she knew exactly who I was looking for.

"Is she expecting you?"

A little, gruff laugh escapes before I can help it. "No, not exactly. But, uh, I need . . . I, uh, I'd really like to just talk to her, for a minute, or a couple of minutes, if that's OK?"

She stares at me, eyes narrowed. Counter Guy flexes his hands, moves all the way out from behind the counter.

"I promise I'm not psycho or anything. I just want to talk to her, and then I'll leave. Promise." I cross my heart.

She lets her hands fall to her sides and suddenly she's even taller. "Does she know you?" Still calm, but less kind and no smile.

How much do I say? "She doesn't know me, but—but . . . my name is Matt Foster. Tell her, yeah . . ." I have to swallow hard to force it out. "Tell her I'm T.J.'s, no, Theo . . . Tell her I'm Theo's brother."

The woman opens her mouth, like she's gonna say something, but then slams it closed.

"Wait here, please."

She turns fast, but slows near the counter, and I can't hear what she says to Counter Guy but he stands down, moving back toward the center of the desk and only shooting looks my way instead of staring.

I really wanted to see Celia's face when I said my name, to see her react. And what if she doesn't know he's gone? She has to know, right? But what if she doesn't, and then I have to tell her, right here in front of everyone? This was the worst damn plan.

I can't move and I can't stand still. My feet keep moving, like they want to go somewhere but my legs aren't cooperating. And my hands, I can feel them, sweaty and sticky, opening and closing reflexively at my side. Do I shake her hand if she comes out? Or hug her? She's kind of like my sister-in-law, except I didn't know she existed, and maybe she didn't know I existed and maybe a hug would freak her out? And I don't think I'm ready to hug her. But a handshake seems weird. Maybe I don't do anything, just stand here. Or maybe I should sit. No, stand, standing is better. Especially because my legs won't move. I'll just stand here and hold my hands out, at my sides, so she can see. *I come in peace.* What the hell am I gonna say?

I can taste puke in my throat, a little, and then kind of like a metal taste. So thirsty. What the fuck am I gonna say?

There she is. It's her. And she's smiling, sort of, maybe. At least, her mouth is kind of curled up, all tight lips, no teeth, but definitely kind of a smile. But her eyes, her eyes are not smiling. And they're big, and kind of wet looking. Please, let her know already.

"Matt?" She has the voice of a famous person. Like a singer, or an actress or something, all smooth and kind of deep.

"Hi," I try to say, but I can't hear the word, so I don't know if I actually said it. I clear my throat and try again. "Hi."

"My God," she says, shaking her head. "I can't believe it's you."

I thought she'd stop when she got close, but she's still coming. She just keeps coming at me until her hands slide over and around my shoulders, pulling me into a hug. It's an awkward hug, mainly because I wasn't expecting it and have no idea what to do with my hands, until she's already pulling back. She sort of holds me at arm's length, studying my face.

Up close she is even prettier, and smaller, than I thought. Her eyes are large and so dark that the difference between iris and pupil is in shades, not colors. The braids are glossy and tight and perfect, like her skin, and I wish I had hugged her when I had the chance.

"You look so much like your brother." Her smile is sad, but also kind of not, and no tears.

Way better than my worst-case scenarios. I feel myself relaxing, limbs losing some of the terror-induced steel, until I might fall down. She doesn't hate me, and she's not scared. And she thinks I look like T.J. Cool.

She laughs a little. "So much like Theo. Especially your smile."

Her hands are still on my arms, and they tighten a little while she struggles to talk, her eyes suddenly even wetter.

"Ah, Matt, we miss him all the time. And I am so sorry we're meeting now, after . . ." She swallows hard and lets go of my arms, like she's just realized she's the one holding on. "You must miss him something awful."

It's like she punched me in the stomach. The sudden, painful need to crumple, holding it in, because if you don't you'll split apart. And yet, the pain is good. It's real. I was starting to think everyone wanted to just forget about him, and that they expected me to forget him, too.

She waves us toward the table.

Negotiating the chairs buys me a few minutes to wipe at my face, swallow the rock in my throat, and remember how to talk. Once seated, she waits for me, hands in front of her on the table.

"Hi," I say again.

"Hi." She laughs.

"Sorry. I guess I already said that."

"What are you doing in Madison?" she asks.

Reasonable question. Obvious question. But I can't find the words to start. I'm not going to say anything about the letter for her, not yet, and it's all I can see in my head. Have to be careful not to say it.

"How did you . . . ?"

"I went through T.J.'s stuff," I blurt, as if this explains everything. "His personal effects?"

Her eyes crinkle at the corners, a little smile, still no teeth.

"I found your letters. And the pictures." I pull out the bags holding them. I leave the one holding the single letter safely inside my backpack for now.

She stares at them, like she's hypnotized or something. Maybe she didn't know we had them, or that T.J. saved them. Or maybe it's just too much for her, seeing them, like it was for me at first, only worse, because they're hers — hers and all wrinkled and worn because he loved them.

I pull the small picture from my pocket and hold it out to her.

Her fingers graze the edge of the picture and then stray near the bag of letters, without touching it, and then back to the photo again. She swallows hard, mouth clamped tight, eyes dry. She eventually picks up the picture and runs her finger around its edges, studying it.

"When I saw the pictures, I wanted to meet you."

Her finger traces the cut edge.

"And her."

Celia looks up fast. Stares at me hard. Perfectly still.

"I mean, if that's OK." Shit. Never occurred to me she might not let me see her. What if she says to go away? Would she just say, "Fuck off?"

She puts the picture down on the table, rubs her hands over her face, leaves one over her mouth. I have no idea what that means. She squints at me. She studies me, then the picture. I sit up straight, smile, try to show her I'm OK.

"Please, don't be mad," I whisper. "But I—I . . . read the letters."

She looks up, her whole face sharp and tight, her eyes huge.

"Sorry. Sorry. I . . ." I'm gonna puke. "I know. But I just . . . wanted to . . ." Can't say I wanted to know more about T.J. "I wanted to know . . . more."

She clears her throat again. "So, um . . ." She stares at the picture.

I'm starting to wonder if I'm gonna get it back, and even though I know I should let her have it, if she wants, I really, really want it back.

"You read the letters," she says.

"Yeah." My face gets hot.

"And looked at"—she pulls the bag of pictures closer to her—"Theo's pictures."

I just nod, staring at the bag of pictures. T.J.'s pictures. Like a half-finished collage.

"And then you . . . came to find . . . me? And . . . Zoe?" She's trying not to cry. And my hands are shaking, my every-thing is shaking. "All the way from Pennsylvania?"

"Yeah."

"How did you . . . ?"

This part is easy. "I saw your address on the envelopes, and then looked through the pictures, and once I saw the one of you and Zoe, and . . . and figured out that, that it was you and, and her . . ." I smile. I can't help it. I did it. I found them. I was right. "I wanted to meet you, and . . . Zoe. Especially Zoe."

She doesn't respond.

"I found you." I laugh with relief. I did it. I found them.

Her face doesn't register anything, and then her eyes close for a long moment, longer than a blink, and then pop open with a new look pasted on her face. My stomach turns. Something about the new look feels wrong, like she's suddenly remembered that she doesn't want anything to do with me, or maybe this is all too much and she wants me to go away.

"Do you have somewhere to stay?" she asks, still stroking the side of the picture with her finger.

"Oh, yeah, got a room at the hostel."

"Where?" She sounds like she thinks I'm lying.

"At the youth hostel? Over by the capitol?"

"Are you OK there? I mean, is it OK?"

"Oh, yeah, except for the no-shoes thing, which, yeah, is a little weird, it's fine. Nice even."

"OK, well, good," she says, letting out her breath. She hands me back the picture. "I still have to finish work, and I'm supposed to be over there behind the desk, so . . . want to come to dinner tonight? Say, around six? You could meet Zoe. And . . . the rest of the family."

Family. "Sure. That'd be great. I want to meet everyone." T.J.'s family.

She starts to give me her address, but I tap the letters. She smiles, and laughs a little, and rubs her face again. Before I leave, she gives me another awkward hug, holding on tight.

I run back toward the car. If I can get there fast, and get back to the hostel, and keep moving, dinner will come faster. And I won't have time to screw this up.

But by the fountain I stop short. The lockout hours — I won't be able to get back into the hostel for hours. And I don't want to waste the gas driving around. And my knees are shaking.

I was right.

Zoe.

That look — Celia's face, her nod. And dinner, to meet the family, and Zoe. I was right. Zoe was — is — T.J.'s. Celia and Zoe were his family. Are kind of *my* family.

My knees buckle. I drop onto the cement steps behind me.

I'm dialing Shauna before I even really think about doing

it. Her voice mail. Shauna's voice, trying to sound all grown up and cool, spoiled by the sudden sounds in the background distracting her. The exasperation clear in the half-laughed next bit telling me to leave a message.

"Hey, Shauna, it's Matt." I laugh. Obviously she'll know it's me. "Anyway, just thought you'd like to know that I met her. Went to the library, and met Celia, and she's totally cool, and I'm gonna have dinner with them tonight, with her and . . . Zoe. And the rest of the family. It's totally cool. I'll, uh, I'll call you tonight, when I get back to the hostel, and tell you everything, but it might be late if we stay up talking and stuff, but, yeah. Shaun . . . thanks. For everything. Talk to you later."

I end the call and stare at the phone. Watch the minutes click by. Hours to kill. And I have no one to tell.

I'm bursting with it, with every detail of seeing Celia, how she talks, what she said, and how she said it. Meeting her races around my head.

Wish I could have at least talked to Shauna, heard her reaction.

Still . . . that look, when I showed Celia the picture, and how she said Zoe's name. The way she hugged me so tight.

I'm smiling so big people are going to think I'm high. Or stupid.

I was right. About everything. About coming here. About coming here alone. About Celia, and Zoe. I. Was. Fucking. Right.

twenty-one

PEOPLE COME AND GO. EVERYONE WITH SOMEWHERE TO BE, or someone to be with. Except me. Can't go back to the hostel. No money to waste. No gas to waste. Only time. And for the first time in . . . ever . . . I'm not running or hiding or scared out of my skull. I'm completely on my own time—no Dad, no school, no work. Not even Shauna.

And I have no idea what to do, but I don't care.

My stomach growls. I'm so thirsty the fountain's looking good. I haven't had anything since this morning, and that was just a soda and some peanut-butter crackers.

I'm pretty sure there's somewhere to get food at the building next to the library—I could smell it while I waited outside.

I follow the sounds of people and the smells of food and end up on a huge patio area next to the lake. Tables and chairs and people everywhere. And a grill. Eight dollars gets me two brats and a huge soda.

My first bite of brat is messy and good. Spicy mustard and spicy-sweet brat, surrounded by just-soft-enough roll.

Juice on my chin, over my hand. After practically inhaling the first one, I force myself to eat the second more slowly, putting it all the way down between bites and consciously chewing each delicious mouthful.

Kids are feeding the ducks at the edge of the lake, splashing a foot or a hand in the water now and then. I wonder if Celia ever brings Zoe down here. If maybe T.J. sat right there, Zoe in his lap, waiting for Celia to get off work.

I wipe brat juice and mustard off my hands, then pull the picture out of my pocket. One of the corners got all bent. I smooth it down, then run my finger around the edges, not quite touching their faces.

Celia looks older now. Fancier, her hair and her clothes. I thought she'd look haunted and broken. Sure, she's sad, but she was totally there. Even when her eyes got all sad talking about Zoe, she was on solid ground. Not broken at all. Strong.

"Matt, right?"

I look up. A girl. Well, a girl-shaped darkness surrounded by the bright sun. She shifts, and then I can mostly see her face.

"Harley," she says. "From the hostel?"

"Oh, uh, hi."

"Mind if I sit?"

With me?

She tilts her head to the side, then laughs at me.

"Sure. Sit." Freaking moron. I push the last bite of the brat to the side. Too messy to eat in front of her.

She ignores the empty chair across from me and grabs

a chair from the table to my right, where some guys are gathering up their stuff to leave. Several of them stop to look at Harley, and I can see why, now that the shock has worn off. She's wearing the shortest shorts I've ever seen. I could palm them and touch skin above and below. Tight pink shirt that barely reaches them. Smallish tits, but nice—could palm those, too.

She reaches behind her to tug her bag off her back. Smooth, tan, sloping belly. A tattoo—some kind of sun, but with lots of colors—circles her belly button. A ring with a sparkly bead in the middle. Hot as hell. I lean over the table to cover the bulge.

She pulls her chair to my side of the table, right next to me, then shifts around until she can face the sun. She smells like suntan lotion. The coconut-smelling kind.

"I love hanging at the Terrace," she says. "Brats. Beer. The lake. Maybe we'll get lucky and some windsurfers will go out later and we can bet on who will fall in the water first." I can't see if she's teasing or serious behind the dark glasses, and I can't move away from the table yet. "One of my favorite summer pastimes: watching windsurfers face-plant in the lake. So, what are you up to?"

I swallow a big gulp of soda to buy time. "You know, seeing campus."

"Sure," she says. "Man, that brat smells good. Ever had their popcorn? Really good."

"No, I, uh, just found this today." I don't know what else

to say, so I slurp at my soda and watch the kids play in the water. "How long have you been in Madison?" I finally ask, for something to say.

"Oh, I come and go." She shifts the angle of her chair again to get all of her pale legs in the sun. "I'm killing some time before I start college in the fall, and I have a lot of friends here. Always someone around."

Starting college in the fall: that helps with the age. I would have guessed seventeen or eighteen, but then she mentioned beer, and they were carding everyone.

"Listen," she says, not even looking at me. "I could really use a drink, but I left the rest of my cash back at the hostel. Could you spot me for a soda? I'll pay you back later."

"Oh, uh, sure." Only a couple of bucks. "Here." I pull a ten out of my wallet.

She ignores it, face toward the sun. "Thanks. I'll take a diet." She tips her head back even farther.

"Oh, OK," I say, getting up from the table.

"And get some popcorn, too. You should try it," she says. "Have to go inside for the popcorn."

"Right." Inside. I look behind me at the long building. "Where?"

She waves her hand. "Just go inside. Head to the right. You'll find it. "

I weave between the tables, dodge little kids with ice-cream cones and a large group following one of those red-shirted clipboards. Once inside, it takes my eyes a few moments to adjust to the dark. Goose bumps climb up my arms in the air-conditioning. Around a corner, and there's a bar, with a big popcorn machine. I wait in line.

Another five dollars down. The journey back is more treacherous. I leave a trail of fallen popcorn behind me; like Hansel, Shauna would say. I shove her out of my head. Too weird while hanging with barely dressed Harley.

Harley is right where I left her. Well, not exactly—she's moved the table and chairs and everything to face the sun again.

With my hands full, I'm having trouble getting around the obstacle course of chairs she's left in my way. I almost trip over my backpack, but manage to push it aside and get to the table without spilling too much.

"Oh, great," she says, sitting up and reaching for the drink first. She tips a bunch of popcorn onto a napkin on the table and starts tossing popcorn into her mouth between sips.

I sip at my own soda and try not to be irritated that she made such a mess of everything while I was inside. Now I'm wedged in between our table and the foreign guys sitting behind us. I think they're talking about her, laughing the way guys do when they can see that much skin. Or maybe they're laughing at me.

She happily eats her popcorn, giving me funny looks, like I amuse her, but not in a cool way.

"What?" I ask when the irritation becomes too much.

"Nothing," she says, still smiling weird. "You're cute when you're all paranoid."

I gulp down my soda, feeling my face go red.

"What are you *really* doing here?" She squints at me, holds a popcorn kernel out and then tosses it into her mouth.

"What, uh, huh?"

She smiles and tosses another popcorn kernel in her mouth, pushes her sunglasses up on top of her head, and folds her arms over the table. Pale eyes intense.

"I was watching you earlier," she says. "Saw you cutting across from Library Mall. Thought you were headed here, but then you went over and stared at College Library for like an hour. So, what's the deal?"

What the hell?

"Relax," she says. "I'm not going to blow your mission. I was just wondering what was up. Ex-girlfriend? New girl-friend? Robbery? Espionage? Private investigation? Stalker? What?"

"Huh?"

She laughs loudly and then settles back in her chair, taking the popcorn with her. "Come on—I'm bored. Share."

No way. "Nothing's going on. I was just . . . looking around. . . ."

"Yeah, not buying that." Harley tosses a kernel at me. "Come on! Tell me something. You have to!"

"No, I don't." I start to stand but she grabs my arm.

"Relax—I'm sorry. I was just curious is all." She nods toward the chair. "Sit. Please?"

My brain is saying go, but my legs aren't moving.

"Pretty please?" she says, pouting, with that bottom lip that makes me have to sit or run.

So I sit. My head is spinning. I should have left. I could still go, in a minute.

"It's just, you looked all weight-of-the-world when you were watching the library. Now you seem totally happy."

I probably look like a dork.

"Totally cute," she says, playing with her straw.

I don't believe her. But then she circles the straw with her tongue and I don't care.

"So . . . you gonna tell me what's up?"

I shake my head, but clamp my lips together. Can't go yet, but I'm not saying anything.

"I am a very good spy," Harley says. "Maybe I can help with whatever is going on. Natasha to your Boris." She tosses another kernel of popcorn into her mouth with an evil smile. "I'd make a very good Natasha. Well, not *good*, but you know what I mean, dahlink?"

Um, no, not so much.

"Oh, come on," she says. "Boris and Natasha? *Rocky and Bullwinkle*? Oh, man, good stuff. The cartoons, not the movies. The movies were bad, even if Rene Russo was seriously hot as Natasha."

I have no idea what she's talking about.

"OK. Clearly, you are not picking up the thread. Natasha is a kick-ass spy. Well, she should be, anyway, if it weren't a cartoon that relies heavily on a moose and squirrel always ending up on top. So, let me be your Natasha and help with the spying or whatever."

She is intently drinking her soda, watching me, with that smile. Nice smile.

"Tell me about the chick with the kick-ass braids."

Whu-huh? "You saw —?"

"Yeah, I did." She shrugs, like she practiced it. "Who is she? Maybe I can help you sweet-talk her or whatever."

My head's saying get up and go, but everywhere else is staying put — except for my stomach, which isn't too happy with the brats.

"Hey, kidding around aside, you seem like a really nice guy," she says, all serious and friendly. "I just want to help if I can."

"I don't need any help."

"Oh, so the first meeting was successful? Or was this a reunion?"

I reach around for my backpack — time to leave.

She grabs my wrist. "Come on, Matt. I can keep a secret." Yeah, I'm sure she can. "And you can't lie for shit." She crosses her heart and holds up three fingers. "Scout's honor."

What could it hurt? And I'm busting to tell someone. And it's not like I'll ever see her again. . . .

"She your girlfriend?"

"No," I spit out, skeeved out by the question. Gross.

"She hugged you pretty hard . . . like she wanted—"

"She was my brother's girlfriend," I blurt. Stupid. I could stop here. But . . . "She didn't know I'm here, and I wanted to surprise her. So . . . I waited. Then . . ."

"*Was* your brother's girlfriend?" She raises her eyebrows. "She's not anymore?"

"Yeah. Uh, he died."

"Oh," she says, all teasing gone. "Sorry. How long?"

Two hundred and three days. "Seven months."

"That sucks. I'm sorry."

"S'OK." I slurp at the watery soda at the bottom of my cup to try to open my closing throat.

"Hey," she says, leaning forward. "I'm really sorry. How can I help?"

I look out at the lake, back at her. "Um, thanks, but, really, there's nothing you need to do." It's done. The hard part's done.

Then I'm holding the picture. I didn't mean to take it out. But I did. So, I just keep it in my hand, play it cool.

Like in slow motion, she reaches over and traces my fingers. She turns my hand over. My fingers tingle, waiting for hers. But she grabs the picture instead.

"No, wait—"

"She's pretty. And the kid's cute." I clench my hands.

"Give it back."

"Sure," she says, nodding, but she's not handing it back.

"Please?" Please. Please. Please.

She puts it in my hand, but then keeps her hand there, covering it. "His kid?" she asks softly.

I pull my hand back, shove the picture in my pocket. Nod. My heart's pounding. I should have left. I'll leave. As soon the dizziness passes.

"Heavy."

"Yeah," I say, calming.

"What's she like?"

"She was nice. Meeting her was—"

"No, the kid. Must be weird to—"

"Haven't met her yet."

"When?"

"Tonight." Why am I still talking? Go, idiot.

"Seriously heavy. But good. Hey." Her hand taps my wrist. Sweet smile. She looks different, nice. "It's very, very cool."

"Thanks," I say, barely. Her hand squeezes mine.

"Very, *very* cool, Matt."

I can't talk, for a lot of reasons, so I just watch her hand.

"OK, well, I have to run." She pushes her sunglasses back onto her face. "But I'm really glad I came over here. Will you stop by and let me know how it goes?"

"Yeah, sure."

"And, for luck." She leans down and kisses my cheek. Her lips pull back and then brush over my mouth. Then she's gone as suddenly as she arrived, weaving between tables and heading in the opposite direction from the one I need to go, taking the last of the popcorn with her, but leaving her soda cup for me to throw out. The foreign guys stare after her, and then look at me like I'm a lab rat. My cheek still tingles where she kissed it. I can't feel my lips.

twenty-two

I PAUSE ON THE BOTTOM STEP OF CELIA'S HOUSE TO BRUSH off my shirt. I had to settle for my least-dirty pair of jeans and the black collared shirt, hung out the window to air out while I showered. I test my breath on my hand. I couldn't find my gum, so I guess it's OK.

Two doors on either end of the porch. I ring the bell for the left door, number 754.

Should I have brought something? I have the letters and pictures—and T.J.'s letter—in my backpack, but should I have brought something else? Like flowers or something? Maybe something for Zoe? Shit. Too late now, I guess. But tomorrow, tomorrow I'll go out and get her something. Like a stuffed animal. That's what uncles do.

"Hi, Matt," Celia says, swinging the door open with one hand, a yellow-and-white dish towel in the other.

"I'm a little early—I know," I say.

"No worries," she says. I can see inside, a short hallway, then a glance of warm-brown-and-gold living room through the open door behind her. "Come on in."

I wipe my feet off on the mat outside her door, twice, then follow her in.

The room is nice. The walls look like they've been covered with brown suede, like if I touched them they'd be soft and plush. Furniture, tables, stuff on the walls. A home.

"Have a seat. I just need to finish one thing for dinner, then we can talk. Can I get you something to drink? Soda? Iced tea? Juice?"

"A soda'd be great, thanks. But, uh . . ." I look around, looking for Zoe.

"Zoe?" Celia asks. "She's at a neighbor's." Missy's, probably. "I thought we should talk first." Celia's face is so serious, cautious, more cautious than at the library even.

"Oh, yeah." I bite my lip to hold down the smile I can feel coming. "OK." Don't act like an idiot.

"And my brother will be home soon, too. So . . ." She stares at me. "He'll come by, when he gets home."

"Great." I try to look cool, but happy, like I'm totally excited to meet her brother. But what if I look too excited, or stupid. Or . . .

"I'll get that soda. Coke OK?" I nod. She waves toward the couch behind me and then heads across the room and through a doorway. I lean my backpack against the side of the couch before sitting down, and then wipe my sweaty palms on my jeans. I can't believe I'm here.

Across the room, near the door, is a long table with lots of pictures on it, including a couple of pictures that look familiar, even from here.

I get up to take a closer look. At the far end of the table is the picture of Celia, T.J., and the other two guys around a table with an umbrella, beach behind them, all of them relaxed and laughing at the camera. Behind it is one of Celia standing next to the lighter-skinned guy from the vacation photo, who's holding Zoe. Could this be her brother? His skin is lighter than Celia's, but they're standing close. Here he is in another one. And another. Must be.

"Here," Celia says, leaning out from the kitchen to hand me a glass with ice and soda, bubbles fleeing up the side of the glass.

"Thanks." The glass is already slick with condensation. I concentrate on not dropping it.

"I'll be right back. Then we can talk."

I turn my attention back to the pictures. I let my eyes slide over them, and slowly move back down the table. A formal picture of a younger Celia in her uniform. One of an older couple — must be Celia's parents. They look nice. Some of other people I don't know. One that looks kind of familiar, Celia holding Zoe, like the picture in my pocket, but with T.J. and the tall, darker-skinned guy from the beach pictures, too. Bet this one was taken the same day. A couple more of just Zoe at various ages.

A big picture of Zoe and Celia's brother. Then a black-and-white one of Celia and her brother at some kind of fancy event—all dressed up and Celia in a fancy dress, holding flowers. Maybe a wedding? Could she and T.J. have gotten married? My heart thuds and speeds up. Was this one from their wedding? I quickly scan all the pictures for their wedding picture, looking just long enough to rule each out before moving on. None. Then back at this one. I pick it up. Needing to see it closer. Something's weird. Celia and her brother, has to be, but when was it taken? Maybe this was at a family wedding, like a cousin's or something? Her arm is linked with his. Maybe they were in the wedding? Her dress is fancy, but not like bride fancy, and she's not wearing a veil.

The front door opens, and a tall guy in a suit shuffles through, juggling some kind of briefcase, two cloth bags, and some other stuff.

"Hi," he says when he looks up and sees me standing there. "You must be Matt, right?"

Oh. Celia's brother. A little older than in the pictures, and with the start of a scruffy beard, and glasses, but definitely him.

"Oh, uh, hi." I carefully put the picture back where it was, adjusting it until it's exactly like I found it. "I was just looking at the pictures."

"I think she has some albums set aside to look through with you," he says, staring at the pictures on the table. "Some pictures of your brother."

I want to say something, but nothing seems right, with

the twisting sick feeling in my stomach and the itching desire to see the pictures she's put aside right now.

"So, you're Celia's brother, right?" I take a large sip of my soda and push my hand out to shake hello.

"Uh, no. I'm Will. Celia's husband."

twenty-three

His hand is stretched out toward me, but my hand falls away before we touch. The bubbles sting my nose. I try to swallow without choking.

"Will?" I sputter and gasp around the burning sensation. "Husband?"

But Will . . . in the letters . . . I thought Will was married to Missy. A different Will? Unless he's not with Missy, or not with her anymore?

"Yeah," he says slowly, drawing the word out. He thrusts his fingers through his hair. "She said she was going to have time to talk with you for a while before I got home. Guess that didn't happen? Damn."

I look back at the picture. At all the pictures. Watching them realign. Yeah, a wedding—theirs: Celia and Will's. But in that picture with her and T.J., the vacation one, he's with them, on vacation. T.J. knew him. She married this guy, not even . . . When? When did she? I look at the wedding picture again. Celia is younger. Will's younger. Oh, God. My eyes fly over the images in frames. Pictures of Will and Celia, Will and Zoe. On the wall above the table, more pictures. One with him holding a tiny baby while Celia looks on.

"Here, Matt, sit down. I'll go get. . . . Just sit."

The glass is removed from my fingers, and I'm nudged toward the couch. But I can't move. The pictures. There are no pictures of just T.J. and Zoe. None of just T.J. and Celia, either. Like . . . almost like . . . Oh, God, I am a fucking moron. Have to leave. Get out, before they come back. Bag. Where's my bag? . . .

"Matt?"

Worried voice. Fast footsteps.

"Oh, God, Matt, I wanted to have a chance to talk before . . . Come on and sit down."

"Sorry." That's my voice. "Sorry—I've made a big mistake. I . . ." Dizzy. "I found the picture, of you and Zoe, in T.J.'s stuff, and the letters . . ." Did they have an affair? God, does Will know? He can't know—he was nice. Shit. Need to leave.

I look at her. Her eyes, wet and sad. But knowing. She knows what I thought. She knew. Before I got here. This afternoon. She knew and she let me come here anyway. She lied to me.

"You thought we were together," she says, "Theo and me, and that Zoe was his." It's gentle, and not even a question, and it burns. "No, we weren't. And Zoe isn't his daughter, but she loved him. She called him Uncle T. Come on and sit down. We need to talk."

What the hell? "Why did you invite me here, if . . . ?" God, she must think I'm really stupid.

"Wait."

Before I can get to the door, she grabs my arm. I shake her off but she reaches again, and her words start to filter through the raging in my head.

"I wanted to be able to talk to you, talk it through. Forgive me, but I didn't think springing all this on you in the library was a good idea."

Something in her tone, and the *all this,* pulls me back. The tingle down my neck. The need to know what *all this* means. "All this?"

"Yes," she says, "all this." She holds out one of the pictures from the table.

I don't want to take it. Not even sure if I trust myself to take it. But she's insistent. As soon as I reach for it, she takes a step back toward the couch. I have to follow. Once seated, she lays the picture frame down on the table in front of me. She reaches her hands toward me, like she's gonna touch me, but stops. I can't help but stare at her hands, still too close to me. She's talking. All these words. Nothing's making sense.

"So, I'm sorry, about Will," she says, then grimaces. "Well, not about him, just that you met him before we could talk."

"Why didn't you just tell me in the library? I mean, how hard would it have been to say . . . ?" I trail off because I don't know what the truth is. Will is Celia's husband. Has been her husband for a while. Man, Will is Zoe's dad. So what were Celia and T.J.? An affair? Do I want to hear this?

"Matt," she says gently, touching my arm. "There are some things you need to understand. I'm not sure I'm the right person to tell you, but it looks like it's mine to handle anyway." She squeezes my arm. "This is actually so much like the both of them, making me do all the hard work so they don't have to."

"What?" Them?

She smiles. It's confusing. "Maybe we should start over."

"How can we start over? Everything, everything is all wrong." I can hear my voice rising as my throat tightens. "What the hell were the letters, the . . . Did he know? Did Will know that you . . . ? Did T.J. know, about Will?"

"Of course he knew," she says gently. Too gently. It pisses me off.

"Then what the hell is with the letters and the love crap? You write all that crap to him when—"

"I didn't write them."

"What?" The hell she didn't. Lying? To protect Will?

"They're not my letters."

Bullshit. I can see them, in my head. The address labels. This address. The *Love you, C.*, on every fucking letter. "You signed them. And the envelopes, the return address. I've *read* them. *All* of them."

"No, I didn't," she says, shaking her head. "I didn't write the letters."

My head spins. *Love You, C.* CELIA CARSON, on the envelopes. "I don't understand."

"I know," she says. After several attempts to say something else, she shifts so she can face me more and starts again. "Your brother could be so stubborn, especially when he was trying to protect someone he cared about. I think he was just trying to protect you."

I can see him, on that last visit, in the half shadows around the fire. "Protect me from what?"

She pushes her braids over her shoulders, stares at her hands. "How much did he talk about his life here?"

I think hard, sorting back through fragments from lots of conversations from the last few years. "Not a lot, I guess. He never seemed to want to talk about Army stuff, so we talked about . . . other things." She nods, but her head dips lower over her clasped hands. "I mean, he talked about some stuff, some friends, and, like . . . I knew where he was when he was stationed at home — Georgia, here, but . . . he never even talked about you. If I hadn't found the letters . . . But if you didn't . . ."

"Theo and my brother did Basic together. After Basic, they got different advanced-training assignments, but by then . . ."

She smiles, shaking her head, but suddenly her mouth snaps tight and pinched. She looks away. When she looks back, she nods toward the picture, forgotten on the table. I pick it up and look at it. Celia holding Zoe, just like the picture in my pocket, but standing next to them is T.J. and the tall guy from the vacation photos. T.J.'s arm slung over his shoulder. Huge smiles.

"That's my brother, Curtis," she says, her finger drifting into my field of vision to point to the guy standing on the other side of T.J. "They met in Basic. With different advanced training assignments, and later different bases, it wasn't easy to get a lot of time together, especially without drawing attention, but they made it work. Eventually Curtis got assigned to an admin post here. Theo visited as much as he could. He spent a lot of time here between his first and second tours. And when he re-upped after his second tour, he got himself assigned to the closest post he could. In the last few years, Theo practically lived here — next door — with Curtis."

My hands shake. I pull my picture of Celia and Zoe out of my pocket. A thin blue line along the edge, clearly part of T.J.'s shirt. My picture is only part of a copy of this one.

Celia's breath hitches. She reaches across me. Her finger traces along the same minuscule line of blue at the edge of my picture. "I guess he cut it down to be able to fit the other piece in his wallet, or somewhere on him. Somewhere close. He'd have kept it close, and hidden."

There's a buzzing in my head, thoughts fighting for dominance like swarming bees. All I can do is stare at T.J.'s arm around that guy, Curtis, and try to understand. They're both smiling, mugging for the camera. Curtis's arm is wrapped around T.J.'s waist. His shoulder pressed into T.J.'s side. T.J.'s fingers gripping Curtis's shoulder, tugging Curtis closer. A hard half hug. I can remember what T.J.'s one-armed half hugs felt like. But T.J.'s fingers, digging into Curtis's arm, are too tight. T.J. never hugged me like that. Like he couldn't get me close enough.

"The letters," Celia says, her voice more steady. "Curtis wrote them. It wasn't safe for them to write each other directly—not with Don't Ask, Don't Tell. Too risky, for both of them. A lot of the guys in Theo's old unit knew, but this last tour he was assigned to a new unit. He didn't really know them yet. A few he especially worried about. One stray letter, one guy who didn't like him, and there could be trouble. And because of his position, Curtis was always going to be a target—all it would take is one jerk who didn't think he got a fair shake . . . So, they used my name instead of his on the envelopes, and Theo sent his letters here."

Buzzing louder, fighting for space with the pounding, tight in my chest, burn creeping up into my throat. It hits me like a punch to the gut.

"No way." I drop the picture with a clatter of metal on wood. I'm on my feet. The room sways. I fight to keep my balance, using the nubby arm of the couch for a crutch. Have to get out of here. "You're a fucking liar."

"Matt, it's a lot to take in, I know. But calm down. We'll talk some more. I'll try to answer any questions. Curtis will be home soon, and then you can talk to him."

"Fuck." I've gotta get out of here. She tries to touch me and my arm flails away, knocking stuff over as I stumble and bounce toward the door. "Don't touch me. I don't believe a word of this crap."

"They loved each other," she says, voice cracking.

"Shut up." I need to get out.

"We kept telling Theo to tell you," she says, talking faster, louder. "We thought he was going to tell you, on his last visit, because he said he was ready—"

"Shut the fuck up." The door won't open. Knob won't turn.

"Curtis is devastated. Can you try to understand that?" she rasps through angry tears. "After Theo was killed, he fell apart. He's really struggled. He's separated from the Army now, and losing Theo . . . He's lost even more than—"

"You're disgusting. Stay away from me." The door! Get it open!

"Even if you don't believe me, if you want to leave, please, just let him have his letters," she pleads. "It would mean so much. . . ."

I get the door open and stumble out into the hall, Celia's voice and then Will's trailing behind. I can't breathe. Need air.

The front door is heavy, and it swings all the way open when I full-body yank on it, slamming into the wall and rattling as I struggle to make it through. Have to get away. Pounding blood in my ears. Burning throat. Fuck.

I crash into a body, hard and tall and rushing at me, so we both sort of collide and rebound, tottering for a moment on the porch.

"Whoa," says a deep voice near my ear. Strong hands grab me and lift me up midfall. "Hey, you OK?"

"Yeah, sorry," I say, reaching out to push off. Need to keep moving.

"Matt?"

"Huh?" I look over my shoulder as I hurry down the steps. Curtis. My legs revolt, locking. I grab the banister, barely able to keep from falling.

"Careful, man," he says, hands reaching out to grab me again.

"Get the fuck away from me!" I stumble backward, my feet searching for solid ground. "Don't touch me!"

"OK, OK," he says, hands up in front of him. "Just calm down."

"I don't wanna calm down. You're a bunch of liars!"

"Hey. I haven't said anything yet. And you don't even know me."

"And I don't want to. There is no way . . ." Pressure in my ears.

He reaches out a hand, palm up. Big hand. Fingers spread wide, palm pinkish and light compared to the darker skin of his arm and the back of his hand. "Let's just go back inside and we can talk, OK?"

Anger surges up, ripping through me, making everything

burn hot and red, turning me. My fist already hard and ready. "Why, so you can tell me some more lies? Fuck off."

"You're so much like your brother." He looks up to the sky, his long neck prominent as he swallows.

I am hurtling toward him, my whole body arching behind the swing of my arm. The impact never comes, and before I know it, I am turned, head forced low, facing the ground. Curtis's pulling my arm behind my back, and I can see in my head how he grabbed the swinging arm and turned me. I kick and fight, but in no time, he has me on my knees with my head almost touching the sidewalk, my arm pulled back as far as it will go. I try to kick out, and he pulls my arm harder until I think it'll pop out of the socket.

"I told Theo to tell you," he breathes in my ear, too close. I try to yank free and he leans pressure on the place where my arm meets my shoulder. "Goddammit, cut it out. I don't want to hurt you, Matt."

I stop struggling, waiting to catch my breath.

"I told him to tell you, but he was so afraid that you might react badly. Wonder where he got that idea."

I push back against him. I can't make any words come, and I need to get away, or I'm gonna puke or cry or something. My stomach hurts. My arm hurts. And there's a panic rising up to strangle me. I push back again, trying to kick at his legs. He pulls me closer until his chest is pressed against my back.

"Just calm down and I'll let you go," he says into my shoulder.

It's too much. He's too close. Fuck. Let go. He has to let go. Don't touch me. I can't make my mouth work.

"I told him to tell you."

Without warning he loosens his hold and pushes me away from him, so I spin toward the street and stumble before I find my feet. When I do, he's standing there facing me, obviously ready if I come back at him. The way he looks at me makes me stop. I take a couple deep breaths, and so does he, relaxing his stance, but not totally relaxed. I watch him. He doesn't even look like a faggot, maybe his clothes, maybe, but he's strong, and he's big. He doesn't sound like a faggot. His hands look strong, not girly at all. No way. No way was T.J. . . . with . . . no way.

"You're lying," I spit out finally.

"Fine," he says, shaking his head and grabbing his bag off the sidewalk. "If that's what you want to believe, fine. Go home to Daddy. Keep believing you knew your brother. Fine by me."

He's halfway up the steps when he turns around and looks at me. "I loved him." His face contorts through an evolution of emotion ending in a gulping sound. A deep breath and he skewers the center of his chest with one rough finger. "And he loved me."

He presses his fists to his eyes, growling out a terrible sound, fury and pain. Then he smooths away all the anguish with his long fingers. Mask back in place, he waves toward the house a couple of times and then sags. "If you want to hear about who your brother really was, come on back, or call. But if you ever take a swing at me again, I'll break your arm."

It's only once I'm back at the car, wiping the puke from my mouth with trembling hands, that I realize — I left my backpack in the house.

twenty-four

MORNING COMES WAY TOO SOON. AT FIRST I'M PISSED AT having to leave the hostel for the lockout period. But once I'm out in the air, it's better than being in that dark, claustrophobic room. I snag a table outside the coffee place away from the crowds at the farmers' market a block up. It's a little wobbly and not all that comfortable, with the woven metal of the chair cutting into my butt and legs, but it lets me sit in the perfect balance of sun and shade, eat my fancy bread, sip my too-strong coffee, and try to make my head stop for five fucking minutes.

I barely slept last night. When I did, I dreamed of T.J., but not my T.J. I dreamed of some other T.J., who was weird and wrong. In one dream, no matter how many times I yelled or got right in his face, he couldn't hear or see me. In another, every time I grabbed at him, pieces fell off in my hand.

After I've torn through the first mini-loaf of bread, butter melting before I can get it in my mouth, my stomach and nerves start to settle. The caffeine starts to do its thing.

There's one clear thought drowning out all the others: I need my backpack. I have to get it back.

They've probably already looked through it and found everything, including the one letter I didn't read—and I know I should just kiss it all good-bye, that they'll never give it back, even if I asked, but I can't. I want it. I want it all.

My brain keeps chanting that I need to get my bag back, with everything inside, like if I don't, I'll die. And I might. The burning awful hole in my gut might really, eventually, get so big that internal organs fall out or get eaten away.

First, above everything else, Shauna's money is in there. What's left of my money is in my wallet in my pocket, but the backup from Shauna is in the small pocket at the back of my bag, and I'm gonna need it to get home.

Second, and almost as important, I need the letters. If I could just read them all again, I could make sense of this. Because there has to be something in them I missed that would make this make sense. I mean, how could I have misread them so badly? If they're telling the truth, why didn't Curtis ever mention Celia, his sister, in his letters? Why do so many talk about Missy and Will? Are there two Wills, or did Will used to be with Missy? So many of them talk about Zoe. And not like she was just someone else's kid he knew.

If I had the other bag of letters from home, and I could find Will's and Missy's, and even Celia's letters—'cause if she's telling the truth, she had to have written him, too, even if I don't remember any letters signed *Celia*—if I could just read them again, would they make more sense? When I get home and dump that bag out, will I find all of Celia's letters, and find in them everything I needed to know not to get this so totally wrong? Or did Celia not write on purpose? 'Cause I know I didn't read all of the other letters, but I'd have noticed if there were some from her in that other bag.

I push the coffee aside, too strong for my acid stomach.

And after last night, there's no way they're gonna give the letters back. It's over. I really should just get on with it. Leave. Go home. Just at the thought of it, the hole gets bigger. And what about the money?

My cell vibrates on the table. I don't need to look at it to know it'll be Shauna again. It's totally uncool that I promised to call her last night and then never did. Bitch-ass move, in fact, but I can't talk to her. I can't even try to explain to her how much the world has fucking changed since my message yesterday afternoon.

I rub my eyes and wait for the telltale beep that means another unanswered voice mail. Not long after the beep, it beeps again. A text.

I flip the phone open and hit the center button. Shauna's text pops up. Worried. A plea to call. I can't. After a bunch of tries to write a meaningful text in return, I finally text back: *All fine. Call 2mr.* I shut the phone off. The first part's a lie, but I'm hoping to keep the promise.

People come and go all around me. Families. Kids. Couples. College students. Old people. A lot of them carry flowers and snacks and bags of stuff from the farmers' market.

The tables around me fill and empty and fill again, people moving the tables and chairs and jockeying to claim them as soon as they are empty. I just sit there. No one talks to me, though some people glare like they'd like me to leave.

I get caught staring at this one guy. The side of his neck and face are covered in tattoos, his earlobe stretched around a black ring, leaving a gaping dime-size hole, so you can look right through it and see his neck. It creeps me out, but I can't look away. When I realize he's staring back, I tense, but he just smiles and asks if I'm using the extra chair at my table.

Then Tattoo Guy waves at someone, and I follow the wave. Two people hurry across the street. A short guy with funky glasses waves back, dodging cars. The guy with him is tall, with really long curly hair. I can't stop staring at the tall guy. Except for the clothes and the obvious lack of tits, I could have thought woman, maybe even pretty woman. But even from across the street, I knew he was a guy.

Tall Guy laughs. The others whisper things that make him laugh more. He flips his hair over his shoulder and then snaps his head to the side to stare directly at me. I can't look away. One of his eyebrows arches slowly up over a wicked smile. Before I realize, I am up and out of my chair and half-way down the block, laughter trailing behind me.

OK, so, gay guys. I get that, them, fine. The clothes. The way they move. Tall Guy's hair and, well, everything. Obviously gay. Once I heard his voice, I knew for sure, but even before talking, just that something that says "gay guy." OK. But Curtis? T.J.? No fucking way. T.J. was strong. He liked hiking and fixing cars and was a big guy. He was in the freaking Army. He wore T-shirts and jeans. His hair was pretty short. He didn't even own any mousse or gel or anything. He never wore jewelry. He hit harder than anyone I've ever met, except Dad. And he was so fierce. He dated girls. Didn't he? In high school?

"Matt?"

I look up at the unfamiliar voice to see Curtis leaning against a car parked just down from the hostel. My feet stop before I can make them keep going toward the front door. Then I remember the hostel is still in lockout time.

"Can we talk?" he asks, still leaning against the car.

"Nothing to say."

"Just a few minutes, then I'll go."

"Why?"

He rubs his hand over his face before answering my question. "Because there are some things I want to say. Because I wanted to apologize for my part of last night and make sure you're OK. Because I thought you might like this back." He reaches into the car through the open window and pulls out my backpack.

I put my hand out for my bag. He holds it close to his body and inclines his head toward the little park across the street.

"Just a few minutes," he says again, so much like what I was planning to say to Celia just about twenty-four hours ago.

Once we're settled on separate benches in the shade of the trees, I wait for him to start.

"This is nice," Curtis says, looking around him. "I've never noticed it before."

I shrug. I like it here, too. But no way I'm gonna tell him that.

Curtis stares out at the street and then down at his hands, hanging loosely between his spread knees. His right hand is all banged up. Red and swollen with scrapes all across the knuckles. Looks a little like my hand after the fight. His chuckle makes me look up from his hand.

"I, uh"—he touches the first two knuckles—"I went a little nuts after you left last night. Beat the hell out of the wall." He shrugs and covers his right hand with his left. "I'm sorry about last night. I could have been less . . . confrontational."

Damn straight, he could. He could have just left me the fuck alone. But I guess he could have been more in my face, too. He could have hit me. I might have, would have, hit him, if he hadn't stopped me.

"Having you show up like that. And then coming home to find you tearing out. It was just, well, too much. I . . ."

He stops talking. I can see his body rippling with tension or anger or something, but not like last night, not like he's gonna hit me or anything. Then, without saying anything else, he reaches down and grabs the backpack and swings his arm out to me.

"Here," he says. "Take it."

I reach for my bag, still not sure if this is some kind of test or trap or something. When my fingers close around it, he lets go all at once. I have to grab it with my other hand to pull it to me. I let my hands trail down, squeezing as I go. I can't believe it. I think the letters and pictures are still in here. I start to unzip it to look, and Curtis makes this huffy sound.

"No," he says, mocking, waving toward the bag, "go ahead. Check it out. But we didn't steal anything. We didn't even look through it. God, what kind of people do you think we are?"

I don't think I'm gonna answer that.

Another huffy laugh. "You're welcome."

"Thanks," I say belatedly, and more out of habit than anything. But I guess it was cool of him to bring me back my bag, even if I'm not sure I believe that they didn't look through it and take anything. I'll be shocked if the letter from T.J. is still in there. But there's nothing I can really do about it if it's not.

"I wasn't sure you were still around," Curtis says, sitting back against the bench. "I called, but they wouldn't tell me."

"Yeah, I, uh, I'll have to leave. Soon."

Curtis nods. "This wasn't the way it was supposed to go." When he sees I'm paying attention, he continues. "None of this. Theo was supposed to tell you. About him. About us."

My hands grip the edge of the bench.

"I wanted to meet you, to get to know you, but not like this—and I sure as hell wasn't supposed to have to tell you, not . . ."

Curtis swallows hard, and his whole body trembles as he

rubs his banged-up knuckles against his mouth. His hand is shaking when he pulls it away. I watch it stutter all the way back to his lap.

"Every time I think it's getting easier, something happens and I'm right back in that hole." I'm not sure he's even talking to me anymore. "It wasn't supposed to be like this. And I'm so damn angry at him, for not being here, for going back when he should have been done, when it would have been so easy for him to get out, to stay . . ."

He wipes roughly at his eyes. Fast, angry swipes. Something lodges in my throat.

"You came all this way to find something," he finally says, voice shaky, "or someone. You just going to walk away because it's not who you thought it'd be?"

I can't answer. I can hardly breathe. There's nothing I can say to this guy, nothing that doesn't suck or sound mean or stupid. I just want him to go away. Go away and leave me alone. Let me have my memories back the way they were. I don't want this.

"I don't know what else to say to you," Curtis says. "I'd be willing to answer any questions you have. I'd love to talk about him. No one really wants to talk about him anymore." He stares at the passing traffic, then looks me in the eyes. "But I don't know what you want or need. So," he says, standing up, "why don't we try dinner 2.0. You come over. We eat some food. You see some pictures of Theo, and we try this again."

"I can't," I say. Even the thought of going back there makes me feel like puking. Not even for pictures.

"We would love to spend some time with you, and I think you'd like Zoe. He loved her. And she really loved him."

I shake my head, because I can't. I can't go there. I can't just let this all be true and then crawl back and pretend it's OK. None of it's OK. If I go back there and pretend it's OK, then . . .

"How about tomorrow?"

"I'm, uh, probably leaving tomorrow." And suddenly, I know it's true. I'll leave tomorrow. If I leave early enough, I could be home by late tomorrow night. But to what? Fuck. Think about that later.

Curtis clamps his lips in a tight line. "We'll be around all day. Come on by before you leave. There are some things I'd like to give you, that I think you should have."

What is this, some kind of trade? I feel my heart pounding. "You just want the letter."

"The letters I sent him? Yeah, I would like them back."

My brain stumbles. Letters. He doesn't know about T.J.'s letter. Unless he's playing dumb because he already took it.

"But that's not what this is about. You don't have to stay if you don't want to. You don't even have to come inside. But I'd like to give you a few things anyway."

I need to look in my bag. And what could he have for me, really? Why would T.J. leave anything for me with him, when he knew I didn't even know Curtis existed?

"Look." Curtis waves a hand, as if trying to pull the words out of the air. "Theo used to talk about you. A lot. For me, well, it feels a little like we've met before, and like I should . . . Maybe it's wishful thinking, but . . . it'd be nice to have someone who really knew him, and who still wants to talk about him."

I force my head not to nod or agree. I can't agree to anything. I need to leave and forget about all this.

"We could e-mail, or talk on the phone, whatever, if you don't want to come by. But think about it, because I think Missy would really like to see you again, make sure you're OK."

My head snaps up. "Missy?"

"Celia," Curtis says with a wave of his hand, like it should have been obvious. "She feels bad about how last night went down. She feels like she messed up. Like she messed things up on Theo. Just, well, just think about stopping by. Even for a minute."

Missy. "I'll, uh, think about it." Missy and Will. They were there, in the letters the whole time. "But I really might have to leave early. I have to get back." I'm pretty sure he knows I'm lying, at least a little.

"Anytime tomorrow." Curtis turns to walk away and then pivots sharply back. "Look, whatever you decide, whether you come by or not, even if I never see or hear from you again, just . . . I'd really like my letters back, OK? You can send them to me, or call me and I'll figure out how to get them from you. But they're mine. And you know they are, because you drove all the way here to give them to me, even if I'm not who you thought I was."

As soon as his car pulls away, I yank the zipper down and pull my backpack open so I can see inside. All three plastic bags are there: the pictures, Curtis's letters, and the single letter from T.J. I check the back pocket near the straps: Shauna's money is still there, too. I pull out T.J.'s letter with a shaking hand. Still in its plastic, label still unbroken over the opening.

He didn't read it.

Or take it.

He really has no idea.

twenty-five

I have no clue what I'm supposed to do next.

I thought I was coming here on a mission, one last thing I could do for T.J., maybe the most important thing anyone could do for him. And I planned and plotted and drove and skulked and it all worked . . . except for the part where I got everything totally 100 percent wrong.

When the lockout time is over, I go back to my room and look through the pictures, trying to see what else I missed. Curtis is in a lot of them, in most of the pictures of Celia. I just didn't really see him, because I was looking at her. In some he's in the background, but he's there. Even the one of her in uniform, he's right there, a step behind her, but there.

I read the letters again, too. Knowing "Missy" is Celia, the words shift and rearrange themselves: some parts more significant, others less. Curtis wrote about Celia, and Will, and about Zoe. I just didn't understand, because he called Celia "Missy."

And Curtis wrote about lots of other people, mostly guy people. And not guys like Joe and Bob and Mike. Guys like

Aiden and Jude and Terrence. He wrote about parties and bars and movies that should have been neon rainbow-colored signs. *West Side Story*, for fuck's sake.

Reading the letters before, the sexy parts were embarrassing, like I was spying on T.J. and Celia. Now I try to skim quickly past parts about kisses and bed and sex. But Curtis wrote about T.J.'s hands. A lot. And when I thought they were from Celia, it was sort of sweet. But now it's not at all sweet. It's fucking all about sex. Now when I read about the rougher feel of T.J.'s fingers, how his hands felt, I know exactly what he meant, where he meant.

He wrote about T.J.'s chest and his shoulders. His back. He wrote about T.J.'s hands on his hips, T.J.'s chin digging into his shoulder, T.J.'s lips on his neck. He wrote about waking up with T.J. breathing in his ear. And when I thought it was Celia's ear, I was OK with that. But Curtis's? Now I wish I didn't know what Curtis looks like. I wish that I could scrub the new images from my brain.

With Curtis calling him Theo, it's almost like he's a totally different person from T.J. But even the parts of me that want to sit in a corner with my ears covered, shouting that everyone is lying, has to give in. Because of Curtis's hand — I know what that beat-up hand meant and how swinging it had to feel, even if he hit a wall instead of a face. And that picture. Not the cut-up piece of crap I've been carrying around. The whole one, the one with all of them, or even the other piece, the piece T.J. kept with him, of just him and Curtis.

That picture is all the evidence I need to know that everything Celia and Curtis said is true, even if I don't want to believe it.

In the instant Celia handed it to me, even before I could process that it was T.J., somewhere deep down I understood T.J.'s one-armed half hug and Curtis's arm around T.J.'s waist. The way they stood and smiled. There wasn't anything "buddy" about it. And somewhere, maybe in the stuff at home, maybe lost because he kept it on him all the time, is the other half of the picture: the one of T.J. and Curtis. I can practically see it, worn and battered and warped from being hidden in some secret place or compartment, soft around the edges from being handled every day. Small enough to risk it. The only one of just the two of them. How much T.J. risked for that one picture.

T.J. lied to me. And, really, that's the part that sucks the most. He had a whole other life, one I'm not sure he was ever gonna tell me about. Was he just gonna come back and move on? Just leave me behind and only come to visit once in a while? Play the part of T.J. a couple weeks here or there and then go back to being Theo?

God, I spent my whole life trying to be brave, and strong, like him. Feeling like a waste of space because I'd never be as good as him. And all that time he was this whole other fucking person.

How many times did he call me, well, maybe not a faggot, but a pussy or weak-ass or a wuss? How many times did he sit there while Dad held him up as the poster boy for macho America, making me feel like shit when I couldn't be as fast or as tough?

My hands clench. And all that time he was a fucking liar!

A knock at the door makes me jump. My heart pounds out of my chest.

"Boris, kweek, opan zee door," Harley says, muffled only a little by the too-thin door.

Maybe she'll just go away if I stay quiet.

Another knock. A kick at the door. "Come on, Matt. I know you're in there."

I hold my breath.

"Don't make me tell the front desk that I think you're a danger to yourself or others in there."

I open the door, ready to get rid of her.

"Hey," she says. She bounces up on her toes and plants a quick kiss on my lips. So fast I'm shocked. Then she laughs and does it again, longer this time. When she pulls back, she ducks under my arm, letting her hand trail across my chest on her way past me. "I was looking for you earlier." She drops her bag onto the chair and pushes some of the letters to the side so she can sit on the end of the bed. "Were you foiled by Moose and Squirrel?" she asks in that weird accent.

"Huh?" My brain is still thinking about the kisses and what the hell just happened.

She rolls her eyes. "How'd it go? Meeting the kid last night?"

"Oh, uh, fine." Not telling her anything, not this time. Then I'm getting rid of her.

"Good. What are you doing?" she asks, gathering up a stack of the letters, flipping through them. My stomach twists.

"Nothing, really. But, uh, I am kind of in the middle of—"

"Hey, are these from her? The girlfriend?"

"Look, Harley, I'm really kind of busy, so—"

"They are!"

She reads, her fingers crumpling the stack she's holding. Drops one onto the wrong pile, shoves a stack off the bed with her knee.

"Wow. How fucking sad." She looks up, waving one at me. "She must be seriously depressed. But meeting your brother's kid went well? Did she call you Uncle Mattie?" she asks with a teasing smile.

I ignore all the wrong and try to figure out how to get her to put the letters down and leave without looking like an idiot.

She whistles. Waves her fingers. "*Caliente.* Seriously, she writes some steamy letters." She clears her throat, tilts her chin to perform. "*. . . I close my eyes and think about your fingers digging into my hips, your lips whispering against my ear, it's almost*—"

"Enough," I say, grabbing the letter from her hand. "What is wrong with you?" My hands are shaking. She has to leave.

Her face goes from entertained to shocked to sad. Her mouth trembles.

"Sorry, Matt. I was just . . ." She looks at the other letters, puts them down on the bed very carefully. "Sorry," she says.

"S'OK." It's not, but I just want her gone. She's part of yesterday, when everything was good.

"And why does this one have its own protective little bag?"

"Give it." I hold my hand out.

Her eyebrows arch up. Then she turns the bag, examining the label.

I lunge at her, but she flails away.

"Stop, or it might rip," she says, batting away my hand.

I watch her, my heart pounding. I clench my hands to keep the anger down.

"Is this . . . It is, isn't it?" Eyes wide, hands still turning it. "It's from him! To *her*!"

"Give it to me." I barely recognize my own voice.

She moves right but then slides across the bed so I can't reach her. Before I can get around the bed, she has a finger under the fold in the bag.

"No!" I slap at her hands, grab her wrist and twist.

"Ow!" she yelps, dropping it.

I pick it up, smooth the edges. The letter is safe in my hand. I shake off the terror and move across the room.

"I wasn't going to hurt it. I just thought—"

"You don't get to think, not about this."

The right side of the label is ripped just a little. I smooth it down, willing it to fix itself.

"I was only kidding."

I walk around the bed and put it into my backpack, then slide my backpack under the bed.

"Seriously, Matt." She walks toward me, and I tense. "I'm sorry. I didn't know you'd flip. I shouldn't have done that."

"It's fine."

"Matt." Her hand on my arm. "I'm so sorry. Let me make it up to you, OK?"

I just want her to leave, so I can think.

"Want to go to a party?" she asks, eyebrows up, crooked smile.

"What?" Is she stupid?

"I'm supposed to meet some friends there. Should be way cool."

Does she not get—?

"Come on. You're obviously upset. It'll do you some good to get out of this room for a while. And it'll give me a chance to make amends. OK?"

"I don't think—"

"Aw, come on. I was just kidding around. It's fine." She waves toward the letter. "All tucked away and safe. So . . . what else are you going to do tonight? Come out with me."

"Harley, I don't want—"

She grabs my hand and bounces next to me. "We don't even have to stay long, but you really need to blow off some steam. And I owe you. So, you should place yourself in my very, very capable hands for the evening." She bites her lower lip and looks up at me through sparkly, spiky lashes. "You won't be sorry."

She pounces on me, throwing her arms around my neck and plastering herself to me.

"Come on, it'll be fun."

Her hands slide over my shoulders and she pulls herself up until her face is close to mine, rubbing her tits up and down my chest.

"Matt? Are you really going to stay here and brood, alone, when you could be out with me? Having fun?" She bites her lower lip again, inches up on her toes. My hands started out warding off her advance, I'm sure, but somewhere along the way they sort of started holding her up.

She shifts closer, until her hips push against me. I try to pull back but she hangs on, grinning bigger.

And then she's kissing me, her lips smashed to mine, her tits squashed between us. Her tongue's in my mouth. She pulls my head down.

And then I'm kissing her back, sort of. My tongue's in the way. She grabs my face, guides me, helping me kiss her better.

Cigarette smoke and strong perfume.

But she's still kissing me, and even wrong smelling, it's good. I'm grabbing her ass.

She guides my hand to her tit. Shit. Total handful. She's

getting into it. She winds her arms around my neck and grinds into me. She's got to feel me, but she pushes up and kisses me harder. Holy shit.

She shoves against me, forcing me to step back. I keep taking steps until my legs hit the bed.

"OK," she says into my mouth. "We'll stay in."

She giggles, smiles up at me. Fuck! Her hands are under my shirt, pushing it up. Whoa! WHOA!

She pushes me down. Paper crinkles, my hand hits paper, too. The letters.

Harley reaches out to sweep a pile off the bed. I grab her arm, but she thinks I'm pulling her in and just pushes another pile out of our way.

Shauna was so careful with the letters. And made the folders and directions and all. Folding the map, holding it to her chest. *You'll have to be nice if you want me to share.*

Harley's in my lap. Her mouth on mine. Not the right mouth.

I yank my face to the side and her lips skip across my cheek. She tries to kiss me again. Part of me wants to — wants to bad — but I shove her off me.

She laughs, but not nice. Mean. Like that first night.

"What's wrong?" she asks, wiping her mouth.

I rub my hand across my mouth and cheek. Hate the taste of her. The cigarette smell that fills my nose.

"You don't . . ." She stands up, tugging her shirt down.

"Sorry." I put more space between us. "I'm sorry. I just . . . I can't."

Maybe I could just shove her out the door.

"I don't get it." She squints up at me. "Felt like you could . . . like you were into it."

"Totally not you." Well, sort of her. "You're hot as hell." Her face goes mad. "And sweet and great. But . . . I can't." Not with her, but I can't tell her that. "I'm sort of . . ." She glares. "There's . . ." I need to get her out of here. "I'm . . . lame. I suck. Sorry. Maybe you should just go."

Maybe she'll be so pissed she'll leave. And I can go back to kicking myself. Again.

But she doesn't move. Just stands there, looking at me. Pissed, I think, but still not moving.

She pulls a pack of gum out of her pocket. She unwraps and then folds a piece into her mouth, chewing and thinking, shaking her head. She fiddles with the pack. A bit of bright pink catches my eye, a blur on the side of the pack as she rolls it between her fingers.

I remember what that pink sticker felt like, when I smoothed it down where it wraps over the edge of the pack, in line at the gas station in Illinois.

The scene on the Terrace flashes back through my head. My backpack wasn't where I left it after I went—no, after she *sent* me—in to find popcorn. She was looking for what? Money? My money was in my wallet, but Shauna's money was in the small, hidden pocket. I checked after Curtis brought it back, but didn't bother counting it. Looked like it was all there and . . . I just knew they didn't take any. If she found it, she didn't take much. Maybe a few bills?

"Listen, can you just drive me to the party?" She sounds different. "It's across town, and I'm running low on cash. I really need to catch up with my friend there." Her voice is different, hurt, something else. And I don't care. I stare at the sticker.

"OK?" she asks.

Curtis and Celia had my backpack. And they didn't take anything. Didn't even look through it.

"Matt?"

I finally look at her face. She looks the same, but not.

"Back for more money?" I ask.

"What? I don't know what you—"

"That's my gum."

She starts to shake her head.

"The price tag. It's mine. From my backpack."

She looks down. Turns the pack over in her hand. "I didn't think you'd mind," she says, flirting again. Fluttery eyes, looking up through her lashes and that crooked smile.

Yeah. No. Not this time. "Save it."

Her innocent smile slides into a smirk. "Ahh." When she looks up, it's like she's someone totally different. Older. Colder. "Got me." She holds it out to me.

"Keep it."

"Great." She shakes her head. Chews. Studies the price tag, flicks at the edge with her nail until it tears. "What are you going to do?" she asks, rubbing her forehead with the side of her hand.

"That's the question, isn't it?"

I open the door and wait. Just before she passes through the door, she turns, but I stare past her into the hall until she leaves. Then I count the money. She only got about thirty dollars, but who knows how much more she would have stolen tonight. I don't think that's all she wanted, but I'm not stupid—it had to be at least part.

I carefully put all the letters back in their envelopes in order and then secure them in their bag and put it in my backpack.

Even after she's long gone, I can't get Harley's smell out of the room—cigarettes and that coconut smell and some kind of perfume. Makes me miss Shauna even more. I haven't turned my phone on since this morning.

I've already broken the only promise I made to Shauna before I left. But I just can't talk to her yet. Not with Harley sort of still here. And not before I know what I'm going to do.

I've lied to her enough. She'll want to know when I'm coming home, and I don't want to make her any more promises I can't keep.

I check T.J.'s letter one more time, just to make sure it's OK.

The bag is still sealed down; the letter's fine. One corner

of the label is just a little bit torn. I'll just tell Curtis it was an accident.

And instantly I can picture it: handing Curtis the letter. *His* letter. The letter I came here to deliver. To *him*, even if I didn't know it.

I can hear Dad's voice in my head, all the things he'd say about Curtis. About *those people*. Before yesterday I would have laughed. Did Dad say that stuff to T.J.? How many times has Dad called me a fairy or a girl? Pretty boy? I know he called T.J. those things, too. I heard it. God. I close my eyes. How many times did I say faggot or homo or fairy in front of T.J.?

Yeah. T.J. lied. By not telling me, by all those years not telling me anything, he lied. But did he lie because he thought I'd hate him? On that hike, in the dark, near the fire, or later, in the tent, when he got quiet, did he want to tell me? Or did he think I was just like Dad?

Curtis said T.J. talked about me, enough that Curtis and Celia acted like they knew me. He couldn't have been planning to just forget about me if he talked about me. Could he?

And Curtis said T.J. was supposed to tell me. About him. About *them*.

My head is pounding. My eyes burn. I just want to sleep, for like a week. But tomorrow I have to face them again.

And the day after, or maybe the day after that, I'll have to face Shauna. And Dad.

twenty-six

I WAKE UP TIRED AFTER A NIGHT OF FITFUL SLEEP AND taunting nightmares. I run upstairs to piss and find some food. Other than someone using one of the showers, the hostel is quiet.

Back in my room with a soda and a pack of peanut-butter crackers from the vending machine, I man up to brave my voice mail. I inhale two of the little cracker-sandwiches and half my soda before the phone even finishes spooling through its waking up. But as soon as it's awake and reconnected to the mother ship, the alerts start popping up: five new voice mails and three new texts.

I put the phone on speaker, hit the buttons for voice mail, punch in my code, and wait. The annoying voice announces my messages in turn.

Matt? Shauna. I almost smile, because she does that a lot, pauses like she's just making sure I'm listening. She huffs into the phone. Frustrated. *You said you would call tonight, so I waited up. But it's late now. Almost three here, so . . . almost two there . . . maybe you're still out? Well, I'm going to sleep. I'll leave the phone on vibrate, so call, if you want.*

If I want. So much in that. I delete the message. Message two. *Hey.* Shauna again. I wince. She's worried, or pissed. Hard to tell. *Where are you?* Pissed. *Call me. I mean it. I need to hear about last night. . . . I hope everything's all right and you're just having fun or something, but . . . if not . . . Just call. Please?*

I close my eyes and hit the delete button. I don't really want to hear the next, but I let it come anyway.

Matt. Hello. This is Roger Anders. I left you a message at home the other day, but I haven't heard from you. Can you please call me as soon as possible? Long pause. *Listen, I need to talk to you. . . .* The second long pause makes my heart stop. Shit. Does he know I lied to him? *It's Sunday morning. Just call me as soon as you can.* Damn.

I press the button to save the message, and while I'm running through scenarios in my head, the next starts to play. It's Shauna again. *Seriously, Matt, way uncool.* Shit. *Call me. You owe me that. I'm starting to worry that I should be, like, I don't know, calling the cops or something. Like we're wasting precious finding-you-alive time, while I'm thinking you're ignoring me. So . . . if you do not call by noon, I am totally dialing 911. Or, you know, whatever number I have to call to get the police in Madison.*

OK. So I'll be calling Shauna. As soon as I've listened to the last one.

Listen. Shauna again. Fuck. *Whatever's going on—your dad was here. He came to my house.* Wow. *Call me.* I think she's hung up when she makes this growly sound and continues.

Deadline still stands. And now I wish I hadn't said dead, because if you are, I'll feel bad, maybe, but, whatever . . . I'm still pissed at you. And I've had to deal with your dad. So, just call me, you big jerk.

Before dialing, I look at the texts, too. A couple of short directives to call and one picture from Friday of Shauna making her I'm-serious face next to a "call me" sign. I feel like laughing, but, like, hysterical laughter. I must be cracking up.

Mr. Anders first, because it's almost ten a.m. there, and I'm not ready to talk to Shauna. My fingers shake as I scroll back through the calls to find his number. He answers on the second ring, before I've even had a chance to brace myself for the conversation.

"Mr. Anders? Hi, uh, this is Matt? Matt Foster?"

"Matt! Thank you for calling me back. Listen, I need you to start early. Tomorrow, if you can. Derek and Pauly were in a car accident, not too serious, but they'll both be off for at least a few weeks. Even with shifting some of the others around, I'm short at least two on the crew working the Southside condo renovation. So, I was hoping you'd be willing to try your hand at some more advanced work."

My head tries to process the information. First, I'm not in trouble or losing my job. But he wants me to start tomorrow, and that's impossible, and so maybe that means I've lost it anyway. But renovation work? He's still talking.

". . . it'll be challenging at times, and the hours can be

somewhat longer, but it's better money, and, well . . . I thought maybe you were ready to give it a shot. If you want, that is."

"Yeah. Yeah! That'd be great. I really appreciate the chance to, uh, do more than paint, to learn, even . . . You really think I can, you know, do more?"

No response. Maybe we got disconnected? "Yes. You do good work, Matt. And I think you're ready to try something more advanced, see if you might like this kind of work."

"Oh, man, Mr. Anders, that'd be great. Really great. You won't be sorry. I'll work really hard and be really, really careful. Promise."

"I'm sure you will—work hard and be careful, that is. So, can you start tomorrow?"

"Uh . . ." I calculate the drive in my head. If I left right now, I could be home by tomorrow morning. But I can't leave just yet. I haven't done what I came here to do.

"Matt?"

"Yeah, yeah . . . I'm here. It's just . . ."

"Are you OK? You're not . . . hurt, are you? Or . . ."

"No, I'm fine, but . . . I'm not at home, and I don't think I can get back in time to start tomorrow."

"Where are you? Are you in trouble?"

Yeah. But not like he thinks. "I'm fine. I'm just . . ." And once Dad is done with me. "Uh, I'm out of town. And it'll take me until tomorrow afternoon, at least, maybe tomorrow night, to get home. Can I start Tuesday instead?"

"Yes. Yes, Tuesday is fine." His breath rushes across the

receiver in a gust. "Tuesday will be great. Just come by the house on Henry and I'll take you over to Southside and introduce you to Raymond. He heads up the crew there. OK?"

"Great. Thanks, Mr. Anders. I really appreciate this. You won't be sorry."

"I know I won't, Matt. I'll see you Tuesday."

My heart is pounding. I realize I'm squeezing my phone in my hand, and the beeping on and off of the speaker phone reminds me I have another call to make.

I steel myself for Shauna. It barely rings before Shauna answers.

"Hello?"

"Hey," I say softly.

"Hey." Short.

"Sorry. About not calling. Things have been . . . Sorry."

I wait for her to yell, or cry, or whatever. I deserve it. But she's not saying anything. I can't actually hear her at all. I look at my phone to make sure the call wasn't dropped. Then I hear something. She's still there, even if she's not talking.

"Shaun . . . I'm sorry." Whiny and stupid, even in my own ears.

"Whatever. Listen, when are you coming back?"

"Tonight."

"Really?" That got her attention.

"Yeah, well, I won't get home until tomorrow sometime, but I'll leave tonight."

"Good." She breathes out hard, like she had been holding her breath. "Good."

"What?"

"Nothing," she says, but it's clearly something.

"What?"

"I just . . . When you didn't call, and wouldn't answer, I just worried . . . that you weren't coming back. And that you'd just leave, and I'd . . ."

"What?"

"Never see you again." Her voice breaks on the last word.

I am such a fucking asshole. "I'll be home tomorrow, promise." Even as I say it I cringe.

"I wouldn't. Come back. If I were you. But if you were gonna leave . . ." She gulps. "And . . . I acted so stupid and . . . said all that crap . . ." Full out tears.

"It's OK," I whisper, pressing my fingers into my eyes.

Her face. Her smile. Everything she did for me, even after she was pissed at me. And she would totally be right here with me, right now, if I had let her.

"I'm not going anywhere," I say. I can't wait to see her, to tell her. And I can picture how she'll look, like when she was reading the letters, but better.

She's still crying, just a little, and trying hard for me not to know. I have to help her out.

"Couldn't let my best friend brave senior year all alone, now, could I?"

She cries harder, and there's nothing I can say but her name and shushing sounds until she calms down.

"I thought," she says, still swallowing tears, "maybe I had screwed that up, too. At Stacy's."

"What?"

"Best friend," she says, like that explains it.

I'm so confused. "I shouldn't have taken off."

"It's OK. I was stupid," she says. "And I know we're not . . . You're not . . . It's OK, as long as we're OK, still . . . friends."

Friends. Like it tastes bad.

"'Cause I couldn't stand it," she says, "if . . . I mean, if you didn't want to even be *friends* anymore." More tears.

"Why wouldn't . . . Shaun?"

"I'm really sorry," she says.

"For what?"

She laughs. "Matt, don't make me say it."

"For. What?"

She huffs into the phone. "Look, I said I'm sorry. Can we move on?"

She didn't do anything. Except wear that freaking insane shirt. And suck the life out of that candy. And smell so freaking good. And try to kiss me.

"But . . . I don't . . . Shaun, I'm the one who bolted. I'm the one who should be apologizing, who—"

"But—"

"For . . . for . . . everything. I should be apologizing for . . . everything . . ."

"But . . ."

I can hear her breathing. I can practically hear her confusion, loud as mine. This is all my fault. I take a deep breath. Time to say what I should have said a long time ago, instead of sulking and giving her a hard time.

"Of course we're friends," I say. "Best friends." I gulp down how much it burns to even think the next part, so that I can say it. "No matter who you date. I know I screwed up, by bolting instead of . . . and I know we can't go back. But . . ."

The lack of sound is loud. I replay what I said. Something's wrong. Did I screw this up again?

"Even if you decide to date Michael again, or whoever, I'll—"

"Stop."

"I can totally—"

"Seriously, just shut up."

Huh?

Silence. Nothing. I look at the phone, but the call hasn't been disconnected.

"Shaun?"

"Yeah," her voice comes through from far away. I put the phone back to my ear. "Yeah . . . When you took off, I thought—"

"I'm a jerk. I should have waited, but I was worried—"

". . . and you said you couldn't bring a friend. A friend—"

"What?"

"You said—"

"Yeah, I know. And I know it pissed you off, that I said—"

"Matt! Shut. Up. And let me . . . let me . . . Shit!"

"OK."

"Shit!" she yells into the air, away from the phone.

"Shaun?"

"When—" she starts, and then stops. I wait. "When you weren't interested, and—"

"Whoa! No 'not interested.' Interested, but—"

"Matt! I was doing everything to . . ." She takes a deep breath. "Shit. I can't believe I'm going to say this."

"Shaun?"

"The shirt. And the makeup. And my stupid hair." She laughs but it's not funny. "Kara did my hair and makeup. Jenna made me wear that stupid shirt. They said I hadn't been sending the right signals, and that if I just . . . That if you were interested, you'd want me to come with you. And if you weren't . . ."

"Signals . . . and . . . Shaun! I had to go on my own. Had to. But that didn't mean I don't, that I didn't . . ."

"But you said 'friend'—it didn't feel right to take a 'friend' along, like I'm—"

"It's not that I didn't want you . . ." Shit. "Or want you to come . . ." Fuck. "I just, I needed to go alone. To prove to myself that I could do this, do anything, by myself."

"Yeah, but I did everything but crawl into your lap! And you didn't, didn't even—*friend,* Matt. You called me—"

"Yeah, but not 'cause I didn't want. I wanted. Hell, I had to get away so I wouldn't . . ."

"Wouldn't?"

"Wouldn't . . . Shaun! You were making me crazy."

"Crazy?"

"Totally." The whole night replays in my head in flashes, but like with a spotlight highlighting things. Her hair hanging in her face. Her eyes all kind of sparkly. That insane shirt. The fucking candy. The way she kept looking at me. "Totally, insanely crazy."

I can hear her breathing. She's breathing hard. Makes me twitch. I go for broke.

"And I liked the shirt." My face is hot, and I can picture it in my head. "Too much." I swallow. "Feel free to wear it anytime." Fuck. "Or pretty much anything else you feel like wearing."

She laughs hard, for real this time, and everything gets hot.

"I'm sorry, Shaun. I'm . . . an idiot."

"Yes, you are," she says, her voice deeper. Damn, I want to kiss her. I'd kiss her right now if she were here. And if she had that shirt on . . . Shit. There are so many things to say, and none of them sounds right, not now, over the phone. And my brain's a little blood deprived. I pinch the skin between my thumb and finger. Take a breath. "So, uh . . . my dad came to your house? What, uh . . . ?"

"It was actually OK," she says, returning to normal. "I

mean, a little weird, and at first I was kind of freaked, but he was . . . it was . . . OK."

"Was he pissed?"

"He's upset," she says carefully, "worried."

"Yeah, I'm sure."

"You know I'm not a fan, but he seemed really worried more than anything else."

"What'd you tell him?"

"I didn't say much. My dad told him you were definitely coming back, because you had my car, and that I had talked to you every day and you were fine."

"He did?" I'm surprised her dad would lie for me.

"Yeah. I didn't tell Mom and Dad that you were blowing off my calls."

"Oh." The guilt trickles through me. Even pissed, and worried, she protected me. "Thanks."

I can practically hear the questions swirling around her brain. I don't even know where to start.

"Matt? What happened? You were so excited and then . . ."

"I . . . Shaun . . . I can't. I just . . ." I clamp down. Wait. Breathe. "There so much to tell you. And I will." I'll tell her everything. Well, almost everything. "Just . . . When I get home. OK?"

"OK." Her voice, somehow warmer than before, makes me shiver. "Take your time. I can wait. In case you haven't noticed, I'm very good at waiting."

There's nothing to say to that, but this kind of hysterical

laughter comes out of me from who knows where. It doesn't even sound like me. She's been waiting, for me, and I've been torturing myself thinking she'd be disgusted if she knew. So fucking stupid.

"Shaun?" I didn't mean to actually say that.

"Yeah?"

Damn. "I, uh . . ." What? I'm sorry I'm so fucked up? I think if I don't kiss you, I'm gonna explode? Please tell me everything's gonna to be OK? "Never mind. I, uh, forget."

"OK," she says, then clears her throat. "OK," she says again, more forcefully. "Just . . . drive carefully. Stop and rest if you get tired. And . . . come straight here?"

I can hear her smile. "OK. Should be midday. I'll call from the road."

I hang up without waiting for her to say anything else, scared of what she might say. Or maybe scared of what I might say.

Picturing Shauna, right now, smiling on her end, or dancing around her room, knowing I'll see her tomorrow, knowing she wants me, too, makes me wish I were already home. Makes me wish all of this was behind me and I could just be with her, her clean, not-too-flowery hair smell, and her grape-candy mouth. The way her nose wrinkles when she laughs. How she feels when she hugs me. Sometimes she looks at me, and I can almost feel it somewhere inside. She's totally gonna let me kiss her. I can almost believe that this time tomorrow, I'll know how her mouth tastes and feels.

Maybe she'll let me touch her, if not tomorrow, soon. God, I want to touch her. Maybe she'll put on the shirt, and then take it off. Fuck.

It doesn't take more than a few minutes to toss all my stuff into my duffel bag and backpack. All packed except for two plastic bags on the bed: one holding Curtis's letters and the other the single letter from T.J.

I pick up the bag holding T.J.'s letter. I want to feel the envelope, the writing, the indentations his pen made. Instead I touch the label holding the bag shut, smooth down the torn edge.

I always thought I'd get to read this one. I couldn't bring myself to open it, but I figured that after Celia read it, maybe she'd be so grateful she'd let me read it, too. But I don't think Curtis will, and I'm not sure I could read it now, knowing T.J. was writing to Curtis. Whatever the letter says, it will only confirm what I already know. I don't need to see T.J.'s words to know it. And even if I believe it, I'm not ready to read any mushy stuff or, worse, sexy parts, in T.J.'s cramped writing, knowing he was thinking about Curtis when he wrote them.

He's already changed enough.

twenty-seven

THE STREET IS STILL ALL TORN UP, SO I PARK MY USUAL blocks away and walk down. I'm almost to the porch before I see Curtis sitting on the front steps. Between his knees, one step down, is Zoe, her hands wrapped around Curtis's outstretched fingers. She's babbling away, and Curtis is so absorbed in her he doesn't see me.

"Uh, hi," I finally say when I'm a few steps away.

Curtis's head pops up and his face breaks into a smile. He looks more like the guy in the picture now. And more like Celia. I had to have been blind not to see it.

Zoe says, "Hi!" and starts to jump from her step, and Curtis wraps an arm around her before she can finish her leap.

"Oh, no, you don't, Baby Girl." Once she is secure under his arm, he looks up again. "Let me just run her inside. Be right back."

He's up and through the door and back before I have time to figure out whether to sit or not.

"Hey." He laughs, rubbing his hand over the back of his head. He walks down a few steps and takes a seat, and then motions for me to sit. "She likes the equipment," he says, waving toward the stuff the road crew left behind. "Can't get enough of it. But she's a daredevil, too, so you've got to watch her every second." He rubs the back of his head again. "I just figured we could talk easier if we didn't have to watch her every move."

I sit down and carefully settle my backpack on the step beside me.

"I'm glad you came by. I was starting to give up hope."

"Yeah, I, uh, had to do some stuff, then check out of the hostel."

"So, you're really leaving today?"

"Yeah. I have to get back."

"Too bad," Curtis says, staring out at the equipment, or maybe at the river across the street. "Would have been nice to show you around. Maybe meet some of our friends. See some of Theo's favorite hangs."

"Like?" I ask. Curtis looks at me. I shrug. "Just curious. I really do have to go, but . . ."

Curtis leans back, resting his elbows on the step behind him, stretching his long legs down over several steps. "Well, starting right here. He loved sitting here, watching that river flow by. He loved to go over and wander up and down the bank, chatting with the people fishing or boating by."

I stare at the water, trying to picture it.

"Friends of ours have a boat. Theo loved to be out on the lake at dawn." Curtis laughs and stretches even farther out with his toes. "He would make us all get up sick-early and get out there, freezing our asses off, so that he could watch the sky get light. Then he'd come back, have a huge breakfast, and sack out for the afternoon."

I can picture it. He loved dawn, and water.

"We hiked a lot. He would chart these hikes . . ." Curtis shakes his head and then swings his face my way. "We'd all be cursing him by the end, you know? Punishing climbs, but spectacular views and just amazing descents. He'd find spots so worth the punishment we couldn't stay mad at him."

"We were talking about doing the Appalachian Trail when he got back," I say, hating how defensive my words sound.

"Yeah," Curtis says, nodding. "I know. He told me." Something in the way he looks at me makes me want to crawl into a corner. "He thought it'd be good for you to get away alone, so you could get to know each other again."

Is what I'm hearing Curtis's own jealousy, like maybe he was mad we were gonna go off for such a long time alone? Or is it that he thought we shouldn't have to get to know each other again? I feel my anger building. I don't need Curtis telling me again that I didn't know my brother.

"Whatever you're thinking," Curtis says, breaking off my inner tirade, "you can forget it. You can't know what I'm thinking, so stop trying."

"But you can know what I'm thinking?"

"Yeah, 'cause I can see it all over your face. Your poker face is for shit."

"So, what am I thinking?"

Curtis's mouth slides up into a knowing grin. "I'm not jealous that he was thinking of hiking the Trail with you. Pu-leaze, like I wanted to go that long without a shower, or electricity, or Ruby Red Cosmos." He rolls his eyes as he laughs in his chest, then points one finger at me. "And don't even start on this 'I knew him better' shit. We both know that's not true. You may have known him longer, true. But I," Curtis says, tenting his fingers over his chest, "I was his future. And Theo over the last seven years? Hmph."

I'm sulking. I know. But . . . seven years? And I still want to know—need to know. "So, tell me, then, what else?"

Curtis leans his head back and thinks. "Well, he loved the everyday things when he was home. Going out for dinner. Sprawling out on the couch and listening to music or reading. Watching movies. Taking Zoe to the park or playing with her in the backyard. As soon as she could walk, we'd take her on these long, slow walks around the block. I'd beg him to just pick her up already, but Theo insisted she be allowed to walk if she wanted, no matter how slow and backbreaking the walk. Last spring, right before he deployed, he taught her to swim, sort of." Curtis smiles a far-off smile. Rubs his neck. "He insisted she was ready to swim, and I guess he was right." He looks at me. "He loved being outside as much as possible, except for in winter. He whined like a baby in winter."

There's a flutter of recognition at that. T.J. always hated the cold.

"Big, strong guy, could dig a trench in no time flat, march across a desert, cart heavy equipment for miles, pretty much do anything he put his mind to, but he hated, *hated* shoveling snow."

Yeah, he really did. Even when we were kids.

"Mainly, when he had time off, we tried to make it last as long as possible. Slowed it down with hikes and movies and dinners and just sitting and talking." Curtis wipes at an eye and turns his face away from me. "He liked to sit on these steps and watch the world go by. Chat with the people who went past. Wherever we went, he was always talking to people. Sometimes I'd get so mad at him, talking up strangers, wasting time, especially when he had no idea how they'd be about us."

We sit in silence. Too many questions float in my head.

"Go ahead," Curtis says, "ask whatever."

"How long—I mean, when?"

"How long did he live here? Or . . ."

"Yeah, or, well, or when . . . when did he . . . ?"

"When did he know he was gay?"

I nod, not trusting my voice.

"Always," Curtis says. "He always knew." He smiles at something only he can see. "He was in such denial when we met. Determined to put 'it' behind him. Be normal. Yeah, like that was going to work."

T.J. was trying not to be like that? And Curtis made him be, or stay, like that?

"The last thing I wanted was to be outed in Basic. Figured the boys would send my black ass home in pieces if they found out. But it was so hard to ignore him. He kept staring. Like he could see right through me."

Like Shauna, and her looks, her stare that can freeze me.

Curtis laughs. "Damn obvious. Hhm-mmm." He smiles, then wipes at his mouth until it's gone. "So, I was keeping as far away from him as I could. But there was something there, even then. And when we got our first night of freedom, well . . ." Curtis's face lights up, then gets serious again.

"Then why didn't he . . . ?" I shift so I can see his face without twisting my neck. "Did he really think, you know, that I would hate him?"

Curtis lets out a long breath, shaking his head. "No. However . . ." He measures his words. "He worried that you wouldn't understand right away, and he couldn't face that he would have to deploy while you were mad or upset and that he wouldn't be here to fix it."

"Did—I mean, the letters, the envelopes—did *anyone* know?"

"The guys in his old unit knew, mostly. And most of them were cool with it. In the unit he deployed with, he wasn't sure who he could trust, at least not at first. Obviously, he told someone, sometime, because someone knew to call . . ." Curtis presses his knuckles against his mouth, takes a shuddering breath, holds it in for a moment, and then exhales through his fingers, calmed again. "It was hard on Theo.

He hated the lying. It tore him up. But he loved the Army." Curtis's eyes squint and tense. "Theo felt he was doing what he was meant to do, and he didn't want to leave anyone short-handed. Even for me. He went back for the third tour, even though I begged him to get out. We fought about it, about . . ." Curtis swallows the thought, shakes it off, and looks at me again. "He'd never let his unit down. Never."

I let that sink in, turning it over in my head.

"He couldn't even be himself, exactly who he was, who we were, but he . . ." Curtis shakes his head. "It wasn't worth losing him."

The silence stretches between us. A group paddles by in canoes and someone waves. Curtis waves back, his face softening.

"Someone called you?" I ask.

"Yeah." His voice is so brittle it almost crackles. "Unofficial, of course. Couldn't acknowledge anything officially. But . . ." He shakes his head with a nasty look. "I kind of went a little crazy. Destroyed my office. I don't really remember it all. They said I yelled at him, the guy who called, called him a bastard. Said they could all go to hell." Curtis shrugs. "Not my finest moment."

I can only imagine what my father would have done, said, if he weren't so busy holding it all in. Curtis says something else, but I can't understand him.

"What?"

He looks at me, clears his throat. "He was going to get

out. After this tour, he was going to get out. We were just starting to talk about what came next, whether to stay here or go somewhere new, together, maybe buy a house, but he was going to get out."

I can hear the pain under the surface of his skin, the tears curdling in his chest.

"It was past time. He'd done his part, more than enough. But I guess I didn't persuade him fast enough." He looks down at his hands, twists a silver ring on his finger. "That's all I could think about. And it felt like they killed him, like all that hiding had robbed him of being free, of being fully him—of letting everyone know how truly amazing he really was. To fight, every day, with everything he had, when . . ."

There's nothing to say. I am instantly angry, but also sad, for Curtis, for me, even for Dad. Not for T.J. He's gone; he doesn't get sad.

"Well and truly outed myself, and destroyed my office— tore it apart. Took two of them to restrain me. After that, the separation from the Army was fast and quiet. I didn't even fight it. I couldn't fight it. And I came home."

"Didn't you want to come to the funeral?"

He grunts like I hit him.

"I mean . . ." I feel like a jerk for asking, and wish I could suck it back in.

He waves me off with the flick of a wrist. "Later, I was—well, really upset doesn't quite cover it. Devastated?" His mouth turns up, but it's not a smile. "I should have been there. But I don't really remember the first few weeks after. I know Will came and got me. I vaguely remember the car ride. That whole week was really hazy. Missy and Will kept me alive. When I could think enough to ask about funerals and everything, well, we heard it had already happened, and . . . it seemed a little too late to do anything official. We had a memorial, later, for everyone here. There are some pictures." He waves back toward the house.

There's nothing to say. It's all too much. My brain has expanded until it's pressing on my skull.

All that time. All the time we were dealing with the funeral and letters and people and so many freaking offers of help that we changed our telephone number to get away, and Curtis was here, with nothing. And later, when he could think, wouldn't he have wondered about the letters? T.J.'s stuff? Maybe he knows where the blanket came from, and why T.J. had that medallion, or the compass.

"Hey," Curtis finally says, sitting up again, folding his long legs to form sharp angles on the steps. "I have some stuff for you. Come on in and I'll show you."

I hesitate for just a step, then follow him through the door, pushing down the wave of sick-feeling nerves that rise at the thought of going into his place, *their* place. I can do this. It's fine.

I expected a replica of next door, but when I follow him in, it's hard to believe that this place fits into roughly the same space as Celia and Will's place.

The walls are sleekly white and smooth, but nearly bare. Everything feels sharp and clean. Dark leather furniture. Silver, gray, and black bits here and there. The room is laid out with a sitting area in the front near the windows and a large table at the other end of the room, where a cutout in the wall shows the kitchen. Deep-red walls and black accents peeking through, like the Chinese restaurant Shauna's sister took us to that time we went to Philadelphia.

A wave of dizziness nearly floors me. This is the room that box in T.J.'s stuff was meant for.

"Yeah, I know, a little much, but be it ever so humble . . ." Curtis waves, walking over to the large leather couch dominating the space facing the front windows.

Between the dining-room table and the rest of the room, there's a long, narrow table covered in picture frames, just like at Celia's, except I don't have to look hard at all to find T.J. here. He's everywhere. Curtis and T.J. at different places. One with Curtis's arms draped around T.J.'s shoulders, T.J.'s hand covering Curtis's on his chest. One of T.J. holding a paddle on a dock, barefoot and sunburned. One of T.J. lying on a beach. One of Curtis in a suit, standing between an older couple, his parents. T.J. and Curtis and Zoe out front. T.J. and Zoe in a pool. T.J. and Curtis sitting on the steps out front, Curtis's legs extended out from behind T.J., who is sitting on the step in front of him, leaning back, his hands on Curtis's knees. They're both smiling at the camera, but it also looks like they were caught midlaugh, like whoever took the picture was laughing with them. T.J. looks so happy. More than that. He looks at home.

"Our friend Alex took that one," Curtis says behind me. "We had just gotten back from a long weekend in Chicago."

"Where was this one taken?" I ask, pointing to a picture of T.J., Curtis, and a bleary-eyed Will, all three holding huge empty glass mugs.

Curtis laughs, maybe the first real laugh I've ever heard from him. "The end of a long night of drinking to celebrate Will's graduation from law school. Will puked three times *during* the graduation ceremony the next day."

I pick up one of T.J. lying on the ground with Zoe, both of them absorbed in whatever they were doing, not even looking at the camera.

"She was crazy about him." Curtis moves down the table and picks up another one, one I've seen before—Zoe facing the camera, her lips pursed. "This one is from the last time he was home. He was trying to teach her to spit for distance, much to Missy's irritation."

"I remember, from the letters."

Curtis carefully places the picture back on the table.

"Everyone keeps telling me to put these away. That it's time to move on. Like it's the pictures that are the problem." He turns one of the photos a little more toward him. "It hasn't even been seven months," he says, like he's talking to someone else.

"At least you have them to put away," I say, before I can

stop myself. "I mean, we've never been real into photo ops, you know?" And Dad got rid of the few we had. "There were just a few of him in his stuff."

"Well, let's see what we can do about that." Curtis sinks down into the couch, his arms and legs neatly arranged, like he's posing for a portrait. He waits for me to sit down, then pulls a small box onto his lap and places its lid on the table in front of him.

"It's not a lot. You probably have much better things, more personal, at home—but there were a few things I thought you might like. Including"—he sifts through the box until he pulls out a small envelope, turning it to slide a small stack of photographs into his hand—"these."

He hands me the stack. I see right away, on top, a copy of the picture that started all of this. The one of Celia, Zoe, T.J., and Curtis. It's a little smaller than Celia's framed copy, but bigger than the one T.J. cut up.

"I thought you might like a whole one."

The next one down is of T.J. in uniform, but not at attention. Relaxed. His shit-eating grin on full display, hand extended toward the camera.

"That one was taken at a charity event. He was so proud in that uniform." Curtis's smile makes my stomach flip, like when I read the sexy parts of the letters. "He strutted and preened like a damn peacock. God, I miss that. His confident strut into a room, knowing everyone's eyes were going to be on him. And they were. Everyone's."

I can't look at it long, but I think, later, I might like it. The next is one of T.J. on some mountain, smiling, a valley spreading out below him.

"I figured," Curtis says, "that with how much you all shared in the hiking, you probably never lugged a camera along. I thought, well, it was the closest one I had to how you must remember him best."

I can't answer. I nod, I think. My fingers touch the edge of the picture. This is the one—this is who he was, to me. I slip it under the others.

A few more shots of T.J. with various people, doing various things. Curtis tells stories I'll never remember. But the pictures are nice, even if they are of times and places I don't know.

The last two are smaller than the rest, and the surface and paper feel different. When I shuffle them to the top of the stack and turn the larger one right-side up, I almost recognize it. Almost.

Curtis sits quietly next to me while I study it. Without even knowing the people, you'd know it was old, older than the others. But I can look at my face, T.J.'s Little League uniform, Mom's flattened-out smile and hollow eyes, and know this was taken right before the end. Nine or ten months, at most, before Mom left. Dad looks the same, really. In my head, I can see him like he is today, a little older, hair a little more flecked with silver, eyes surrounded by crevices instead of lines. But the hard, steady look, giving nothing away, is the same. His body, strong and steel-straight, the same. His clothes are even nondescript enough not to stand out, not like the rest of us.

"T.J. said this was the last picture he could find of all four of you," Curtis says quietly. "He kept it close, and when he deployed, he put it in the box with some other stuff he didn't want to lose."

I'm only half listening, already turning to the last photo. This one I don't recognize at all. Well, I recognize Dad, younger than in the other, thinner, his hair even shorter, and in uniform. It's hard to look away from that alone. But I force my eyes to slide to the left, to the woman who is clearly Mom, but not like I've ever seen her. She's smiling, her eyes are alive, and her hair is all done up. She's wearing a dress and gloves. She's really pretty. I'd never thought of her as pretty before. Dad's holding T.J. He's missing his two front teeth. Dad's holding him so proudly, and his arm is around Mom, and T.J.'s arm is around Dad's neck. They're all smiling. Happy. What, three years before me? Maybe four? And they're all happy.

"Theo said this was taken the day your dad got promoted to staff sergeant," Curtis says beside me.

"I don't even know where this was taken." The cinderblock wall screams base housing, somewhere, and I could probably figure it out if I could think.

"North Carolina. Theo said your family lived on base until he was almost ten."

I shake my head, mouth suddenly dry. I can't stop staring at Mom. "I've never seen her look like this. She was really beautiful."

"I know," Curtis says. "Theo said she used to set her hair on rollers, and sometimes she would let him play with the curls before she brushed them out." His eyelids flutter at the thought. "I can picture it, you know? Little Theo, one thing when your dad was away, another when he was home. . . . Must have been hell to have to pull it all in every time he came home."

I try to remember, to see it. But I can't. "I don't remember Mom in rollers or T.J. any different or . . ."

"You wouldn't," Curtis says, his voice firm but not harsh. "You were a baby when your dad got out and moved you all to Pennsylvania. And by the time you were older, well, I'm sure Theo had learned to be what your dad needed him to be. He'd have had to. And your mom . . ."

"Was a fucking mess. Nothing like this." I barely resist the urge to crumple the picture in my hand. "Toward the end, most days we were lucky if she showered. Funny, Dad washes out of the Army, and Mom stops washing at all."

"He didn't wash out, Matt. Your mom couldn't handle it."

My stomach drops. "Handle what?"

"Any of it. Life on base. The long absences. Taking care of herself, much less you and your brother. She was falling apart. Theo said she'd always been a little . . . up and down. But after her father died, she never seemed to get back on track. Just before Theo's tenth birthday, she had a little break-down at one of those wives' events. There was a meeting. Your dad didn't really have a choice. So, he got out and moved you all to Pennsylvania, where he could have a regular job, and he thought your grandmother could help keep it together."

"Then Grandma died. I don't remember, but I know that's what happened."

And then Mom fucked it all up anyway. What, three, three and a half years later? She took off. And before she left, in that house on Mulberry, she was always such a mess. And he was always so angry. My memories of the fights shift in my head. Maybe when he was yelling about none of it being worth it, he didn't mean me, or us, so much as her, or the move, or getting out.

I look at the two pictures again. Mom was so beauti-ful once, but Dad's always been pretty much the same, and maybe that's all he could be. And T.J., then, didn't seem scared of him, but Curtis said T.J. was different when it was just T.J. and Mom. Maybe when Dad was around all the time, T.J. stopped getting along with him?

T.J. must have taken these with him from home, but I wouldn't even know where to look for more. Does Dad have boxes of stuff somewhere? Or did he chuck them all at some point after T.J. took these? What else don't I know?

"Anyway," Curtis says, bringing me back to the present, "he had some stuff here, some clothes and things. I've kept them . . . you can look through them if you want, now or . . .

but there are some things I think you should have now, some stuff he had on his desk here that I think he'd want you to have. His favorite hiking gadgets — his compass, fire starter, pocketknife. Some papers. I've pulled them together so you can take them with you now. You can look through them later. Along with these. These are from me."

I turn to look at Curtis, who's picked up a stack of stuff and is holding it to his chest, a small smile on his face. He holds the pose for just a few seconds and then swings his arms out, pushing a stack of envelopes into my hands. My fingers fumble around the shifting papers, trying not to drop them all. Once I've gathered them in, I turn them until one rises to the surface, faceup. An envelope. Everything slows down. Hot and cold. Something pounds in my ears. T.J.'s handwriting. Celia's address. I look up for confirmation.

"It's just a few, I know, but I thought you might like some of his letters. I picked a few that seemed . . . I don't know . . . most Theo-like, if that makes any sense, and more, huh-hhmm, brother friendly, if you get my drift," he says, tucking his chin into his chest and raising his eyebrows. "Didn't want to scar you for life or anything." He flutters his eyes, long lashes over a slanted-chin pose. My face gets hot.

I can't speak. I can't move. He has just handed me a piece of my brother back. Curtis, who yesterday I wished didn't exist.

"I . . ." I swallow, try again. "I don't know what to say."

"Thank you will do just fine." Another pointed smile.

"Thank you," I say as enthusiastically as I can. "Seriously, oh, man, this means . . . this means so much to me. Just . . . thank you."

"You're very welcome," he says, pleased. Not happy. He's not happy. Neither am I. But I think maybe we both are as close to it as we have been in a very long time.

I carefully shuffle the letters into an orderly stack. Curtis didn't have to do this. Later, I'll read them, and it will help. I know it will. God, T.J.'s letters.

"I didn't even say good-bye," I say, surprising myself.

"When?"

"The last time he was home." I can see it. That last night, before heading to bed, we grabbed right hands and T.J. pulled me into a sort of rough hug, but it wasn't really good-bye—at least, not a good-bye that you say to your brother when he's walking into danger, when you might never see him again. He came by my door early in the morning, and I pretended to be asleep because I didn't trust myself not to spaz or something. I was being selfish: I didn't want to ruin the high of the trip or look like a wuss. Now sometimes it's all I can think about. "I didn't even say good-bye. Not really."

Curtis makes this sound, like the last dregs of a killer cough. "I *never* said good-bye. Thought it would jinx him. Guess maybe I got that wrong."

I look at him, his face struggling to hold back the pain. He gets it. This . . . thing, inside me, choking me, hating me.

"I hate him sometimes," I whisper. "He just . . . I know it's stupid, but he left, and I hate that he's never coming back."

"So do I," he says. "But I love him all the time. Still. And I miss him. There's this huge, gaping hole . . . And sometimes I can't tell which I'm feeling."

Yeah. Exactly. Only ten times worse, because now I feel like I never knew him at all.

"He was proud of you," Curtis says with a crooked half smile. "It was always, 'Matt this' and 'Matt that' . . . Whatever fear he had, that this would . . ." He waves between us, shaking his head. "He loved you. And he was so proud of you. Know that."

I close my eyes. If I move, if I breathe, all the pieces of me will shatter and fly away. Dizzy dark splotches, but I can't breathe yet. If I breathe, I'll explode.

A knock at the door breaks the moment, and we both exhale loudly. Curtis puts the box on the table and opens the door.

"Hi," Celia says, looking first at Curtis with sweet sisterly eyes, and then, once satisfied, at me, less sweet but not hard. "Everything OK?"

"Uh, yes. Right?" Curtis asks, turning to me, hand planted on his hip.

"Yeah," I say after a beat. "Good."

"Good," Celia says with a genuine smile. "We thought we'd grill out." She takes a cautious step inside, hands clasped in front of her. "Matt, will you join us?"

"I really should head out." I'm not sure I can take much more. I have this insane feeling that if I don't leave right now, this will all go to hell again.

"You've got to eat," she says, moving a little closer, looking at Curtis, maybe for backup. "We could eat soon? Anytime really."

Curtis shrugs at me. "It's up to you, but might be good to get a good meal into you before you hit the road."

"And I thought you might still like to meet Zoe?" Celia asks.

Zoe. Not his daughter, but T.J. loved her, played with her, taught her stuff. Yeah, I'd like to meet her.

"OK. Sure," I say. "Thanks."

"Great. Come out back when you're ready and we'll throw the food on," she says, hurrying out the door.

Curtis's smile follows her out. "Carson family motto: When in doubt, feed."

It's now or never. "Uh, I have something for you, too." I reach for my bag.

He sits back down on the very edge of the sofa, clenching his hands between his knees as if to keep himself from grabbing it from my hands.

"First, I thought you should have these back." I hand him his letters. He sinks back and clutches them to his chest. Then he looks at me warily, maybe hearing the "first" in his head.

My hand shakes as I pull out the other letter, and I hold it to my own chest before slowly extending my arm and handing it to him. His eyes slide over it and he moves his face to be able to see it better, but continues to clutch at the letters held to his chest. I can tell the moment he understands what I am handing him. His whole body jerks from someplace deep inside. He drops the bag of letters onto his lap before covering his mouth with trembling hands. He rocks back and forth a few times before finally gaining enough control to reach out a shaky hand and take the letter.

It shudders between his fingers, the plastic bag making small crinkling sounds. His hands shake so much I am surprised he doesn't drop it. He turns it over and back and then over again. His fingers trace the label holding the bag shut. He looks up at me with wide, wet, pained eyes.

I shrug, answering the silent question. With a sudden inspiration, I try to save us both. "What kind of guy do you think I am?" Tears race over his face, but his smile says he got it.

I gather my letters and photos, and slide them back into the box, trying to ignore the awful sounds radiating out of Curtis.

His gulping sobs slow. His hands shake when they wipe at his cheeks. Deep breaths to calm himself. He shakes his head and flutters his hand between us. I get his thank-you even without the not-quite smile. But I can also see something else brewing. When he turns to look at me, his face is shuttered.

"This is . . . more than I hoped. But . . ."

"What?"

"I don't know if you've gone through all of Theo's stuff yet, and I think he would have had it on him, but . . . he had a medallion. I got it for him in Rome. If you—"

The floor falls away. I nod. Try not to react. "In the stuff they gave Dad just before the funeral." I swallow. "There was a medallion on a cord. A saint?"

"Yes. Saint Sebastian." Curtis laughs quietly, like to some private joke between him and T.J. "Pretty much Theo's personal guardian, as the patron saint of soldiers, athletes, and queers. Not to mention credited with bringing the gift of speech to a girl named Zoe."

I can't speak.

"But, yeah, I'd . . . I'd really like it back, if there's any way. I'm sure your dad . . ."

"No. Sure. I'll look for it. When I get home." I can't tell him, not yet, not until I've looked everywhere.

"If your dad could—"

"I'll send it to you." I'll have to find it first, but if I have to tear into the walls or, hell, even fight it out with Dad, I will. Please let it just be somewhere hidden, still to be found. "I promise."

Curtis nods through a new wave of tears and clutches the letter close again. I'll find it. And I know just the box to put it in when I do.

I slide the whole box of stuff into my backpack. I'll read T.J.'s letters later. Maybe I'll even wait until I get home. I'm not ready yet. And knowing they're mine, to keep, the urgency's gone. Curtis must feel the same, because he smooths the bag holding the envelope from T.J. and carefully lays it in the center of the table, the small curving of his lips a silent promise. I'm sure I'll always wonder what the letter says, but I don't think I'll ever doubt that I did the right thing.

twenty-eight

DINNER IS NICE. I CAN'T REALLY SAY FUN, BECAUSE THERE'S
a heaviness hanging over everything, and we all try a little too
hard to pretend we can't feel it.

When we first came out into the backyard, Celia pulled
Curtis close. I turned and watched Will slap brats and
burgers on the grill to ignore their murmured conversation.
After, Curtis disappeared inside and Celia slid her arm over
my shoulders and led me closer to the grill. She patted my
back while she talked.

During dinner, Celia and Will tell me more stories about
T.J. At one point, Zoe chimes in with her own version, something about ice cream and big spoons. I never quite get it all,
but she smiles and says "Uncle T." and I can see a little more
what he had here.

Curtis is quiet over dinner, kind of not even there. He
smiles in the right places and answers when Will or Celia
prod him to tell a bit of a story. But his eyes are unfocused
and his body tense, like he's waiting for this part to be over.
How many days did I come home from school and I couldn't
remember anything about the day? I'd bet that right now

he wants to be upstairs with that letter, and the hurt. I get that. I can't let myself feel it yet—too far to drive first—but I get it anyway and know exactly how it will feel when I let myself feel it.

I stay later than I intended. And then this feeling comes over me, like it's time to go home. Not just to leave, but to take myself back to my home.

We exchange telephone numbers and e-mails. I write down my address and e-mail in Celia's address book, and then put my cell number into Curtis's phone.

Celia and Will give me a bag of snacks and sodas for the road. Will shakes my hand. Celia gives me another of those too-tight hugs, but this time I'm ready and I hug back, feeling the ends of her slick-shiny braids under my fingers before I let go. They both extend "anytime" invites for visits and say to call if I need anything. Anything at all.

Zoe gives me a sticky-wet kiss on the cheek and hands me her plastic frog to take with me. She tells me his name is Froggy. I stick him in my pocket and then pat it with my hand to make sure he is secure. She takes my hand and walks me to the side yard before Celia intervenes. The look Zoe gives me is like an adult's, in her little-kid face. And then she hugs my leg. Celia hurries away with Zoe, but I see her tears.

Curtis walks me down the block to the car. Once there, he nudges the tire with his shoe while I toss my backpack and the snacks onto the passenger-side seat.

"Listen," he finally says in a rush, "do you have enough money? For gas and . . . whatever?"

Before I can answer, he is digging into his pocket and pulling out a wad of cash.

"Here." He pushes his hand toward me. "Take it."

"No, really, I'm fine," I say, backing up and pulling my hands behind my back.

"I'm sure you could use it. Take it," he says again, pushing it at me.

"No, I'm good. Promise."

He seems to struggle with what to do, before dropping his hand to his side, but he doesn't put it back in his pocket. Instead, his fingers rotate the bundle over and over.

"You sure?"

"Positive." There's nothing else to say. Well, at least nothing here, now, next to the car. "Well, I guess I should go."

"If, uh, you . . ." He stops and starts again. More determined this time. "If you want to talk, or if you ever need anything . . . you have our numbers and e-mails. Just . . . drop us a line now and then. Let us know how you are. It'd be nice, to have someone who understands, when it's hard."

I nod, because I don't think I can talk. I open the door and look back to say good-bye again. Curtis's right there. He grabs my shoulder and then tugs me into a hug. It's weird, and awkward, and I tense with the shock of it, but then I'm hugging him back and it's OK.

"Go," he says, pushing me away. "Before we both make

idiots of ourselves. Text or e-mail me, to let me know you got home OK."

I get into the car and fasten the seat belt and put it in gear. I pause to look out at him. It feels like I've been here for months, like it's been weeks, not two days, since I met him. I can hardly believe the guy who tried to hit him was me.

He smiles and waves again. But before I can pull out, he stops me with a hand on the door frame.

"Just in case," he says, tossing the wad of cash through the open window and onto the far side of the passenger seat. "Don't be stubborn. Now, go."

He takes off at a loping run back toward the house. I turn the car toward home. At least, I think I do. It may take me a while to find my way out of this crazy-ass town and get turned toward home.

Home.

twenty-nine

CROSSING BACK INTO PENNSYLVANIA FROM OHIO, PANIC starts to set in.

For most of the night, I was flying along I-80 in the center lane, just me and the truckers. But around four a.m., the traffic picked up, and since then I've had to start paying attention again. Cars weave in and out, faster and slower, getting in my way and bugging me, making it harder to drive at a steady speed.

I stop for my third infusion of caffeine since midnight. If I cut myself right now, I'd probably bleed coffee.

The sky is starting to slide toward purple, pink, and gray as the sun rises. My whole body is tense and tight from the strain of driving for so many hours in a row, and each adjustment of speed or shifting lanes takes all my strength and focus.

But when I see the signs for McConnells Mill State Park, I have to detour. Takes about half an hour, and then I'm there, not too far in, but parked near an overlook, staring out over a gorge. Not too far from where we might have gone, if T.J. had come home.

★　★　★

Before the hike itself, but after the detour to talk, T.J. buzzed with energy, seemingly caught in the pure joy and fantasy of freedom. Grooving along, tapping out the wrong beat, and only singing some of the words to the songs on the radio. Pulling into Raccoon Creek State Park, he grinned like an idiot at the ranger manning the station.

But on our last night, in front of the fire, he got quiet. Poking at the flames with a stick, staring at nothing. So much of that trip was a blur, but that last night is burned into my skull, even though nothing really happened.

"You OK?" It was a stupid question. I even knew then it was a stupid question. But it was as close to what I really wanted to know as I could let myself get. When he focused on me, T.J.'s look was kind of confused, so I tried again. "You were just staring, but . . . are you OK, I mean, being up here?"

His mouth succeeded in making the shape of a smile, and at the time the tension in me eased just a little, but it wasn't a happy face. The pops of burning wood sounded loud while he tried to answer, starting and stopping a few times before actually getting anything out.

"Yeah, being up here is great. It's just . . ." He leaned back again, and I lost his face in the shadows. "I don't know, too quiet, I guess. Head gets heavy. You know?"

"Like a headache?"

He rolled onto his side and his face disappeared into the darkness. I was relieved when he rolled back into the firelight and I could see him again.

"No, like the quiet invites all the thoughts you usually drown out with noise, and they all start asking to be heard, and I don't know, your head just gets . . ."

"Heavy. Yeah, I get that." But I didn't. Not really. Not then.

"Even when it's quiet, over there, it's never this quiet. There's always something else to focus on, if the thoughts get too loud. Even the *tick-tick* of the truck, or the breathing of the guy next to you. Something to focus on to make all the inside stuff quiet down."

I made a big deal of clearing my throat, sitting up straighter, trying so hard to be more than his kid brother. And he did look at me — really look at me — for one long beat. But then his eyes and face changed, and his look became kind, like he was looking at a kid. Too kind. So kind it felt more like a slap. And then his face settled back into a flat mask.

He never told me what was in his head, being loud. And I didn't ask. Instead, I started talking about school, and Shauna, and Dad, and whatever came into my head. Nothing that was really important. Nothing that mattered. And I knew right away that he was somewhere else again, somewhere heavy. I didn't even bother to stop. I just rambled. Occasionally he would nod or make a sound, but he didn't even really hear what I was saying.

Maybe if I had waited. If I had stayed quiet. If I hadn't

filled the space with bullshit, maybe he would have said it. Maybe he would have told me the truth.

Ultimately, a heaviness settled around both of us, like the words I was saying were trapped in the smoke from the fire, creating a haze. At the time, I worried that whatever he was hearing in his head was about the war. And up there, in the dark, I was scared. Scared to know what he had seen, what he had done. Maybe even a little scared of him. Even scared for me. I didn't want to know what I might have to do if I gave in to Dad. So I didn't ask the right questions, and he never told me what was clouding his eyes and making his head heavy.

He was probably thinking about Curtis, maybe even regretting that he was wasting five minutes of leave with me, instead of being in Madison with Curtis. But maybe he was trying to figure out if he could tell me, or if he should tell me, or how. Maybe he was already getting ready to leave for good, leave me behind, and didn't know how to tell me that. Whatever it was, I didn't ask because I figured, ultimately, whatever was in his head was about death.

It never occurred to me it could be about life.

thirty

DAD'S TRUCK ISN'T IN THE DRIVEWAY. I KNEW IT PROBABLY wouldn't be. He's never home in the middle of the day. But I still feel a weird mix of relief and disappointment at seeing the empty driveway.

Maybe I knew deep down this was a trial run, but I've been talking myself into the confrontation with Dad for the last hour, maybe even the last twenty-four hours. Now it seems like a waste of effort. Still, home, even with whatever's about to happen hanging over me, looks pretty good. I need to curl up for a week, or at least a weekend, in my cave of a bedroom, dark, and a little too warm, and mine. Not yet, I know, but that much closer. Soon.

I let myself in the side door, halfway between the kitchen and my room, and hold my breath. "Dad?" I wait for any signs of movement. "Da-ad?" Nothing. Nothing at all. I relax a little, but not all the way, not until I'm sure.

I stop dead one step into the kitchen and drop my duffel on the floor. The sight is incredible.

All over the kitchen table, in no apparent order, hundreds of pieces of paper, all different colors and sizes, with all these folds, so they don't lay flat. And envelopes, all these envelopes, one on the floor next to the table, with one of those red-white-and-blue return labels winking up at me. The empty box on the floor makes my stomach flip.

I can hardly understand, let alone believe, that Dad did this. I sidestep my way to the closet in the hallway, never taking my eyes off the table, littered with failed condolences. I open the hallway closet slowly, and see exactly what I expected to see: nothing. The empty box in the kitchen, the letters . . . Dad opened them. He opened them all.

I rest my forehead against the closet door. I turn my head and glance into the living room. My knees go weak. I can't move closer, and I can't back away.

Dad's TV is in pieces. It's on the floor, on its side. The screen isn't just broken: it has a hole in the middle of it, and the glass all around it is crackled and ragged, like he put his foot through it, or maybe a bat or something. The TV stand is in pieces, too. And whatever used to be on the hutch in the corner is now scattered debris next to and around it, and the hutch door is hanging by one hinge. All around the living room, stuff is broken and in pieces on the floor. There's a fist-size hole in the far wall.

I backpedal into the kitchen, like if I turn my back on the destruction, or take my eyes off the TV, something will attack me.

Once back in the kitchen, I'm confronted again by the letters. I don't know which came first or when: his decision to beat the TV down and generally smash everything of value in the living room, or the decision to open and read seven months' worth of condolence letters, mostly from strangers.

I can only hope he read the letters second—and recently, because they're all in one piece, and so is the kitchen.

thirty-one

"Thank God you're here."

Shauna catapults herself out of the house and at me before I can even close the car door. We stumble back into the side of the car with the full weight of her body thrown against mine. But when she steps back, her forehead is furrowed with worry. She shrinks in front of me, wrapping her arms around herself as if to hold her body together.

"Where have you been?"

"I had to go home first."

Her eyes narrow to slits. "And?"

"He wasn't home." I don't tell her about the state of the house.

A glimmer of softening in her eyes, but the moment and the glimmer fades fast. It's now or never.

"Shaun, I'm sorry." For everything. I need to tell her now, before anything else, that I am so fucking sorry for everything I've ever put her through, starting with ignoring her calls and working backward from there. "After the shit storm has settled, I'll make it up to you." I don't promise, not to her, but I'm determined. I will make it all up to her.

I wait. She doesn't move for a long time, but then her serious face appears. Means she has demands.

"I don't want you to go home."

"I know you don't." I brace for her outburst. "But I have to."

"No, you don't. I talked to Mom." Shit. I should have seen this coming. "She said you can totally stay here until you work things out with your dad." Shauna with a plan. "I already made up Stacy's old room, and—"

"Shauna—"

"You can't go back there!"

"I'll be fine."

"Yeah, like you've been fine your whole freaking life? Like all the times he's—?"

"Shauna, stop!" She jumps. I force my voice to be as soothing as I can. "Really, I appreciate it, all of it. But I have to face him. Today."

"And if he beats the shit out of you?"

"He won't." I promised myself I wouldn't lie to her anymore. "And if he does, he does. But I have to do this."

The anger melts away, leaving fear. "Please, for me, just stay here, at least tonight. Please?" Tears slide over her cheeks.

For the first time in a very long time, I know exactly what to do for her. I pull her into my arms and hold her as tight as I can. She turns her face against my shoulder and lets go, crying so hard her body shakes against mine. I just hold her, waiting for the waves of tears to pass. She soaks my shirt. I try not to think about how good it feels to hold her, even with the tears.

Her hair smells so good. Like Shauna, her familiar smell, and so, so good. I press a soft kiss to the top of her head and rest my face against her hair, breathing her in.

When her tears stop, I can hear the questions swirling around her brain. I run my hands over her back, feeling her shiver until I hug her tighter to keep her still. I need to do this now, before all the shit gets in the way again.

Her hands on my back soothe away the last of my doubts. I just start talking.

I tell her about Will, and Missy, and Zoe.

I tell her about Curtis. I have to close my eyes so I can keep going when her eyes go wide and wet. I tell her about the T.J. who lived there—about the pictures on the table—in that black-and-white apartment. About the pictures in my bag, of the family I never knew. About the letters in my bag, waiting to be read.

And before I can lose my nerve, I tell her everything else. I edit out Harley with a quick, decisive cut. But I hold nothing else back.

I tell her about the stalking, and how much of a stupid idiot I was when I met Celia in the library. How I floated around all afternoon, so proud of myself, like a moron. I tell her about Will's coming home, and about cursing out Celia, and trying to hit Curtis. I tell her about thinking about leaving, and Curtis's bringing my bag back, with everything inside.

I describe every screwup, every look, every stupid thing I did. It just pours out of me until I run dry.

I try to tell her about that last night with T.J., when I did everything wrong, but the strangling ache in my throat cuts me off.

She starts shushing and trying to talk over me, but I can't let her until I say what she really needs to hear.

"God, Shauna . . . I'm such a fuckup."

"No, you're not."

"Yeah, I am." I've fucked everything up. Everything. And no matter what I do, it's just gonna get more fucked up. "I can't . . ." The air catches in my chest.

"Shh." Soft breath against my skin. Her hand curls into my shirt over my heart, anchoring her to me. "You'll work it out. I'll help you."

"I've been an asshole, and I know I screwed up, and I have no idea what I'm gonna do, and you're—"

"It's going to get better. Maybe not tomorrow, or next week, but eventually, it'll be better. And I'll be here, but you've got to deal with it—with . . . T.J."

I flinch.

"He's gone. And I know it sucks. But you can't keep trying to pretend that everything's OK. *That*'s fucked up." She smiles. "And not that Pinscher didn't have it coming . . ." She bobs and weaves until I feel my mouth turning up. "But if you keep trying to pretend that everything's OK, you're gonna explode again."

"Or turn into my dad." Fuck. I can feel the panic coming. I try to pull away, but she won't let go, so I hide my face in her hair.

She pulls back and tugs at my shoulders until I meet her eyes.

"You're not him." She leans up closer. "You are *nothing* like him."

I want to believe her.

"Nothing," she whispers.

I shiver. My fingers won't stop rubbing at the worn-soft denim of her jeans. My palms mold over the curves of her hips, fingers pressing in.

A slow smile lights up her face. She shifts up on her toes. "Trust me," she says, her lips moving against my chin. Her breath flutters over my lips. I gulp it in, my gut lurching with the breath. "Kiss me?"

It takes only a little tug at her arm to pull her close. I bend my neck to press my mouth to hers. Harder. She makes this sound, like humming in her throat, and opens her mouth. And then I don't know who is kissing who. But she tastes kind of sweet—not grape, more like honey. The spark of contact sends an electric current straight through me. My hands clutch at her hips. I'm kissing too hard. Teeth. Her fingers on my jaw, guiding my mouth. I let her lead. Quick kisses, moving like a dance. Then there's a rhythm, a give and pull to it, and her fingers slide into my hair. When she breaks the kiss to breathe, she blushes to the curls around her face.

"Wow," she whispers.

I can't form words, too focused on breathing and dealing with the hot, heavy ache.

A car door slams. We jump apart.

I frantically look around, bracing already for my or Shauna's dad. But after several gasping breaths, it's clear no one is here. My pounding pulse is slowing, nothing like the pulsing pleasure-heat-pressure of before.

Her laughter floats around me, soft, gentle, warm like her hands. Her fingers roughly rub at her overheated face. I tug at my jeans. A mischievous smile forces her cheeks to curl up toward her eyes.

My stomach growls loudly. I can't remember the last time I ate. And it's getting late. "Listen, I really think it'll be OK at home, but just in case, can I hang on to the car for one more night?"

"Sure." She steps a little closer and her fingers reach out, as if to take my hand, but she just touches a bit of my shirt instead. "You'll bring it by tomorrow?"

"I have to work, so it would have to be before or after."

"After's fine," she says, before taking another halting step closer and sort of leaning toward me. "Mom and Dad have to go visit my aunt. They'll stay in Jersey for the night. So come by anytime after work. We could hang out." Her eyes flicker up to mine. "Or something. Maybe order in some Chinese for dinner?" Her face is red. She's studying something on my shirt now, her fingers still worrying the edge of it.

"Sure," I say, but the word gets mangled, what with the lack of air and all the blood diverted from my head. "Sounds good."

"OK." She is so happy. And beautiful.

She holds my stare. A slight tilt, chin higher, angled perfectly, and it's all the invitation I need. This time I have to break the kiss or lose it, right there in her driveway. She buries her face in my shirt before pushing away from me.

"Go." Her hands slide down my arms and away. "And call me later." Her serious face is very serious, but she can't hang on to it, and the big smile ruins it. But I will—I'll call her, right before bed. Can't wait.

Back in the car, I give her one final wave. She pushes her hair off her face, then tucks her hands into her back pockets. A huge grin on her face. I've known her practically my whole life. I know her sounds, her smiles, the way she moves and talks. Now I know how she tastes and feels: better than every good dream and fantasy I've ever had. Nothing bitter or wrong. I'll go home, where fucking anything could happen. But tomorrow night I'll be back here. With Shauna.

thirty-two

Standing on the back porch, I stare through the window in the door at my father sitting at the kitchen table.

The letters have been organized into neater stacks around him, and he's hunched over the table, staring down at something in front of him.

I am weirdly calm. Scared shitless, but calm. Maybe this is what it feels like to be bracing for war.

He looks up when I close the door, but doesn't turn his head until I'm even with him. His first look morphs lightning fast, too fast to understand, stealing my calm.

"Where you been?"

"Got back earlier. Stopped home. Then ran by Shauna's . . . in case she needed the car."

He stares at me. Unmoving.

On the table in front of him, framed by his hands, is the red bag and T.J.'s stuff from the morning of the funeral. Everything's laid out in a neat row, including the medallion.

I force myself to look at him.

The silence is dense.

I focus on the medallion.

"Where'd you go?" he asks.

"Madison, Wisconsin."

"Why?"

His voice is too calm, makes me shiver. "Deliver a letter."

"To?"

"T.J.'s boyfriend."

He jolts in his chair. I go on before I can lose my nerve.

"I mean, I thought it was a letter to a girlfriend, and there were all these other letters that I thought were from her, and I thought . . . but when I got out there, it was for her brother . . ." I swallow. "Curtis." Dad flinches. "His name is Curtis."

His fingers flex, but he doesn't lift his hands from around the stuff. Too calm. It hits me.

"You knew." Pounding in my ears. "You knew, didn't you?"

He looks away, his jaw clenches and releases. "I didn't *know*."

"But you . . . suspected?"

"When he was a kid, I thought maybe, and then later, but . . ." He sits back a little and rubs his hand over his face before continuing. "Your brother never said anything."

"And you didn't ask."

"No."

"Why?"

He stares at me. Shifts his jaw. Then answers. "I didn't want to know."

"But why, why did you think, I mean, what . . . ?"

He leans all the way back in his seat, folds his arms over his chest. Just when I think he won't answer, he does. "Dan."

"Dan?" I rack my brain, flip through my memories, trying to see it. Dan and T.J. were friends forever, as long as I can remember. But even in all those times they kicked me out of the room or I sat in the hallway trying to hear through the door, there's nothing that I can say would have tipped me off, even now.

Dad's chair creaks. "Few weeks before T.J. enlisted. I saw them. Together."

My eyes bug out.

"Not like that," Dad says roughly, disgusted. "Nothing like that. Just . . ." He exhales hard, waving his hand in front of him, then drops it back to the table.

"What did you do?"

"Nothing."

"Nothing?"

He shrugs, like I just asked what he had for lunch. "He knew I had seen them."

"But you didn't talk about it? You didn't ask? You—"

He shakes his head.

"Why? Why would you—?"

"I figured the Army would take care of it, and if not . . ."

"Take care of it?" Shit. "Like what, knock the gay out of him?"

He drops his chin into his chest. "And if not, I didn't want to know."

"And later, all those times he was home on leave? Leaving again, going back to war, when he might never come back?" My voice cracks, and I grip the counter behind me to steady myself. "You didn't even ask? To try to understand? For him?"

Tension flows through him. He slowly shakes his head from side to side.

"And now?"

The silence stretches between us. Finally, he opens his mouth. "If he chose to be . . . like that, then I didn't want to know. But . . ." Dad turns his face away from me. His shoulders tremble. When he turns to face me again, he looks so old: eyes sunken, face lined, lips thinned out and pale. His hand strays as if he's gonna touch something, but his fingers fall to the table and stop a couple of inches from T.J.'s dog tags. He swallows hard. "Knowing anything would be better than . . ."

I can't look. His hitching breaths ignite the terror at the base of my skull, but everything else screams for calm. I'm not going anywhere. From the corner of my eye, I see him touch the tags.

"I'm not going to enlist." His hand jerks, fingers pushing the dog tags out of line. "No matter what you do, I'm not doing it. So, if you're thinking about kicking my ass every day until I do, we might as well start now. But I'm never going to do it."

He gently lifts the dog tags and lays them on the table back in their place, straightens the chain and pats it down.

He tilts his head, strokes the chain. Shakes his head, like he's arguing with himself. Or making up my side of the fight. My heart pounds, pulse loud in the quiet kitchen. A week ago I'd have been ready to bolt. Now I have to stay.

He finally stops muttering to himself. But his clenched jaw says the fight is far from over.

"I'm not enlisting," I say again, stronger.

"Then what—?"

"I don't know. But not that."

I tense for it, whatever is gonna happen now. Hoping I don't run as soon as he moves.

I hold my ground. "I'm not enlisting. And I'm not going to college, either," I say, going for broke.

"Then—"

"At least, not right away," I add fast. "Maybe later. I don't know. But not right away."

His hands clench. Unclench. Clench. He glares. I don't look away.

He's not backing down. But he's not trying to kill me, either. I'm not stupid; he's not giving up. But I said it, and I'm still here.

His chair scrapes back from the table and I shudder with the sound, but my feet stay rooted to the floor.

He leans back in his chair. Then nods to the chair next to him.

I take the three long steps across the kitchen and sink into it. My legs tremble under the table.

He stares at me, like he's just realized I'm sitting there.

"I'm not going." Anywhere.

He wraps his arms across his chest. A rumble of sneering, sad laughter. "What, then? Because you're in serious danger of pissing your life away."

"I was thinking maybe building? Construction? Something like that?"

"You're pissing away your chances and gonna have fuck-all to show for—"

"I'm not." I flinch and lean away, then look. He's puffed up but not swinging. "I'm not gonna just be some loser. But . . ."

"And your girlfriend? Think she's gonna be happy working all her life? Both of you busting your butts just to make ends meet?"

The question hits me like a fist.

"Whatever else, Shauna has a chance to make something of herself. You gonna hold her back? Make her struggle while you work a series of dead-end jobs? Seriously, Matt. Where is your head? You're on a one-way ticket to nowhere, and I am not gonna let that happen."

His fist hits the table. I jump.

"I'm not," I say. "I'm gonna figure something out. Maybe talk to Mr. Anders. Something. Something that I'd be good at that wouldn't make me want to kill myself."

I hold still under his scrutiny.

"Dad . . . I'm not T.J. And I'm not you." I don't know who I am yet. "Can't you see that? And just let me . . . let me have a couple years to . . . figure it out? Figure out . . ."

We sit in silence. Me waiting, him having some conversation in his head.

"You *are* going to pick it up next year," he says finally. "Come up with a plan, a plan that gives you a future. And you're gonna have to hustle to make sure you have enough credits to graduate, since you failed Spanish."

"Huh? I thought . . . the hold, since I didn't pay yet, I didn't think . . . They sent my report card? Or . . ."

"I paid for the case," Dad says, nodding his head to the side. "All of it. Told Pendergrast you were visiting family for a few weeks. That you needed a break."

Wow.

"Don't get used to it. You screw up again, and you can clean up your own mess. And you'll be handing over every single paycheck until you pay me back. You hear?"

"Yeah." Wow. Failed Spanish, not surprising, but does that mean I passed everything else? "So, my report card?"

"On your desk. And clean that room. It's a sty. If you want to be treated like a man, start acting like one. Take responsibility. Follow through. And don't think I'm gonna let up on you. Not for one minute. I'm not gonna let you float through next year and then get some job after graduation and piss away your money and live here free. You can forget that."

God, I hope I'm not still living here a year from now. That will be priority number one: find a job that pays well enough so I don't have to live here.

"Understand?"

"Yes."

"And I'm not going to let up about college, either. You *are* going to make something of yourself, if I have to stay on your case twenty-four/seven. Got it?"

"Yes, sir." I've taken the battle, but the war's far from over, and next time he'll have reinforcements and maybe even forget that he's happy I'm home. Yeah. I get it: *Embrace the suck.*

I stare at the stuff in front of Dad. A few weeks ago, I would have done pretty much anything just to hold this stuff, maybe have the knife, the dog tags. Now as much as I'd still like to have these things, they're nothing compared to what I already have. Except for one thing. And it's not for me.

I reach out and pick up the medallion from in front of Dad. Close my fist around it so the cord hangs free but the medallion presses into my palm.

His hand slaps over my wrist like a vise.

I don't let go.

"Drop it."

No. Not even when it starts to hurt.

When he twists my wrist, I yank back, hurtling out of my chair, which clatters to the floor behind me.

"We owe it to him," I say, trying to hold my ground. "To T.J. and to Curtis."

"I don't owe that . . ." He swallows the rest, but doesn't let go.

"What, Dad? That fag?"

"Shut your mouth."

He wrenches my arm, tries to get it behind me, but I won't let him, twisting with him, like T.J. taught me to. It hurts. It hurts like hell. But I'm not letting go.

Too much. I yelp.

Dad lets go. I stumble to the table, the medallion still in my hand. I stand up, catching my breath, looking at the medallion on my palm.

He leaps at me but I jump back, clutching it.

"Don't make me fight you, old man."

He stops cold, and stares like he's seeing me for the first time.

"I will, if I have to, for T.J." I shift my feet, try to get a better stance. And when I realize he's not coming at me, I carefully put the medallion in my pocket. He watches my hand and then looks at my face again, blinking a dozen times.

"It doesn't mean anything to us," I say. "But it will to him." And so will that box, black-and-white, meant for that apartment in Madison.

Dad deflates. And I'm still standing.

The clock in the living room dongs, and time starts again.

My stomach growls loud enough for even Dad to hear.

He shakes his head. Laughs a little. Then his face shifts into a sneer. A growl rumbles deep in his throat. "I can still take you. Anytime I want. Don't think I can't."

I laugh, out loud, for the first time in this house in as long as I can remember—maybe since T.J. last sat here at this table with us—because the thought never crossed my mind.

Dad's hand lands on my shoulder. His grip is too hard, his fingers too rough, but it doesn't make me flinch. Not at all.

Pizza has never tasted so good. Not even the silence at the counter, both of us eating standing up, can ruin it. And when Dad retreats to the living room, I hear him pause, curse under his breath, and then head upstairs. I bet he gets a new TV tomorrow.

I drag my duffel and backpack down to my room. I could sleep for a week. But I'm only gonna get the one night. Gotta work in the morning. And before sleep, I've gotta call Shauna.

But before all that, there's one more thing I have to do.

I dig through my backpack until I find the envelope of pictures from Curtis. I flip through them until I get to the one of T.J., on the hike, looking so much like he did on that mountain fourteen months ago.

I walk over to my desk and turn on the light. I fish three

of the pushpins out of my drawer. I push the green one back into its ghost-hole at the start of the trail in Georgia. I trace my finger over the trail of holes up the map, and then push the red pin into the hole marking the end of the trek in Maine.

Next to it, I tack the picture of T.J.

Acknowledgments

A debut novel is a milestone, an event to be savored and shared. I am grateful for the love, encouragement, and support of many, many people, most of whom know who they are. Special thanks are due as follows:

First, I wish to thank all those who have served in our armed forces, and their families. I especially wish to thank those LGBTQ service members who served under "Don't Ask, Don't Tell," including the over 13,000 military personnel who were discharged because their sexual orientation became known. I owe special thanks to those who have written and spoken publicly about their experience serving under "Don't Ask, Don't Tell." I also thank those who have shared their experiences, publicly and privately, as casualty assistance officers, casualty notification officers, staff of the Joint Personal Effects Depot, and as the family or friends of deceased service members. They helped me understand the amazing work done by those charged with handling the persons and effects, as well as notifying and assisting the families of service members killed in action. They have my profound gratitude for their work, for their service, for their sacrifices, and for their willingness to share their experiences. While I have made every effort to accurately reflect how T.J.'s family would have been notified of his death, how his remains and effects would have been handled, and to show (within Matt's very limited point of view) some of the assistance that would have been offered to his family, I have, of course, fictionalized those events. Any errors, shortcomings, or aberrations are mine.

My agent, Chris Richman, Michael Stearns, and everyone else at Upstart Crow Literary.

Everyone at Candlewick Press, most especially my editor, Andrea Tompa; Pam Consolazio, who designed the cover; Nathan Pyritz, who designed the interior; my copyeditor, Kate Herrmann; the copy chief, Hannah Mahoney; and the entire marketing and sales teams.

My critique group while I was writing *Personal Effects:* Kashmira Sheth, Judy Bryan, Georgia Beaverson, and Bridget Zinn. (Bridget won't get to read this note, but she knew how much I valued her friendship, her unique worldview, and her support. I wish she were here for this last step and for the celebratory cake).

My early readers, including Robin Smith, Dean Schneider, and Andrew Medlar.

All of my writing friends, with special thanks to my friends at the Absolute Write forums (especially all those who have shared the journey in Purgatory), my fellow members of the Wisconsin Chapter of the Society of Children's Book Writers and Illustrators, and the members of the Apocalypsies.

My family's love and encouragement makes everything about this sweeter. Thank you, Mom, Dad, Scott, Mary, Amanda, Peg, and Ian—and even Tyler, Emily Ruth, Douglas, and Samuel, who I hope someday, when they are older, will read this book.

Finally, K.T., there are not words enough to say thank you, for all you do and all you are. Every day and for many reasons, I am thankful for having you in my life. (And, because it really must be said, thank you for enduring countless reads of slightly tweaked paragraphs without asking *too* often, "What's different?")